The Watery Grave

THE LADY MORTICIAN'S VISIONS SERIES

HELEN GOLTZ

ATLAS PRODUCTIONS

The Watery Grave – The Lady Mortician's Visions, book 6.

PUBLISHED BY: Atlas Productions

First published 2024.

Cover design, as always, by the wonderful Karri Klawiter, Art by Karri.

PLEASE NOTE: This book is written in British-Australian English.

Dear reader...

For dog and animal lovers everywhere

PLEASE KNOW THAT NO animals, including Julius's big hound Rufus, ever get harmed, dog-napped, threatened, injured or die in these stories. Rufus lives on forever. So, rest assured, dear reader, and read on in peace.

I proudly support the WSPA (World Society for the Protection of Animals), RSPCA, and Animals Australia. I thank them for their continued efforts to make the world kinder to animals.

PLEASE NOTE: This book is written in British-Australian English.

Chapter 1

Brisbane, Australia. Monday 4th May, 1891. Mostly fine, scattered showers, 25 degrees.

The Courier – afternoon edition.

A FASHIONABLE WEDDING
By Lilly Lewis, reporter and wedding guest

Miss Violet Forrester, only daughter of the late Edward Forrester, married Mr Julius Astin, eldest son of the late Montague Astin of Auchenflower, at St Thomas's Church, Toowong, on Saturday afternoon. The Rev. J. McWain officiated, and Mr Thomas Forrester gave his sister away.

The wedding was intended to be a very intimate affair with only relatives of the bride and bridegroom and a few close friends invited, including Detectives Harland Stone and Gilbert Payne and Lady Palmer, godmother to the groom and a dear friend of his grandmother, Mrs Maria Astin. However, long before the appointed hour, the church and grounds were thronged with people keen to see one of Brisbane's most eligible sons and businessmen marry. The Astin family is well known in our fair city and has shared many of the community's life experiences as proprietors of *The Economic Undertaker* mortuary service. Several of the wedding guests had to be escorted to get into the church.

The bride, an accomplished seamstress and employee of the Astin family, wore a beautiful gown designed and made by Miss Mary Pollard. The bodice and court train were of white brocade, the skirt of white crepe de chine arranged in three gatherings, down each of which, from the waist to the hem, were spays of myrtle, orange blossom, and lily of the valley. The same flowers trimmed the edge of the corset, bodice, and basque, which was finished with a gathering of crêpe de chine and featured transparent sleeves of the same fabric. The bride wore a coronet of bridal flowers and a long tulle veil and carried a superb bouquet of white blossoms.

The attendant was Mrs Vivian Allen, fondly known to the bride as Aunty Viv, though of no blood relation. Mrs Allen wore a handsome gown of light blue silk poplin. Mr Ambrose Astin attended the bridegroom as best man.

After the ceremony, Mr and Mrs J. M. Astin entertained their guests at a small garden party on the grounds of Lady Palmer's estate nearby. Many of the grand old trees at the stately home lent valuable aid in beautifying the scene, and a large marquee had been erected at one end of the garden, whence the time-honoured bridal cake and other refreshments were served.

Mr and Mrs Astin left Brisbane by the afternoon train for Toowoomba, where they will spend their honeymoon visiting the region. The bride's travelling gown was made of blue crepe, with a silver-embroidered vest, cuffs, and collar.

Chapter 2

ONE WEEK LATER...

Silver-haired, handsome Randolph Astin, the patriarch of the Astin family, was last to join his family and Mrs Dobbs for the afternoon tea break, having seen a client out the door of *The Economic Undertaker* and noted their order. He sat and sighed, weary and looking forward to Julius's return tomorrow.

'I am sorry they could not holiday for longer, but I, for one, will be happy to have Julius back,' Randolph said, sipping his tea.

'I can't believe they are to return already,' Ambrose said of his eldest brother and new sister-in-law. 'The week flew by; I feel like I was only at the wedding yesterday.'

'I believe Violet was anxious about leaving Tom alone for too long, and Julius was no doubt anxious to return to the business,'

Phoebe said with a knowing smile to her grandfather and a glance at her brother, Ambrose.

'We only lost one body while he was away,' Ambrose said, looking very pleased with himself but hastily adding, 'it might be best that we don't mention that to Julius. All ended well.'

Phoebe couldn't help but laugh, and Randolph shook his head at his grandson while Mrs Dobbs blessed herself, as she often did in the company of the Astin family.

'It was a lovely wedding ceremony and afternoon,' she said, slicing her apple tea cake and serving it, before taking a seat to enjoy a cup of tea. Mrs Dobbs joined *The Economic Undertaker* business after the Astin family buried her husband, and she found herself at a loss to fill her day. She quickly made herself indispensable by offering to manage the kitchen and look after the bereaved with refreshments.

'It was a wonderful day, and I must say a very emotional one for Maria and me,' Randolph said, and all eyes turned to him.

'Why, Grandpa? Did you think Julius would never marry?' Ambrose asked. 'Sure, he's grumpy, moody and aloof, but the ladies never seemed to mind that, given he is almost as handsome as I am.'

Phoebe elbowed him, and he laughed. 'Oh, fine then, he might be slightly more handsome if you like those tall, brooding types that feature in the ladies' novels.'

'All of my grandchildren are most handsome,' Randolph said with a smile. 'I knew Julius would have no problem finding a wife, but I wanted him to make a love match, like your parents and grandparents,' he said, including himself and Maria. 'I confess Julius has always been a bit of a mystery to me.'

'How so?' Phoebe asked, fascinated, given her close relationship with her eldest brother.

'Well, I remember when he was the happiest of boys and after that terrible accident,' Randolph referred to the death of his son and daughter-in-law, parents of Julius, Ambrose and Phoebe, 'he was never the same. His boyhood was stolen, and once he was back on track—after a brief rebellious period—Julius took his responsibilities too seriously.'

'So much for a young man to bear,' Mrs Dobbs said.

'Indeed, Mrs Dobbs, it worried me,' Randolph agreed. 'Maria and I tried to get him to enjoy his childhood, to leave the worry to us. We were fortunate that you two were young enough not to understand the full implications of that day,' he said to Ambrose and Phoebe.

'We did not see their deaths firsthand,' Phoebe said, 'unlike Julius.'

'True,' Randolph nodded. 'That boy worked so hard. He had a paper run, gave his earnings to his grandmother, studied and secured himself a school scholarship, and looked after you two; he still does. He looks after us all now. Forgive me for saying so because I love you two no less, but he is the grandchild I most wanted to see settled.'

'Amen to that,' Mrs Dobbs said, filling their teacups again.

'It has all turned out well,' Ambrose said in his normal fashion of lightening the mood. 'Violet must put up with him now, and hopefully, he'll come into work cheery every day, with a smile on his face, well fed and rested.'

The small party exchanged looks and smiles, knowing it was not Julius's nature and no one expected marriage to change him to that degree.

Ambrose cleared his throat. 'As well as the lost body, which we found, perhaps we should not mention that we accidentally buried one of the customers in the wrong timber coffin as well.'

'I am sure, as they are dead, they will not know the difference between cedar and mahogany from six feet under,' Phoebe agreed.

'And their family did not notice,' Randolph agreed. 'It was an upgrade of sorts.'

'Exactly,' Ambrose said. 'As for the two missing shrouds...'

'I'm sure they'll show up,' Randolph said, and Ambrose nodded.

'Good then, to the happy couple.' Ambrose raised his teacup. 'I confess, I'm looking forward to seeing Julius. I missed him at our jobs this week. Good Lord, who would have thought?'

'Who would have thought indeed?' Randolph said with a smile, knowing full well how close his grandchildren were. He, too, was looking forward to Julius's return, not just to share the load but also to have the family reunited.

As luck would have it, Mr and Mrs Julius Astin's return came at the perfect time.

At dusk, several miles away in South Brisbane, Detective Harland Stone hurriedly alighted from the omnibus and, with large strides, headed to the waterfront, his partner Detective Gilbert Payne extending his stride to keep up. Harland groaned when he saw the hundreds of people around the river's edge, many in a state of heightened distress. The detectives would not normally be called to the scene of a ferry accident, but accusations that the vessel had been deliberately struck or sunk saw them issued with orders to get to the Brisbane River with haste and investigate.

'If only it had happened earlier in the day when fewer people might have been onboard,' Gilbert said as they gingerly made their way through the crowd.

Harland agreed. 'The ferry will be full of after-work commuters. I hope most have been rescued. Excuse me, police, please let us through,' he said as politely as possible while moving towards the two uniformed policemen at the river's edge.

'Sirs,' one of the young constables greeted them, recognising the Roma Street Police Headquarters' newest pair of detectives. Despite their success in solving several complex cases over the past year, they were still considered oddities, and Detective Gilbert Payne was not well regarded, given his acceleration through the ranks had more to do with his family's connection with the commissioner than his skills. He carried that burden in every job.

'Constable. What have you then?' Harland said, stopping and surveying the area.

'A disaster, Sir,' he said, pushing his hat back on his forehead. 'The bridge is closed after the recent flood as the authorities said it was not safe to cross, so there are a lot more water vessels ferrying people across the river.'

'And what has happened?' Harland pushed him to get to the point.

'It's the *River Lady*, Sir. She's a small wooden steamboat, 58 feet long and with a maximum of 10 horsepower,' he rattled off to Harland's great annoyance and Gilbert's delight; the younger detective liked facts and figures.

The constable continued, 'It was one of several small boats pressed into service this afternoon, Sir, and it has sunk,' he said, getting to the point and looking out at the water where there was no sign of the ferry. 'There are lots of people missing.'

Harland realised the young man was overwhelmed and reined in his impatience.

'It's all right, Constable. We will all do our best to assist during this tragedy; it is all we can do.'

'Yes, Sir. Thank you, Sir.'

'Who is the ferry captain, and is he alive?' Harland asked.

'Captain Gordon Crouch is his name, Sir, and he is alive. We tried to speak with him, but he was quite incoherent and said it was an accident, that the tide was too strong, and he could do nothing to stop it drifting into another boat.'

'So, he did not believe it was a criminal matter that caused the capsizing?' Gilbert asked.

'He did not say so, but there have been cries to have his head,' the constable said. 'One survivor said the captain had been imbibing.'

Harland groaned. 'Where is he now?'

'When he returned, he was taken to hospital as a precaution, Sir.'

'Returned from where?' Gilbert asked, confused.

'He went home and changed.'

The detectives exchanged looks, and Harland scanned the area, spotting journalist Lilly Lewis and her tall partner, Fergus Griffiths, along the river's edge. They were not the only faces he recognised from *The Courier* newspaper; a large staff had been dispatched to cover the various angles of the story.

'How many on board, Constable?' Gilbert asked.

'No one knows, Detective,' the young man answered, 'but it is estimated to be eighty or so. It was quite crowded but not at capacity, I was told.'

'And how many have been recovered or found alive?' Harland asked, dreading the answer.

'About thirty, Sir. The rest are lost out there,' he said, nodding to the swirling waters.

Harland thanked the young constable and, with Gilbert, moved closer to the site of those receiving aid. People gathered at the water's edge, wailing and calling names as if their friends or family members might surface from the water upon hearing themselves summonsed. As Harland scanned the area, another body was spotted floating nearby, and a rescue party moved to retrieve it.

'Detectives!' Lilly Lewis arrived beside them, slightly breathless from hurrying over the embankment. 'It is odd to see you here. Do you believe the sinking is not an accident?'

'Hello, Miss Lewis,' Harland said, greeting her soberly. It had been at least a month since they had crossed paths, and she, too, was solemn of face.

'We don't know yet,' Gilbert said, 'but there was talk of it. Have you discovered anything untoward?'

'No,' she said, 'but if it were a crime, would you let me work the case with you and report exclusively?'

Harland was always amazed at her single-focused outlook, even amidst tragedy.

'If we abide by our normal terms and conditions,' Harland said, offering her a small smile, which was returned.

Lilly told the two detectives, 'Thus far, I have discovered that the tragedy happened at 5pm and the *River Lady* took only three minutes to sink. The captain survived and was taken to the hospital, but one of the surviving passengers told me he was under the weather and quite reckless.'

'Drinking?' Gilbert confirmed, and Lilly gave a small nod.

'That is unsubstantiated,' she said.

'And that, if true, is the worst of crimes,' Harland said.

Chapter 3

THE NEXT MORNING, JULIUS Astin barely had time to receive a heartfelt welcome back from his family and staff when the employees of *The Economic Undertaker* had to brace for the impact of a maritime tragedy. His wife, Violet, proprietress of Julius's business, *In Mourning – Attire for the Family,* rushed in to join the family for an emergency meeting, as did cousin, Lucian, whose carpentry business—of which Julius was part-owner—made the coffins for *The Economic Undertaker.* Even Rufus, the recently inherited large black dog found in the cemetery who adopted Julius, looked serious as he lay near his master's feet.

'Thank goodness you are back today, Julius,' Randolph said, 'though I am sorry that a tragedy has greeted you.'

'I am glad I am here to assist, Grandpa,' Julius said, looking at the faces of the staff—both family and hired—around the table or seated on chairs around the room.

'You don't look any different,' Ambrose observed. Julius was momentarily lost for words before ignoring his brother and addressing his grandfather.

'What is the latest on the ferry sinking?'

Randolph tapped the newspaper in front of him. 'What a terrible thing. An estimated eighty people might have been on board, including women and children; 34 people have been recovered and are alive and well. Twelve bodies were retrieved at sundown; however, that leaves many unaccounted for, and according to the newspaper, another six were found in the water overnight. They were removed by police wagon to the morgue for identification this morning. We are bound to get many enquiries shortly, and it will be a busy few days if we get 15 or more to bury as well as our usual business.'

Julius agreed. 'We may have up to four burials a day if that is the case – twice our normal load. Should this occur, Claude and I will manage two funerals per day, and Ambrose and Will can take the other two. You need to remember that any bodies that have been in the water for some time are likely to be even heavier than normal, so take care when lifting the stretchers.'

Ambrose groaned. 'Let us hope they were not big people to begin with, or we will have our work cut out for us.'

Julius continued. 'Charlie, as Will and Claude will be on funeral duty, I will hire some stable hands to assist you, but you will need to manage the coming and going of our horses and hearse and stocking the vehicles as needed.'

'I can do that, Sir,' Charlie said most earnestly, delighted for the responsibility.

'I know several boys who can work with Charlie and do that work capably,' cousin Lucian offered, and Julius accepted gratefully. He looked to their kitchen manager.

'Mrs Dobbs, I am afraid you will be run off your feet, but please do not take on more than you can handle. I can hire a tea lady to assist you.'

'Goodness, no, Mr Astin. I am not afraid of a little hard work,' she assured him.

'Thank you. It is best you order supplies now. Charlie can take you in the trap this morning to collect your needs. Lucian, we need at least a dozen of the coffins in storage brought here ready to deploy.'

'You can store the excess in my room if needed,' Phoebe said.

'I shall get my boys onto it immediately,' Lucian agreed.

Julius continued, 'Phoebe, given the manner of death, there may be fewer requests for a viewing or open casket,' he said as delicately as possible, thinking of the bloated bodies. 'But if you are inundated, Charlie, will you assist, and we'll hire more stable hands.'

The young man nodded solemnly, and Phoebe gave him a look of encouragement.

'Between the two of us, we will be just fine,' she said.

Julius continued issuing orders. 'If we get very few requests for viewings, Phoebe, could you assist Grandpa with bookings and quotes? I will assist you as well, Grandpa.'

'Absolutely,' Phoebe agreed.

'I can also assist at the front desk as needed,' Mrs Dobbs said, having now stood in on several occasions.

'That would be most appreciated, Mrs Dobbs,' Julius said, then looked to his wife. 'Violet, could you and the ladies pre-make as much as you can today and tomorrow?'

'We will pre-cut garments in loose fittings; it is easy to adjust to size then as needed,' Violet agreed.

Claude raised his hand, and Julius invited him to ask his question.

'What happens if we don't have a body to bury but the family still wants a funeral?' the tall, young man who had been with the business for several years asked.

'That may well be the case for over a dozen or more victims,' Randolph said. 'The families may elect to have a memorial service. We will not be required as there is no body to bury.'

'This will not be an easy time,' Julius said with uncharacteristic emotion, and Ambrose's eyes widened. Perhaps having a wife has made him a little more emotional. 'If we have the honour of burying the deceased, their families will be extremely distressed; they have had no time to prepare for these deaths, and if you feel overwhelmed, please let me, Grandpa, or Ambrose know. We will step up.'

'We shall open early for business then, Julius, if you are finished?' Randolph said.

Julius nodded. 'Let's get to work.'

Chapter 4

THE ETHEREAL AND TALENTED mortician from *The Economic Undertaker*, Miss Phoebe Astin, was no stranger to talking with spirits. She had inherited the skill from her mother and was humbled to help those who needed assistance moving on to the afterlife. Phoebe had helped several souls right a wrong and assisted the police, notably her new beau, Detective Harland Stone, in seeking justice.

While conservative and introverted by nature, she was not averse to expressing herself with her own style – wearing her long blonde hair loose or tied at the back with a ribbon and favouring the loose garments of the aesthetic dress style rather than the corseted requirements that society preferred. While Ambrose and Phoebe had blue eyes and Phoebe was fair like her mother's side of the family, she was by nature more like her brother, Julius, who took after her father's side with his dark looks and eyes – neither sought much company to feel satisfied. In contrast, Ambrose and cousin Lucian always sought their next entertainment. Fortunately, she believed Detective Harland Stone was like herself in nature.

Descending the stairs after the urgent staff meeting, Phoebe felt her brother's unease. Julius was rarely stressed, but the coming week would be demanding. They knew from experience—they had stepped up to assist the community in past tragedies—that they would be part of many families' history as they buried their dead. Phoebe stopped suddenly, her breath hitching.

'Oh, my goodness,' she said and hurried down the last few stairs. At least a dozen spirits stood waiting for her. Some sat on chairs, some spoke quietly with each other, and several paced.

'I am Miss Phoebe Astin; I am sorry I have kept you waiting, but you have not arrived as yet… in body, that is,' she added, with a quick look around her workroom.

Several spirits started talking at once, and then one of the mature ladies held up her hand.

'Miss Astin, forgive us. We do not mean to overwhelm you. Perhaps one at a time?' she said, looking around. Heads nodded, and the lady speaking continued. 'We were on the ferry that sank. Several of us are still missing; we had hoped to provide information about our whereabouts. Some would like to get a last message to loved ones if possible.'

Phoebe nodded. 'I will do my best, but I am not a clairvoyant or psychic. Your loved one must be receptive to my message.'

'That will never do,' a cranky older man said. 'My lot doesn't believe in that. But can you find my body?' he asked, and Phoebe took down his name and where he was floating as such.

'Forgive me, Miss Astin; my father will also not believe a message has come from the afterlife,' said another man, younger this time and with more manners. He provided his name and the location of his body.

'That far!' Phoebe exclaimed to the handsome young man.

'Yes, the tide was most fierce, and apparently, I am a very good floater,' he said with a smile and a bow before disappearing.

'Miss Astin,' a young, determined lady said, 'Good morning to you. I am Miss Ida Nielsen, and you will find my body in the Hamilton Reach, but I believe my hat—a small black hat with yellow and black feathers, my favourite—is on its way to Manly.'

'Goodness!' Phoebe exclaimed at the distance it had travelled. 'Rest assured, Miss Nielsen, I will ensure you are recovered, along with your hat, if possible.'

'That is very kind. I would like to be buried in it. A selfish last wish, but I would like to go to the afterlife looking respectable,' she said with a note of melancholy acceptance.

'I understand, Miss Nielsen, and I shall do my best to ensure you do,' Phoebe said.

'Thank you, Miss Astin. You are very beautiful, but I imagine everyone tells you that,' Ida said with a smile and vanished.

Phoebe smiled self-consciously and moved on to the next person waiting. She took down the details of where their body was drifting, and in the end, one young lady remained.

'I am Mrs Ernest Rowe; please call me Elizabeth,' she said, offering her Christian name.

'Hello Elizabeth, thank you for waiting so patiently,' Phoebe said, and Elizabeth laughed.

'It's my pleasure. Besides, I am not in a hurry anymore, as I don't know what to expect now.'

'I hope it is peaceful and you will be content, Elizabeth. Please call me Phoebe. How might I help you? Do you know where your body is?' she asked, looking at her list.

When Elizabeth did not initially speak, Phoebe looked up to study the beautiful woman before her. She was of similar age to Phoebe, in her early twenties, with large almond eyes, soft brown hair tied back in a bun, and a fitted cream dress. Her skin was pale, and her lips were full and pale.

'Phoebe, my body has been found, and I believe it is on its way to you for burial. I, too, was found in the river. But I was not on the ferry, and I did not die in the ferry accident. My murderer took my life with his hands and wants it to look as if I were a passenger that day.' She detailed how she had been left to float in the turbulent water.

'Can you help me get justice, Phoebe? Please say you will?'

Photographer Miss Kate Kirby could not believe her luck if you considered witnessing a tragedy good fortune. But on this occasion, the photographs might be crucial to a police investigation or accompany a story by her good friend and fellow *Vexed Vixen*, reporter Lilly Lewis.

The willowy red-haired woman with a smattering of freckles had stayed late at her studio to develop them; her father, arriving, worried for her and walked Kate home.

This morning, having sent an urgent message to Lilly, Kate hurried in, keen to study each photograph. The images were harrowing, to say the least, and had earned her father's praise, which was hard won.

The door burst open, and Lilly rushed in, a small bell announcing her arrival.

'Hello!' Kate said, 'they are ready. Come and see.'

Lilly hurried to Kate's side and gasped. 'Oh, Kate, these are amazing. There it is as it struck the other craft, and that man leaping off the deck is so tragic. Look at the debris in the water.'

'It is swirling and full of rubbish from the recent flood; the victims never stood a chance if they could not swim or were weak swimmers. Can you use them? I will also give them to the police as they might assist if there is a formal investigation into the cause of the tragedy.'

Lilly looked up from the photos. 'Of course I can use them, and I will ensure you receive the proper acknowledgement. I will select a half dozen and return them as soon as possible.'

Kate nodded. 'I'll let Phoebe know, and she can notify her detective if the photographs can assist.'

'Oh, my,' Lilly said, moving from one harrowing image to the next, her hand on her heart at some of the raw emotion captured forever. 'May I interview you, Kate? The editor has all his reporters working on the story and getting as many angles as possible. With these photos, I am sure it will be the story of the day.'

'Yes, of course. I am not sure what to tell you, but...'

'I will lead you with my questions. Can I do so now, if that is convenient?' Lilly reached into her bag, withdrawing her pen and pad as Kate indicated the table and chairs near the window. When settled, Lilly began, 'You have captured the shock of the onlookers so graphically. It was the perfect place to be at the time. Why were you there?'

Kate smiled and looked a little guilty. 'I wished to capture some images of our beautiful city, so I thought sunset at the busy wharf with everyone heading home from their day of industry would be interesting. I am trying to create a gallery of images.' Kate leaned forward. 'Do not put this in your story, but it was Ambrose's last day in charge before Julius returned from his honeymoon, so he skipped out early and met me there.'

'Good grief, so he witnessed the tragedy too?' Lilly asked.

'No. As soon as it began, he realised what was developing and went back to warn his grandpa of the pending calamity. I suspect I won't see him for a few days now,' she mused.

Lilly smiled. 'Your secret is safe with me. Now, paint the picture for me,' she said and fired away with questions.

Unbeknown to Kate, a clue captured in one of her photographs would assist Mrs Elizabeth Rowe, who was currently visiting Phoebe and beseeching her help.

Lilly knew she would impress her editor with the offering of Kate's photographs for the late edition, and she was not disappointed; Mr Cowan gave her one of his rare smiles. After conferring with her writing partner, Fergus, she hurriedly finished her copy to rush off and catch the detectives before lunch.

PHOTOGRAPHER CAPTURES TRAGEDY
FIRST-HAND ACCOUNT BY WITNESS
An exclusive report by Lilly Lewis
Photographs by Kate Kirby, Kirby Studios.

The terrible tragedy of the *River Lady* Ferry sinking took place late Monday afternoon when workers made their way home. On the nearby hill was professional photographer Miss Kate Kirby, 22, who had set up her camera to capture the sunset over the river and city. Instead, Miss Kirby captured a maritime disaster.

'At first, I could not believe my eyes,' Miss Kirby said. 'It seemed to happen so slowly and also so quickly; it was most distressing. I took a photograph of the boats on the river and thought that the *River Lady* was very brave or foolish trying to get through the gap between two larger boats to get to the other side. I was transfixed watching it; I took a second photograph of the attempt.

'Then it seemed to float towards one of them, and the passengers on the deck pointed and yelled to the captain, but it was too late. The ferry struck with an awful grinding noise.'

Miss Kirby said she watched momentarily and then returned to photographing the incident because she thought the images might be important.

'The shrieks and screams startled me and made me feel giddy; it was easier for me to photograph the scene rather than watch it directly. The ferry was right against the sharp nose of the other boat and almost cut in two, with steam escaping from it.

'I saw a few panicked people jump from one boat to another. If the ferry had settled, they might have all been rescued, but I captured when the ferry gave a turn and slid on her side, the steam hissing out of it.'

Miss Kirby said it was then that dozens of people slipped off and were swept into the swirling brown waters, and the ferry began to sink.

'It went under so quickly. To describe what happened is almost impossible; the photographs best represent the dreadful trauma of the event,' she said.

'I saw about twenty persons—men, women, and children—fighting with the debris in the rushing waters and sinking from exhaustion. People were running along the shore calling out to them to grab something, but it was so rough in the water, and their wet clothing must have been very heavy.'

One of Miss Kirby's photographs features three women clinging to a lifebuoy; we are pleased to report that the three ladies survived. Another lady captured by the camera while floating on a piece of timber was not so fortunate. She was pulled to shore but was quite dead on arrival.

Miss Kirby's photographs also depict a young boy floundering in the water, and there are several close-ups of distressed people watching from the nearby banks of the river, their faces masked in horror.

Miss Kirby said, 'I saw a man trying to save a woman, and his hand almost reached hers, but then she disappeared below the waterline. I felt most sad for another woman I saw rushing to catch the ferry before it departed. If only she had missed it, but instead, she climbed aboard. I saw her fall into the water, but she was not retrieved.

'I shall never forget, to my dying day, the sight of the poor creatures perishing before my very eyes. Capturing their last moments seems disrespectful, but if the photographs can assist in understanding what happened, I hope that might honour their memory,' Miss Kirby said.

Chapter 5

DETECTIVE HARLAND STONE RECOGNISED Phoebe's handwriting on the front of the envelope waiting on his desk and grabbed it. He opened the envelope to find two sheets of paper – a list of names and locations where the bodies of ferry victims might be found.

'Good Lord,' he mumbled, turning over the pages. On reading it, he was disappointed she had not sent a message requesting his presence, but perhaps they were too busy with the deceased ferry clients. Nor did she add her name or any personal comments, which he understood was for fear the note might fall into the wrong hands and be hard to explain.

Ten bodies, one floating as far away as Moreton Bay. He shook his head in disbelief. He looked inside the envelope, and upon seeing a small card, smiled. Phoebe requested his company at his convenience – there was the possibility a crime had occurred and suggested the list of bodies might be best in Lilly's hands if he had no objections. He did not.

'What is it, Sir?' Gilbert asked, entering the room carrying two cups of tea and placing one in front of his superior. He looked particularly neat and chipper this morning. Harland had observed that his protégé's joy in life had increased considerably since he started wooing Phoebe's friend, Miss Emily Yalden of the *Miss Emily Yalden School of Deportment.* He imagined them speaking about etiquette to their hearts' content.

Harland showed him the list. 'Phoebe must be inundated,' he said.

'Good gracious, Sir, a body as far as Moreton Bay! What do we do? It would be hard for us to explain how this list came into our possession and how we found these bodies, especially as no crime is afoot.'

'Agreed,' Harland said. 'But perhaps Miss Lilly Lewis might be of service. She can lead the police to find the bodies—tell them she has been tipped off—and write her copy at the same time.'

'Excellent idea, Sir.'

'It was Phoebe's suggestion, and she has requested our company. I am keen to know what she has unearthed and if she believes a crime is in the making. We shall go as soon as we finish our tea.'

As if they had conjured the lady reporter, John, the desk sergeant, rapped on their door, announcing, 'Miss Lewis, gentlemen.'

'Ah, speak of the devil, and he is sure to appear,' Harland said with a smile at the intrepid young lady as she entered their joint office.

'Detective Stone! I have been called many things, but that is a first,' Lilly grinned. She looked resplendent in a pale lime dress, her brunette hair neatly tied back in a knot at her collar, and her blue eyes alive with the excitement of the chase of a good story. 'Hello, Detective Payne.'

'Miss Lewis,' Gilbert acknowledged her with a smile.

'May I ask why you were speaking of me?'

'We were discussing slipping a story to you of a most serious nature,' Gilbert said.

'Oh, and here I was seeking you out in the desperate hope you had charged the ferry driver or had a crime for me to report on.'

'Not as yet, but this is quite sensitive,' Harland said, handing her the note and watching Lilly's surprise as realisation dawned on what she was reading. 'Would you be interested in retrieving them and reporting without identifying your source?'

'Without a doubt. Thank you. I shall get onto it immediately, and should I be asked, I will say members of the public tipped me off,' she said. 'Gracious me, as far as Moreton Bay!' she was as shocked as the detectives.

'We too were amazed,' Harland said. 'I shall come with you and let the sergeant know at the desk that you might know the location of a few bodies; he will assign some constables to you to help retrieve them.'

'That would be wonderful,' Lilly said and thanked him again.

'Miss Lewis, please be warned. A body that has been floating is a fearsome sight. Do avoid getting close if you can,' Harland said. 'It is an image you will not forget. Please take your fellow reporter, Mr Griffiths, with you.'

'Thank you for your concern, Detective. I will collect Fergus on my way. So, do you have a case you are working on?'

'I may have, Miss Lewis,' he said, waving a second piece of paper at her. He grabbed his hat to depart for *The Economic Undertaker*. 'I shall inform you should it be something you might report on. Gilbert, your hat. We shall see you out, Miss Lewis, and assure you are assigned the necessary resources.'

Ambrose Astin was too old to sulk, but he was doing a very good impersonation of a sulking person. He missed working with Julius, the comfortable camaraderie, teasing his eldest brother, and being with family. The work felt more like a job when they were not partnered. It surprised him how much he had missed his honeymooning brother, and now Julius was back and had partnered with Claude due to the workload. Ambrose understood that logic; having an Astin family member attend every funeral was best, but he didn't have to like it.

It was Ambrose's second funeral for the day as the family grappled with the influx of flood victims and the demand for burials. He would be very happy when the backlog was worked through and life returned to normal. Father Morris was officiating at his third funeral.

'I knocked one over earlier for Julius,' he told Ambrose with a wink. 'I am looking forward to my well-earned glass of port tonight.'

'I might raise a glass myself even though it is out of character,' Ambrose said in jest, making Father Morris chuckle. Having seen the body enter the grave and the gravediggers shovel the earth upon it, Ambrose and Will began the journey back to the office of *The Economic Undertaker*.

'I wonder how Claude is going with Julius,' Ambrose mused.

'Am I not serious enough for you?' Will asked with a light-hearted laugh. 'I could try to look a little more sober and tell you to be quiet if it might help you miss your brother less.'

Ambrose laughed. 'Very amusing, Will. You are fine company; it is just that I have never gone this long without seeing Julius. Quite odd, really, and to be expected as we get older and our paths diverge.'

'They might never diverge if you continue to work together. You will have the joy of seeing each other every day,' Will said, grinning at Ambrose's expression.

'I did not say it was a joy to be in his company; I just said I temporarily missed him.'

'I, for one, am pleased Julius partnered with Claude. I like your brother, but he is imposing. We are lucky if Claude utters half a dozen words daily, so the pair are perfectly matched.'

'Not too perfect, I hope. I don't want Julius replacing me with Claude for good.' Ambrose smiled. 'What am I saying? I am irreplaceable. I am sure he misses me as much.'

Will chuckled. 'No doubt.'

As they arrived in the yard at the back of the business, Charlie came out to meet them, assisted by two hired young men who began to unhook the horses from the hearse.

'There are more collections,' Charlie said. 'I've prepared the wagon and put the cover over it if you want to go now.'

Ambrose sighed. 'I was dying for a cup of tea and some of Mrs Dobbs's cake. Perhaps the dead can wait ten minutes. Are Julius and Claude back?'

He had no sooner said the words when the second hearse came into the yard behind Ambrose.

'Yes, just back now,' Charlie said with a grin. His teasing earned him a playful clip from Ambrose. The two men looked equally weary, and Julius passed the reins to one of the young hired helpers.

'Did you miss me, brother?' Ambrose asked, and Julius smiled.

'Was I not just saying that, Claude?' Julius asked.

'You did say it was quiet and sober as a funeral should be,' Claude recalled.

'There you go then,' Julius said, slapping Ambrose on the back.

'Hardly a glowing testimony of brotherhood,' Ambrose said with a grimace.

'Why is the wagon ready?' Julius asked, turning to Charlie amongst the men.

'More collections, Sir,' Charlie said, refusing to call Julius by his first name.

'Ah, right, well done. I shall go. You three head in and have a break,' Julius offered.

'I will come with you,' Ambrose said, swinging into the trap and taking the reins. 'No doubt you are dying to tell me about your honeymoon and how much you missed me.'

'I did come up with a few new business plans while away,' Julius said.

Ambrose's wry expression said that was not what he hoped to hear, and the other men present could not help but grin as they departed for a cup of tea.

'Have you been to see Miss Kirby?' Julius asked as Ambrose turned the horses and wagon out of the grounds onto the busy street.

'Not since Monday evening when I last saw her at—' Ambrose hesitated, and Julius turned to look at him. 'I finished early and met her at South Brisbane to take some sunset photographs.'

'Ah, that's when she captured the ferry disaster,' Julius said, ignoring that Ambrose left early.

'I only left thirty minutes early.'

'I am sure you earned it, given that you managed the workload for the week. I think you should drop in and see her very soon.'

'Why?' Ambrose asked, alarmed.

Julius frowned at him. 'Have you not seen the afternoon edition of *The Courier*? She has captured some very graphic images; there is every chance she is quite shaken.'

'Of course,' Ambrose said, taking the street that led to the morgue. 'I am so used to Phoebe working with the dead that I forget not everyone is as familiar with it as we are. Thank you, Brother. Have you seen Uncle Reggie since your return?'

Julius looked at Ambrose sternly. 'Do not start trying to trap me, Ambrose. I have told you I do not wish to see the spirits like Phoebe, and I am confessing nothing.'

Ambrose sighed. 'Very well then. But Grandpa and I believe you do see them, so when you are prepared to admit it, I assure you we will not be shocked.'

They stopped to collect the two bodies of victims from the morgue and loaded them with dignity, Ambrose subtly watching his brother. If the spirits of the deceased were nearby, Julius did a very good job of ignoring them. They tied down their load securely and climbed back onto the trap.

'I can see why you missed me now,' Julius said as he reached for the reins to drive on the return trip. 'You have had no one to annoy for an entire week.'

'It has been most frustrating. I even asked Phoebe if I could join the *Vexed Vixens* as an honorary member to vex about it.'

Julius grinned, a rare sight, and Ambrose smiled at his brother.

'Welcome back, Brother.'

'It's good to be back,' Julius said, and they headed to *The Economic Undertaker* with the two bodies onboard.

Chapter 6

DETECTIVE HARLAND STONE HESITATED, his hand on the door handle and unable to see through the frosted glass, took a deep breath and slowly opened the door of *The Economic Undertaker*. Looking in, he saw an elderly couple sitting in black attire in the reception area, and greeted them solemnly. Detective Gilbert Payne did the same as he entered. Harland could hear Randolph Astin's gentle and dulcet tone from the meeting room, and Mrs Dobbs appeared with a cup of tea in hand for the waiting party.

'Good day to you, Mrs Dobbs,' Harland said. 'Miss Astin has requested our presence.'

'Of course, detectives. She is in her room if you will make your way there.'

They thanked her, and Harland heard one of the people in the reception waiting area exclaim, 'Detectives?' Mrs Dobbs explained that sometimes the bodies arrive here before the detectives can conclude an investigation. It was a reasonable stretch of the truth and protected Phoebe's skill.

Descending the stairs, he saw his beloved applying make-up to a young woman who did not look water-affected; perhaps she had not been submerged for long. Another body under a shroud was on a nearby table.

'Harland, Detective Payne,' Phoebe said, looking up at them with a smile.

Harland was sure Miss Phoebe Astin was the most beautiful woman he had ever seen, with her blonde-white hair, fair skin, blue eyes, and slight figure. Today, she looked most feminine in a pale pink dress. He desperately wanted to protect her from all the evil in the world and to call her his wife one day soon.

'Phoebe, I hope you are not too exhausted by the unfolding tragedy,' Harland said.

'It is a terrible time for you, Miss Astin, and our community,' Gilbert agreed.

'Thank you both, but do not be concerned on my behalf. I am not as busy as my brothers, and victims of drownings rarely need open caskets.' She placed the shroud over the face of the lady she had been preparing not to alarm the two men.

'I believe it affects us all, even if we do not know any victim personally,' Gilbert said.

Phoebe agreed, giving the empathetic Gilbert Payne a small smile. 'If I might say without embarrassing you, Detective Payne, the orchid you sent Emily was happily received.'

'I am delighted to hear that news, Miss Astin,' Gilbert said, trying not to appear too delighted given the surroundings and their mission.

'She does love a challenge, and an orchid will certainly be that.' Phoebe looked at Harland and smiled. 'Please do not get me an orchid, should you think I am hinting for one. I have neither the patience nor skills like Emily to keep it alive.'

Harland grinned. 'But Florence is looking well,' he said, referring to the thriving green plant sitting under the window that he had gifted Phoebe.

'Dear Florence thrives in a cool room with a modicum of conversation and a little water now and then. I believe we are similar,' Phoebe joked. 'You received my note?'

'Yes, thank you,' Harland said, pleased she understood time was of the essence. 'We took up your suggestion, and Miss Lewis has the list of bodies and is currently working with several constables to retrieve them.'

'How taxing that must have been for you, Miss Astin,' Gilbert said.

'I confess, Detective Payne, it was a little daunting to come down the stairs and find my room full of people. But they were all very polite and orderly. One lady, though, wishes to be brought to your attention.' Phoebe pulled back the shroud of the body she had been working on. 'This is Mrs Elizabeth Rowe.'

The detectives moved to Phoebe's side to observe Mrs Rowe.

'She is a great beauty,' Gilbert said, stating a fact.

'Yes, she was very beautiful,' Phoebe agreed, 'and so young to have lost her life.'

Harland did not comment on the young woman's appearance before Phoebe but added, 'She does not appear to have been in the water very long.'

'No, I believe Elizabeth was found and retrieved quite quickly, hence her mother's desire for an open viewing to remember her beautiful daughter.'

'That is a nasty wound on her head,' Gilbert said, studying the cut toward the back of Elizabeth Rowe's skull. 'She must have hit the ferry when falling or was hit by debris.'

'Elizabeth—Mrs Rowe—visited me. She said she was not on that ferry and was quite alive when the ferry sank. The blow was made afterwards.'

'A clever ruse if it was murder,' Harland said in a low voice, studying the wound more closely and turning the body on the side.

'There is bruising around the back of her neck, too, Sir,' Gilbert observed.

Phoebe continued. 'Elizabeth said she felt a sharp blow and then a hand pressing her down into the water, but she could not identify her assailant. She was with a gentleman friend at the time, whom she believed could not be responsible.' Phoebe pre-empted Harland's question. 'She would not name him.'

'We will find out if needed,' Harland said.

'Elizabeth and her male friend had moved to the riverbank to assist the ferry victims when she found herself completely immersed in the river.'

'She could not swim?' Harland asked.

'No, and with the weight of her clothes, she sank very quickly. There are two oddities I should bring to your attention, if I may?'

'Please do,' Harland said, buoyed by her growing confidence and trust in him.

Phoebe gave him a grateful look. 'Firstly, Elizabeth said something very odd to me.' She had the detectives' attention now. 'That she was not meant to die that day, and she wants her husband investigated.'

'How odd,' Gilbert said. 'As if she knew when she was going to die and was taken by surprise.'

'Exactly so, Detective Payne,' Phoebe agreed, her hand touching her throat.

'Did her husband say she was on the ferry and claim she was a victim?' Harland asked.

'I could not say, however, she is on the passenger and victim list.'

'Her husband can easily claim she was on the ferry, and no one is likely to remember in all the panic that ensued,' Harland said.

'The only chance we have of proving her story is if someone witnessed her after the ferry sank or saw her husband in the act,' Gilbert said. 'In all that turmoil, that is quite unlikely.'

'Indeed, Gilbert,' Harland said and looked at Phoebe. 'She is not here now, by any chance?'

"No, she has not returned. The second oddity is a tin found in Elizabeth's possession.' Phoebe elaborated, 'After Elizabeth was brought in, her mother arrived with a change of clothing so I could dress Elizabeth in her Sunday best. When I removed the other dress the river had dirtied, I found this tin in her pocket. It should be returned to the family, but the contents are puzzling.' She handed the object to Harland, who pried open the small tobacco tin.

'Good Lord,' he said, showing Gilbert the contents – a roll of fifty-pound notes tied with string and a large diamond and ruby ring of considerable value were within. Harland opened a folded piece of paper lining the bottom and read aloud, *Deed Done. E.R.*'

'And this was found in Mrs Rowe's dress?' Gilbert clarified.

'Yes, Detective.'

'Do you know Mr Rowe's Christian name?' Harland asked.

'Yes, he is listed as next of kin,' she said, reaching for a list on her table. 'It is Ernest – E.R.'

Deed done. E.R.' Harland repeated the words and looked at the large sum of money. 'If he did kill his wife or pay to have her murdered, why was this tin in his wife's possession?'

'Perhaps he dropped it, and she retrieved or discovered it,' Phoebe offered. 'I shall ask her if I get the chance.'

Harland nodded towards Elizabeth's covered body. 'Is Mrs Rowe wearing her engagement and wedding rings now?'

'No,' Phoebe answered without having to look. 'But that is quite normal. Most personal items are removed and returned to the family before I receive the body. That well may be her ring,' Phoebe said with a nod to the tin.

Harland nodded. 'Thank you, Phoebe. Unfortunately, with the debris in the water and the stress the coroner—Tavish—is under, there would be little point in sending the body back to him. If, as Mrs Rowe claims, she was struck on the head, it would be hard to prove given her wound is consistent with the flotsam and jetsam at the site of the sinking.'

'Of course,' Phoebe agreed.

'However,' Harland continued, 'we will call on Mr Rowe and ask him a few pertinent questions if I may take the tin?'

'Please do. Can I proceed with her preparation and burial?'

'Yes, I see no reason not to do so. We may need to speak with her parents as well,' Harland said, 'but do not alarm them at this time. Let them grieve her as if it were accidental until we hear what the husband has to say.'

'One more matter, a little trivial but not to the victim,' Phoebe said, flushing slightly as she returned the list to her desk. 'Should you in your travels come across any hats recovered from the victims, Miss Ida Nielsen wants to be buried in the small black hat with yellow and black feathers that she was wearing at the time of her death. A little thing but important to her.'

'It would be nice to do that for her,' Gilbert said earnestly.

'I do hope I can, Detective,' Phoebe agreed, giving him a warm smile.

'We shall give Tavish notice to keep any hats that come his way, and we'll let the desk sergeant know as well,' Harland said.

Phoebe laughed. 'Thank you. I may end up with a millinery in my workroom.'

'Or a great many spirits returning to claim them,' Gilbert joined in.

With that, the pair bid Phoebe good day. Given the trauma underway, there was pressure to bear on all of them, and the best Harland could do was look back from the top of the staircase and give Phoebe a smile. He made a mental note not to send her an orchid and to stick to the roses that seemed to be well received.

The Courier – Afternoon edition.

TWO HATS FOUND ON NUDGEE BEACH
THE SEARCH FOR BODIES CONTINUES
An exclusive report by Lilly Lewis and Fergus Griffiths.

Great diligence and sympathy have been shown by the public and the police in maintaining a systematic search for the bodies of the drowned in the *River Lady* ferry tragedy, the river being patrolled as far down as Lytton. With the assistance of the water police and your journalists, an additional seven bodies were found floating in the water and were taken to the General Hospital morgue. Several were badly decomposed, but the police believed they would be identifiable by their jewellery. The body of Miss Maggie Gether was found near Bribie Island, 53 miles from the scene of the disaster.

Several bodies bore marks about the head as if they had been struck by substances, possibly debris in the water, and all were completely dressed with the exception of one woman, believed to be a capable swimmer, who may have removed layers to improve her chances of survival in the swirling tides. Unfortunately, her life was extinguished.

Certificates of burial were given to the relatives by the police, and several of the bodies were yesterday removed from the morgue to the homes of the deceased or collected by undertakers. Police have interviewed the ferry captain, and an inquiry is pending.

Sergeant Primrose of the Roma Street Police Station, in the company of your journalists, found two ladies' straw hats nearly 15 miles away on Nudgee Beach. They were identified as belonging to victims of the *River Lady* ferry disaster. One hat is a black and white check straw hat, and the other is a lady's small black hat with yellow and black feathers.

The following dramatic two-page photographic spread features additional images captured by professional photographer Miss Kate Kirby from Kirby Studios at the scene of the disaster.

Chapter 7

MRS VIOLET ASTIN, NEE Forrester, was hosting her inaugural *Vexed Vixens* dinner in Julius's home, now her residence. She assumed Lilly's newspaper deadlines with the ferry accident would delay her, but Lilly arrived on time with the other ladies, keen for a night of relaxation with dear friends. Violet's brother, Tom, had made plans for the night, and Julius hurriedly departed to have dinner with private investigator Bennet Martin, the coroner Dr Tavish McGregor, and Harland if the detective's workload allowed it.

The ladies looked forward to the monthly gathering. The clever, independent group of women included Violet, the newest member; her sister-in-law Phoebe; Emily Yalden from the *Miss Emily Yalden School of Deportment;* photographer Kate Kirby; and reporter Lilly Lewis.

'I am so grateful to your grandmother, Phoebe,' Violet said to the ladies as they sat to enjoy the meal in the large dining room.

'Our grandmother now,' Phoebe said with a smile, and Violet laughed.

'Of course. I wanted to host my first dinner and cook, but it was impossible with our workload since the ferry accident. Our grandmother insisted on cooking. And mind you, my cooking would not come close,' Violet said, looking at the dishes with appreciation and hunger.

'Thank goodness for Mrs Astin senior,' Lilly said, acknowledging the newly minted Mrs Astin present. 'I am starving. It has been a frantic and dramatic week, and I have been concerned for you, Kate.'

'Me?' Kate said, taken by surprise.

'I know you have worked with the police before, photographing death scenes, but capturing a tragedy in progress would have been most traumatic,' Lilly said.

'Oh, yes, thank you, Lilly. I confess it has been unsettling. I found some of the faces haunting me, and I have not slept well since the accident. I am sure it will pass. Ambrose dropped in this very afternoon to check on me,' she said with a small smile.

'How thoughtful,' Phoebe said, surprised by the burgeoning romance and his consideration. 'They were amazing photographs, Kate. You have captured history and real-life suffering, and I am sorry it has been at your expense.'

'I feel foolish being so weak when you deal with death every day,' Kate said humbly.

Phoebe shook her head in the negative while accepting the bowl of vegetables, thus confusing Emily.

'Sorry, yes, I will have the vegetables, please, and no, Kate, it is not the same,' Phoebe assured her. 'I deal in death, but my victims are at rest when they are brought to me. The family has had some time to come to terms with their loved one's death and is preparing to send them off. You captured people desperate in the last throes of life. Dreadful.'

'Then let's be cheery so I can forget,' Kate said, accepting a slice of pie from Lilly.

'On that note, I should step up as hostess then and welcome you all,' Violet said. 'Please forgive the state of disorganisation you might find. Ambrose kindly assisted Tom with moving in our few chattels while I was on my honeymoon, but with the ferry accident, I have not had time to put anything away, and boxes are scattered everywhere. I am sure Julius is wondering if he should rescind the offer.'

The ladies laughed.

'Nonsense,' Phoebe chuckled. 'I am sure he cannot wait to come home to his new family every night, including Rufus,' she said, glancing at the large black dog who stretched on a rug in the lounge room, looking most at home having been fed and patted.

Lilly agreed. 'It will be lovely when things are back to normal, and you can go home together at the end of each day.'

'It will. With Rufus sitting between us,' Violet laughed, looking at the large dog. 'I do love that big hound.'

'Do tell us something romantic about your honeymoon,' Kate pleaded and looked at Phoebe. 'You can cover your ears if you prefer not to hear about your brother.'

Phoebe laughed. 'I'm keen to hear something romantic about Julius, too! Was he romantic?'

'Oh, very,' Violet said with a happy sigh. 'He was such a gentleman and always looked out for my comfort. I could have stayed in our room and looked at the park view for the entire week.'

'I bet you could have,' Lilly teased, 'and I'm sure that wasn't the view you were looking at. You've broken many women's hearts taking Mr Julius Astin off the market.'

Violet looked far from repentant with her wide smile. 'The most exciting thing I discovered on our honeymoon—'

Phoebe covered her ears, and Violet grabbed her arm, pulling it down. 'Do not fear, I won't be that indiscreet.'

'That is a relief,' Phoebe joked.

'I discovered we have a mutual passion for developing ideas and creating new ventures. My grandfather, when he was alive, would challenge me to suggest wild inventions, and we used to have such fun,' Violet said, smiling as she thought of her beloved grandpa.

'Julius would love to be challenged as such, I am sure,' Phoebe agreed.

'He did. Julius's wonder about everything was infectious. Perhaps because he did not have to deal with day-to-day business needs, it freed his mind to see potential in a number of ideas. For example, after our train ride up the mountain to Toowoomba, he suggested a mortuary train that took the coffin and mourners to the cemetery directly would be a wonderful asset or even several carriages of a regular train reserved for that purpose. He was disappointed in talking with the station master and learning it is already done down south but not yet in Brisbane.'

'That is clever,' Emily agreed, 'and would be less stressful for the mourners if they could all travel together right to the cemetery gates.'

'Indeed,' Violet said. 'In confidence, Julius is also interested in exploring a bridal wear shop. We intend to discuss it with my staff.'

'Really?' Phoebe exclaimed, and the girls praised Violet's wedding dress, which junior dressmaker Miss Mary Pollard made.

'Well, mourning wear sales have been declining,' Violet explained. 'People are mourning for less time, and the expanded mourning wear section at Finney and Isles in the city is taking away some of our customers. Mary displayed such talent in making my dress, and Julius saw an opportunity. Mary, Nellie and I would love to work with white fabric for a change.'

'Your dress was stunning,' Emily said. 'But do not Finney and Isles make bridal wear as well?'

'They do,' Violet agreed, 'but many a lady does not want to buy their dress from a department store. They want an original design.'

'I would,' Kate agreed. 'I have my dress designed in my head, ready to go!'

'Then you will all be sisters,' Lilly proclaimed. 'Emily and I will have to stick together as we will be on the outer.'

The ladies teased Phoebe at the thought that she might lose her name but gain two more Mrs Astins – Violet and Kate.

Emily concluded, 'Well, it sounds like an inspired honeymoon, dear Violet, if not a little unromantic with all that business talk, but I am sure that good couples have shared interests.'

'Yes, I very much enjoyed and encouraged it. In fact, I impressed Julius with my own idea, which involves you, Phoebe,' Violet said, looking most pleased with herself.

'Oh dear. Will I be doing bridal make-up next?' Phoebe asked, biting her lip.

'No,' Violet laughed, 'your work will always be in demand. But the hotel had a very good dumb waiter device that delivered food and drinks to our room without interrupting us. I mentioned to Julius that a similar pulley system would be advantageous for delivering bodies from your workroom directly to the viewing room. He was most interested in the idea and surprised he had not thought of it himself. I suggested perhaps I was the more inventive of both of us, which set forward many challenges for the rest of the trip.'

Phoebe laughed. 'Oh, I am sure it did, knowing Julius. But that is an excellent idea.'

'Thank you, Sister,' Violet teased. 'Enough from me. I am not vexed, having just returned from a lovely week away. So, now that we are all served, who would like to begin with a vexation?'

'Please allow me,' Emily said, 'since Kate needs to be cheered up.'

'I do love to hear of the pupils of the *Miss Emily Yalden School of Deportment* and their adventures,' Kate agreed, smiling at the thought.

'Well, for the last lesson of the week, I allow forty-five minutes for questions before we finish class. It is often fun, and we have a few laughs. It also gives me an insight into the girls' personalities and intelligence. I am sorry to report that my current class has little of the latter.'

The ladies laughed. 'I am sure that is not true,' Violet said. 'Perhaps they just don't like to show off in front of their friends.'

'You are too kind, Violet,' Emily said with a smile at the hostess. 'But I have decided my current batch of girls are the silliest girls in Australia.'

After another round of laughs and insisting on examples, Emily said, 'As you wish, here are some questions I received last week. After enduring a lunchtime of the girls giggling and gossiping, I reminded them of the notable saying, "It is better to remain silent and be thought a fool than to speak and to remove all doubt", whereby one student enquires, "Would it not be better to leave them in no doubt, Miss? I think honesty is the best policy".'

As the ladies laughed, Emily continued, 'As I teach young ladies about the dangers of being overly familiar with young men, I introduce the subject by asking, "What happens to young women as they mature?" One of my misses quickly responded, "They require new clothing." So very helpful.'

Emily raised her voice above the laughter and continued. 'And one last example – one of my students is terribly nosy and has asked me and her fellow students numerous personal questions. When she asked who my roses were from, I asked, "Do you know what 'minding your own business' means, Mabel?" to which another of my students called out, "I do! So, who are they from, Miss Yalden?" I reminded both of them I was not seeking a definition but suggesting that they apply it.' She rolled her eyes dramatically, and the *Vexed Vixens* laughed.

'Oh, I can hear your tone when you say that,' Phoebe grinned. 'So, were the roses lovely?'

'Beautiful. And the orchid is still alive, thank goodness! So, who is next?'

'I shall go next,' Lilly said. 'I am vexed as I have not had a chance to see Bennet at all this week,' she said of the private investigator she had begun courting. 'He braved meeting my parents and five brothers to seek my father's approval to court me, and mind you, my father almost threw me at him, but with the ferry disaster and my editor's insatiable demand for stories, I have had to turn him away from collecting me at the office twice.'

'I am very pleased that you miss him,' Phoebe said. 'That bodes well.'

'I guess so,' Lilly said. 'Hopefully, our lives will all return to normal soon. Oh, I must know...' Lilly turned to Phoebe.

'What?' Phoebe asked, surprised.

'Lady Palmer hosting Violet and Julius's wedding breakfast! Goodness, that was a surprise. I wrote in my article that she was Julius's godmother and a dear family friend, but you never mentioned you were so well connected.'

Phoebe smiled. 'I guess we forget that Lady Palmer is considered well-to-do. She is my grandmother's best friend, and they both had sons within months of each other – my father being one of those boys. She was his godmother and very close to him. Hence her being asked to godmother his firstborn son, Julius.'

'And she kindly insisted on hosting our wedding breakfast,' Violet said. 'We were only too happy to accept. I only wish my family could have been there, but enough about that. My dear brother, Tom, was there and looked so grown up giving me away.' She smiled at the happy memory and began passing around dishes for second servings.

'I am sure they would be so happy for you, dear Violet,' Phoebe said.

Kate agreed. 'It was so beautiful in Lady Palmer's grounds. I would love a garden like that, but I do hate gardening. So, what of you, Phoebe? What vexes you?'

'I have a murder case, but the vexing thing is, I fear it will be impossible to prove,' Phoebe said in a low voice.

'Ooh, do tell,' Lilly said. 'There may be a story in it, hopefully.' The other ladies leaned forward with interest.

'Perhaps so, Lilly. I told the detectives about it today, so we should know more soon,' Phoebe assured. 'I had a visit from a young lady, Mrs Elizabeth Rowe. She is our age and very beautiful.'

'Forgive the possibly silly question,' Kate said with a glance at Emily – proprietor of silly questions, 'but is she dead?'

'Very much so,' Phoebe said. 'Sorry, I should have said I had a spirit visit. But she claims she did not die in the ferry accident, but it was made to look as if she did.'

'Goodness gracious!' Violet exclaimed. 'I outfitted her mother with a mourning gown. Does she know her daughter was not onboard the ferry?'

'No, not yet, and Harland fears it will be very hard to prove and get her justice.'

'Oh, the poor thing,' Kate said.

'There is more,' Phoebe said and told of the tin and its contents found in the pocket of Mrs Rowe's dress. 'It is now in the possession of the detectives.'

'Ooh, that could be a very good story, Phoebe. Can we discuss it in depth tomorrow?' Lilly asked, trying to be sympathetic and not appear too excited.

'Of course. Mrs Rowe's viewing is at 11.30 tomorrow if that is of interest to you. She will be buried mid-afternoon.'

'It certainly is of interest, thank you, and a sniff of a story will do, just so I have something to say to the editor in the morning,' Lilly said. 'I shall also see what the detectives have to say about the tin and its contents. How exciting! Of course, not for your spirit lady.'

'If you can prove she was murdered, I am sure she will welcome your enthusiasm,' Phoebe teased Lilly. 'Besides, I owe you a favour now.'

'How can that be? I am sure the tab is still in your favour,' Lilly said.

'I read in the paper that you came across the hat of one of the ferry victims and my client, Ida Nielsen, on Nudgee Beach.'

'Did it travel that far?' Emily exclaimed, shocked.

'Yes, incredible, is it not?' Lilly agreed. 'We found two hats. Which one is Miss Nielsen's?'

'It is a small black hat with yellow and black feathers. She wishes to be buried in it. It is her favourite,' Phoebe said.

'Then that gives me a valid excuse to drop in to see you tomorrow,' Lilly said, looking pleased. 'It is a little worse for wear.'

'We will fix it for you, Phoebe,' Violet said.

'Thank you both,' Phoebe smiled. 'At least one of my visiting spirits will be happy. As for Mrs Elizabeth Rowe, let us see what you can turn up, Lilly, but justice would be appreciated.'

Chapter 8

LILLY LEWIS—OUTFITTED IN A sea blue dress that brought out her blue eyes—walked out of the front door of her family home the next morning, patting her brunette hair into place while juggling her bag and notebook in her other hand. She looked up to find a very handsome, tall, blonde gentleman leaning against a waiting carriage.

'Bennet!' she exclaimed with delight.

He removed his hat and gave a small bow. 'I cannot bear it any longer, and since you are too busy to go out, I shall accompany you to the office and spend that precious time with you.'

Lilly beamed. 'How lovely. Did you wish to dash in and greet the family?'

'I wouldn't dream of imposing on your mother at this hour,' he said, opening the carriage door for her and offering his hand.

Lilly climbed up, and he hurried in, sitting right beside her and holding her hand. With a tap on the roof, the driver nudged the horses and moved forward at no great pace, as instructed by the hirer, to the offices of *The Courier*.

'Have you missed me?' Lilly teased.

'As much as you have missed me, I'm sure,' he responded with a cheeky smile.

'Desperately then!'

Bennet grinned with delight before sobering and asking, 'Is it over yet? Surely, you can have nothing further to write about the ferry's sinking.'

'I think it has run its course even though over a dozen people are still unaccounted for and several bodies are unidentified. Only yesterday afternoon, two more bodies were found in the river near the Meat Works at Eagle Farm, both men.'

'The waiting must be terrible for the families,' Bennet said.

'Yes, unimaginable. But you will be pleased to know our editor was assigning different jobs last night, so his focus is changing,' Lilly brightened. 'I may have a story to pitch to him. I will drop in on Phoebe today and the detectives.'

'A spirit crying foul?' Bennet asked.

'Yes, a victim of the ferry disaster, Mrs Elizabeth Rowe, who says she was not on the ferry. But proving that will be a challenge. She claims she was murdered.'

'Dastardly clever,' Bennet said, sitting back and thinking.

Lilly hit his arm.

'What?' he asked, surprised.

'Do not get any ideas, Mr Bennet Martin! If you wish to stop seeing me or dispose of me should we marry, then you need only declare it over, not knock me off and pretend it was an accident.'

Bennet chuckled. 'Trust me, I do not want to be rid of you ever. But you must admit it is a clever way to perform a murder.'

'I will admit to no such thing,' Lilly said. 'However, it is not a bad way to get rid of a husband,' she mused before laughing at his playful, shocked expression. 'And what are you working on?'

'Well, our paths may cross with our workloads as the ferry's insurance company has asked me to investigate where fault might lie for the accident.'

'Is that so?' Lilly asked, surprised. 'I thought you were not accepting any more insurance work. Your clerk, Mr Dutton, told me you had so much of it, and he had to turn it down to his great disappointment.'

'Yes, he is most annoyed at turning away the work, but it is too boring. However, I will accept this one as it interests me and puts me in your path.'

'Ah,' she said and smiled. 'You are romantic in an odd way.' She gave him a wry look. 'So, are they not accepting the captain's word that the rough waters drove the ferry off course?'

'No. He is standing by his statement that it was not his fault, that the ferry was forced up the chains of the nearby steamer due to the current, and he did all he could to navigate it through the two anchored boats,' Bennet said. 'Witnesses and survivors disagree.'

'And the insurance company wishes you to find fault with him?'

'Yes. They will not pay if he was wilfully reckless. There will be an inquest, and I will report my findings. Late yesterday, a diver confirmed where the wreck of the *River Lady* is, and it will soon be brought to shore.'

Ever the curious journalist, Lilly asked, 'Where is it?'

'Just off Hancock's wharf, South Brisbane. When it is recovered, we will see if it tells us anything.'

'That is rather exciting. Can I report on your investigation?' she asked.

'I will check with the insurance company, but I can't imagine we could stop you from doing so. If they don't wish me to comment, then we will work around it,' he said, giving her a wink.

'Lewis and Martin,' she said with a firm nod, offering her hand to shake, which he promptly took and kissed.

'I hope you do not do that with all your business partners,' she teased.

'Of course I do; that's why I am so in-demand.'

Lilly could not help but laugh, and as *The Courier* came into sight, she thanked him.

'This has been my best journey to work ever,' she teased.

'Are you sure you will not stay in the cab with me and we could ride off into the sunset?'

'Given that it is not yet 9am, that is a lot of riding. Good day, my fair prince, and thank you for a most comfortable and entertaining ride.'

Bennet jumped down as the carriage stopped and offered his hand for her descent. 'I may see you at the police station. I have to catch up with the detectives, too. If not, I shall see you very soon.'

'Soon,' she agreed. Pulling her hand from Bennet's, given that he had not unhanded her, Lilly hurried in to talk with Fergus about their potential murder story and onward to see if the detectives might have enough to make a case of it.

Arriving around 9.30am at the marital home of Mr Ernest Rowe and the late Mrs Elizabeth Rowe, Detectives Harland Stone and Gilbert Payne were surprised to find so many people present, spilling out of the house and into the garden. The small home with the white picket fence was crowded with mourners of all ages dressed in black, some openly weeping, others sitting in quiet contemplation, and a small group of ladies bustling around with teapots and plates of cake and sandwiches. A large black wreath hung on the front door, and a man sat on a bench under a not-in-bloom jacaranda tree, surrounded by people with whom he did not interact. Harland presumed it was Mr Ernest Rowe.

A tall, young man, who looked very similar to the affected man, whom Harland guessed to be his brother, met them at the gate.

'Gentlemen, thank you for coming. Are you an acquaintance of Ernest or the late Mrs Rowe?' he asked.

Harland introduced himself and Gilbert. 'We understand this is a very hard time for the family, but may we speak privately with Mr Rowe?'

'My brother, Ernest,' the young man confirmed, introducing himself as Leslie Rowe. 'If you come with me, I will take you to the study and bring him separately.'

The detectives followed, observing the house as they made their way into the study. Leslie closed the door behind him as he departed to get his brother.

'There are several elderly people in the sitting room,' Gilbert said, 'perhaps the parents of both Mr and Mrs Rowe.'

'Yes, I would like to speak with Mrs Rowe's parents, but we will tread very carefully. There is no point in alarming or distressing them if we have no evidence.'

'It is kinder to believe a loved one died in an accident than a murder,' Gilbert agreed.

The door opened, and Leslie entered with his brother, Ernest, who was half a head taller and looked as if he had not slept for a week. His gaze, when it fell upon the detectives, was glazed, and Harland thought if the man was a murderer, he was certainly taking his wife's death very much to heart.

'My elder brother, detectives,' Leslie said, directing Ernest to the couch near the window. He invited the detectives to sit and, at Harland's request, left them to speak in private.

'Mr Rowe, forgive the intrusion at this painful time, but we need your assistance,' Harland began, taking the tact the men had determined while travelling to the interview this morning.

'My help? What do you mean?' Ernest Rowe asked.

'Can you tell me if your wife was wearing her engagement and wedding rings when you recovered her body?'

'Yes, of course she was. I have them in my possession,' he said. He pulled a tobacco tin from his pocket and opened it. The only items in the tin were two rings and a strand of her hair tied with a white ribbon.

Gilbert moved slightly to observe the brand on the tin – *Old Judge Tobacco*.

'You probably think it is odd I am carrying her rings with me, but it is all I have of her now,' Ernest said.

'It is not strange at all, Mr Rowe,' Gilbert said. 'I would do exactly the same thing.'

'Did your wife only possess one diamond ring, Sir?' Harland asked.

'No, Detective. She was widowed before we married and no doubt has that ring in her possession.' Then, as if it were an afterthought, Ernest asked, 'Why? Is jewellery being stolen from the corpses?'

'No, nothing so offensive,' Harland assured him. 'Brace yourself, Mr Rowe, but it has come to our attention that a number of the victims were, in fact, not on the ferry, *The River Lady*, but met their deaths before or after the accident and were dumped in the river to appear to be victims of the ferry disaster.'

'Oh my, that is appalling,' Ernest said, but Harland thought he now looked sharper and more sober.

'We believe your wife was one of these victims.'

Harland waited, and Ernest said nothing. He stared at Harland, then moved his gaze to Gilbert and returned it to Harland again.

'Sir?' Gilbert said quietly, looking at his superior.

'Gilbert, see if there is a doctor in the house,' Harland said, rising and moving to Mr Rowe's side. There would be no further questioning of Mr Rowe, who seemed to have gone into shock. They waited until a medical attendant was found before departing the room.

Harland pulled the younger brother, Leslie, aside. 'I have a request to make of you; it may seem odd, but it is very important.'

'How can I help, Detective?' Leslie asked.

'Could you discreetly see if you can find Mrs Rowe's jewellery? I need to know if her first wedding and engagement rings are still in her possession. We shall wait by the gate.'

With a slightly bemused look, Leslie agreed as the detectives made their way outside, and he undertook the odd request. An elderly lady came down the front stairs and walked towards the men. She was dressed in a large mourning dress that seemed to hang on her frame and provided a striking contrast to her white hair and skin. From the similarity of their noses and mouths, there was little doubt she was Elizabeth Rowe's mother.

She confirmed it a moment later. 'I am Mrs Jenkins, Elizabeth's mother.'

'Madam, may we offer our condolences? Detectives Stone and Payne,' Harland said, introducing them both.

'My sincere condolences, Mrs Jenkins,' Gilbert said, bowing his head.

'Thank you, thank you both,' she said, clasping her hands before her, a white lace handkerchief webbing through her fingers. 'We are departing shortly for the viewing of my daughter at the funeral home. You will not delay us, I assume?'

'No, not at all,' Harland assured her.

'She should be here, but Ernest could not bear to have Elizabeth dead in the house.' She shook her head as if the notion was absurd but showed no emotion as one would expect. 'I attended to my son-in-law after you left the room, and he was muttering something about Elizabeth not being on that ferry.' Her tone implied she held no great affection for Ernest Rowe.

Harland lowered his voice. 'We are here to ensure your daughter's wedding and engagement ring are returned to her husband. We have found an engagement ring and believe it to be hers.'

'And that is what detectives do these days?' she said curtly. Harland realised she was no fool and would not be taken for one.

'Only when the ring is accompanied by a large amount of cash and an ominous note,' Harland said.

'Ah,' she said with a small nod of understanding and turned to look at the mourners. 'Elizabeth did not have a great many friends. She was rather a selfish girl. But she chose Ernest against our wishes. I did not believe he was good enough for her, but you can trust me on this, Detective: he loved her to the point of being a lap dog. He would never do her harm.'

'Thank you, Mrs Jenkins,' Harland said, 'that is a useful insight. If your daughter had few friends, who are these people?'

'Friends of the family on both sides doing their duty.' She moved away as Leslie Rowe approached the detectives.

'Her first marriage jewellery is present, tied with a ribbon and a small portrait of her first husband, along with a pearl necklace. May I ask what this is about, Detective?'

'A broad investigation at this stage, Mr Rowe. Please do not concern yourself or allow your brother to be overwhelmed. Should we need to speak with him again, we will come after the burial.'

'Thank you,' Leslie Rowe said, and the detectives departed, walking down the street before hailing a hansom cab. Once inside, Harland asked, 'The tin, Gilbert, did you see it?'

'Yes, Sir. It was the same brand as that found in Mrs Rowe's possession. I shall stop at a tobacconist and see how common that brand is amongst smokers.'

'Good idea. Let us hope it is rare,' Harland said and sighed. 'So, we have a tin found on Mrs Rowe's body that is the same brand as that kept in their house, and it includes a diamond ring, which was not hers, and a large wad of money.'

'Plus, the words, "*Deed done. E.R.*", but what deed?' Gilbert mused. 'Mr Ernest Rowe seemed genuinely shocked and, from what his mother-in-law said, incapable of harming her.'

'Yet, I have seen the mildest of men in the heat of passion or rage of jealousy strike out,' Harland said. 'But in this instance, I agree with you. He seems placid and shocked by her death.'

As they arrived at the Roma Street Police Station, Harland stopped at the desk and asked Sergeant Henderson, 'Have you had any reports of missing engagement rings, Sergeant?'

'Goodness, not for some time,' he said and fished under the desk for a large book. The sergeant flicked to the section marked "Missing" just after the "Stolen" section and scanned to the last entry. 'I thought so, about four weeks ago, ' he said, turning the book around.

Gilbert read the description of the ring. 'That sounds very much like it, Sir. The large ruby in the centre. I shall get the owner's details.'

'Thank you, Sergeant and Gilbert,' Harland said, leaving the pair and heading towards his office feeling most dissatisfied. He didn't like letting Phoebe down, but he would need much more meat on this case to justify its pursuit.

Chapter 9

PHOEBE HAD HOPED TO set eyes on Mrs Elizabeth Rowe again, but she had not reappeared. The deceased lady's viewing was today, and the brother of the widower, Mr Leslie Rowe, requested to have it in-house rather than at his brother's residence, who was indisposed with grief. Phoebe could only imagine how distraught the man must be losing his bride only a few years into their marriage. Unless, of course, he took his wife's life – *"Deed Done. E.R."*. So engrossed was Phoebe in that thought that she did not hear Julius until he was almost upon her.

'Goodness, you startled me. Why can you not be as noisy as Ambrose?' she asked crossly. 'Are you sure you are not a spirit?'

Julius smiled. 'Sorry, Phoebe. And yes, I am very much alive.'

Phoebe exhaled. 'Well, that is a relief. Should you depart before me, I suspect you would be quite a nuisance.'

'You can count on that. I will oversee everything from the other side and won't need sleep or tea breaks.'

Phoebe grinned at his silliness.

Julius added, 'I shall call out or cough loudly next time I come down the stairs or bring Rufus.'

'Where is the dear big hound?' Phoebe asked with affection.

'Asleep in the sun in the coffin showroom. Being a guard dog is exhausting, he would have us believe.'

Phoebe laughed and, hearing a cough, both turned to see Uncle Reggie lounging on the couch near the stairs. A handsome man like his brother, Randolph—grandfather to Julius, Ambrose and Phoebe—Reggie was killed in a riding accident aged forty and cut a fine figure in his riding gear.

'Thank you, Uncle Reggie, for announcing your arrival,' Phoebe said with a nod to her brother. 'See, Julius, that is how it is done.'

'And how are my favourite niece and nephew, and Ambrose, of course, who is not present?' Reggie asked.

'In good form, thank you, Uncle,' Julius said. He did not ask about his uncle's health as there was little point in asking the dead how they were today. Julius moved towards the covered body in the corner. 'May I?' he asked Phoebe.

'Of course, you need not ask.' Turning to inform her uncle, she added, 'It is Mrs Elizabeth Rowe, one of the ferry accident victims, although she claims otherwise.'

Julius lifted the shroud and studied the young woman. Reggie joined him.

'My, she is a beauty,' Reggie said. 'A terrible waste.'

'You have done a very good job, Phoebe. It was fortunate she was not in the water for too long,' Julius said, studying the corpse.

'Why are you carrying measuring instruments?' Phoebe asked.

'I would not have thought you were the handy type, Julius. Academic, yes, but good with a hammer and nail, well...' Reggie said.

'Fear not, Uncle, I will ask Lucian to build what I have in mind, but I wanted to see if it were feasible first. Violet had an excellent idea while we were on our honeymoon.'

'She told me her idea at our *Vexed Vixens'* dinner,' Phoebe said. 'A dumb waiter as such to move the body from my room straight to the viewing room. Why had you not thought of that before?'

'I can't imagine,' Julius said, not realising Phoebe was joking and looking slightly bemused that he had not. 'I will be happy for Grandpa not to be on the end of a stretcher carrying bodies upstairs anymore. He insists on helping, but it is too much.'

'Yes, he thinks he is still a young man,' Phoebe agreed.

'Ah, my dear older brother,' Reggie said and sighed.

Phoebe was about to respond when Mrs Elizabeth Rowe's spirit appeared, and Reggie disappeared. He was reticent to reveal himself to the recently departed unless they inundated him with questions and became clingy. Julius turned, ignoring her, and moved to measure up the area in question.

'I am so pleased you have returned, Elizabeth,' Phoebe said, relieved.

'Thank you, Phoebe. I believe my viewing is today. May I see myself?'

'Of course. Please come this way.' Phoebe returned to Mrs Rowe's body and lifted the shroud to reveal the body to the spirit nearby her. She was pleased to see the young woman smile. Laying on the table, Elizabeth Rowe looked as pretty as a picture. Her hair was loose and glossy, falling softly over each shoulder. She wore the dress supplied by her mother, and her skin looked dewy and feminine.

'Oh, thank you,' the spirit said, pleased and surprised. 'I expected the worst from my time in the water, but I look most pretty and restful. I do love that dress.'

'Your mother kindly brought it in for you, and I imagine it would be very hard to make you appear any other way,' Phoebe said.

'Goodness, is that your husband? He is strikingly handsome,' Elizabeth gushed, studying Julius, who was undertaking measurements in the corner and ignoring the pair.

'My brother, Julius,' Phoebe said. 'He is indeed very handsome.'

'If only I were not dead, but how would our paths ever cross so I might meet him,' she mused sadly.

'Julius is recently married and met his wife at her grandmother's funeral. We had the honour of burying her.'

'A sad but fortunate day for her,' Elizabeth said, still admiring Julius.

'If I may talk about your recent request of me,' Phoebe started. 'I spoke with the detective on your behalf, but we need your help.' She disappeared.

'Elizabeth!'

Julius looked around. 'Well, that was interesting. It does not bode well for her case if she is unwilling to help you further.'

'That was odd,' Phoebe agreed. 'Why ask for my help and then not offer it? Is she so frightened of her husband even in death?'

'Perhaps she feels there will be repercussions for her family,' Julius suggested.

'Something is not right, Julius. I feel it in my bones,' Phoebe said with a small shudder.

'See if Uncle Reggie can dig up anything, so to speak. But if you are worried, walk away from this; you owe Mrs Rowe nothing.'

'Thank you for your concern, but no. I want to get to the bottom of this, and I shall.'

She heard Julius mutter something about determined women before giving her a wink and heading upstairs again with his measurements, leaving Phoebe to ponder what had become of Elizabeth Rowe.

As they did each time before entering the office of *The Courier* editor, Lilly and her reporting partner, Fergus, took a large gulp of fresh air. The smoky den that Mr Alex Cowan favoured—also known as the editor's office—was hazy no matter the hour. He nodded toward a seat, and the young pair sat down. It was hard to pinpoint Alex Cowan's age, somewhere around the forties the pair had guessed based on his experience and receding hairline, and while he was perpetually gruff, he was a fair man.

'I'm keeping Lawrence on the ferry stories; everyone else is off them,' Mr Cowan said, placing his cigar in the ashtray by his side and gathering some papers on his desk. 'As for you two—'

'We have a story to pitch to you, Mr Cowan,' Lilly said, pleased to see the editor give a small smile, even if it was fleeting. She felt as if he had humoured her initially. However, when Lilly and Fergus started having considerable success with their news stories and paper sales increased from their dramatic headlines, the look became more like a happy indulgence.

Alex Cowan sat back, webbed his fingers across his stomach and said, 'Let's hear it then.'

'It is a potential murder story, and we are working with the detectives again.' Lilly set it up. 'But it is indirectly related to the ferry accident.'

He gave a small snort of disinterest, and Fergus hurriedly continued from Lilly.

'A beautiful young woman who was found dead and believed to be a passenger on the ferry may not have been on board at all,' Fergus said.

'Her husband is the likely suspect, and it is possible he bumped her off after the ferry accident and placed her body in the river so she would be found like all the other victims.' They watched as his chin went up.

'Beautiful, you say?'

'Yes, about my age, Mr Cowan; I'm sure she will have a lovely wedding portrait to feature with the story,' Lilly said, not knowing if Mrs Rowe did or not. 'There is also another angle,' Lilly hurried on. 'An insurance company has hired a good acquaintance of mine to find fault with the captain rather than the ferry. I am sure it will all come out at the inquest, but we could feature some interesting angles before the inquest and beat other outlets to the story.'

Lilly knew the editor saw right through her, but she was prepared to tempt him with whatever means possible to report her own story... professional means, that is.

Alex Cowan chuckled at her attempt to persuade him. 'All right, there might be a yarn amongst that lot. Let's see what you can come up with, but I'm expecting regular copy. If it gets dull, you're off it, right?'

'Yes, Sir,' they both said and hurried to their feet to depart.

'First story tomorrow for the late edition,' he barked after them as they departed his office.

'Good Lord, tomorrow,' Fergus said under his breath.

Lilly looked at him with equal astonishment. 'Best to get to it then. I shall visit Phoebe and then the detectives. The deceased has her viewing this morning at 11.30, before her burial later today. If I am in luck, there might be a confession.'

Fergus gave a huff of laughter. 'Should we be so lucky? I shall take the coroner and see if there are any other suspicious deaths, and if this behaviour is common with tragedies – that will give us a fallback story. I will ask if he saw the lady's body and her injuries and try to get a comment.'

'Excellent. I shall see you back here early afternoon, Fergus,' Lilly said. Grabbing their pads, pens, and hats, the pair departed with great haste, Lilly muttering, 'Tomorrow late edition,' under her breath.

Moments later, she returned and grabbed Miss Ida Nielsen's hat she had found washed up on the shore when directing the constable where the bodies were; she promised to give it to Phoebe.

'Nice hat, Lilly. I'm partial to feathers,' one of her fellow journalists teased her as she hurried past.

'Thanks, Frank, but it belongs to one of the ferry's dead.' That stopped their teasing and laughter immediately.

Chapter 10

THE *In Mourning—Attire for the Family* store had only been open for an hour, and the ladies had assisted half a dozen customers. Violet sat back and sighed as the door closed behind a customer, providing a short reprieve.

'We must be almost at the end of the demand,' she said. 'I am exhausted.'

'It has been most wearing,' Mrs Nellie Shaw agreed. The mature woman in her late forties was the breadwinner as her husband, Harold, was poorly. 'I, for one, will be glad to return to our normal routine, even though I was very grateful for the bonus Mr Astin gave us last week. Harold needs some new shoes, so that will secure him a good pair.'

'It was a lovely surprise,' young Mary said from her desk, overlooking the comings and goings in the street and the next-door entry to *The Economic Undertaker*. She looked particularly pretty with her large brown doe eyes and light brown wavy hair worn tied back. Mary wore a pale green dress of her own making. 'I have to get used to calling you Mrs Astin now, Miss,' she said to Violet with a laugh.

'I will answer to either, and you may call me Violet,' Mrs Violet Astin said, even though Mary had refused to do so before. 'Besides, it was not a bonus; it was hours earned. We worked under great pressure this past week. To cheer you both up, I may have exciting news soon.'

'Oh, you are—'

Violet cut Nellie Shaw off mid-sentence. 'Business news!'

Nellie laughed. 'Oh, well, that is good too.'

'I love surprises,' Mary said. 'Can you give us a hint, Miss, um, Mrs Astin?'

'Yes. And please call me Violet. Mrs Astin sounds terribly formal. I must insist on it, Mary,' Violet said.

'You will get used to it if you say it often enough, Mary,' Nellie said encouragingly. 'So, practice right now.'

Mary blushed. 'Very well then, Violet,' she said, not making eye contact, 'but I will not call you anything but Mrs Shaw,' she told Nellie.

'So be it, given I am so much more your senior,' Nellie said with a pretend sigh. 'Now, Violet, do tell us, what is this good news?'

'It is an idea that Julius had on our honeymoon, he will explain, but it has to do with our business and what we produce.'

'We are not moving, are we?' Mary said. 'I love my position in the window.'

'We might be, but I am sure you will be pleased, Mary, and I will ensure you have a window view.'

'Ooh, sounds intriguing. When will Mr Astin come to speak with us then?' Nellie asked.

'As soon as this rush ends, I will ask him to drop in. Half a dozen finished dresses must be collected today; he has three funerals. I believe our workload will ease starting tomorrow,' Violet said.

'There he is now,' Mary proclaimed as she saw Julius coming out of his business. 'He is on his way, Miss, I mean, Mrs, I mean, Violet.' Nellie chuckled.

'We will get there,' Violet said with a laugh. 'He must have a spare moment.' She watched her husband walk past the windows, his stride confident, his appearance so handsome that Violet almost sighed.

Glancing in, Julius opened the door to the dressmaking store, and as Mary was in his sight, she said, 'It is clear, Mr Astin.'

'Thank you, Miss Pollard,' he said, entering. 'Good morning to you and Mrs Shaw,' he said, closing the door. 'And to my wife.'

All three ladies smiled as he moved towards his wife's desk and sat on the corner she patted, inviting him to do so.

'Good morning, Julius,' Violet said. 'Your ears must have been burning; we were just speaking of you. I was telling the ladies all about our honeymoon.'

Julius looked horrified, Nellie laughed, and Mary shook her head, blushing.

'I am teasing,' Violet said. 'We barely had time to speak; six customers have visited this morning already.'

'That is a relief. Not about the customers but about...' Julius relaxed. 'I am sure the ladies would not want to hear of our adventures.'

'Well, I did mention that you might have an exciting idea to tell us about shortly. We needed some buoying after such a heavy demand on our time.'

'Thank you for the bonus, Mr Astin,' Mary said hushedly. She was quite nervous in the company of the imposing Julius Astin.

'Indeed, it was a most welcome surprise, thank you, Mr Astin,' Nellie added.

'No, thank you, ladies. It was earned, not a bonus, for your hours and labour. Thank you for managing this extra workload and the heightened emotions of our customers. We shall all be glad when the dead are buried and the families are appropriately dressed. Ambrose believes he will expire soon if it does not stop.'

They laughed, imagining the dramatics of the younger Astin brother.

'Has Violet told you anything about our business concept?' he asked.

'No, Violet said you might explain,' Nellie said.

Julius looked at his wife and smiled. 'I shall leave her to discuss in detail, but...' he turned his attention to Mary, who watched him with fascination – she had never seen more handsome men than the Astin brothers. 'You inspired it, Miss Pollard.'

'Me!' she said, shocked.

'Yes, the wedding dress you designed and made was one of a kind; I am sure my wife was the most beautiful bride that ever walked.'

'How romantic,' Mary said and smiled at Violet, who laughed a little at the pair of them.

Julius continued, 'So, we thought, would you like to work with white fabric rather than black?'

The detectives arrived and just as quickly departed from the small worker's cottage address of Miss Charlotte Glasson, conveniently close to the main street of industry in South Brisbane.

'She's gone to work, gentlemen,' her mother said. 'She's a shop assistant, works just down the road a bit,' she pointed in the direction. 'Charlotte's not in any trouble, is she?'

'Not at all, Madam,' Gilbert assured her, 'We understood she lost her engagement ring and—'

'Yes, she did, and it will be that good-for-nothing ex-fiancé who stole it, mark my words!'

'Mrs Glasson, do you know a gentleman by the name of Mr Ernest Rowe?' Harland asked, keen to find out why her daughter's ring was in the possession of Mr Rowe's deceased wife, Elizabeth.

'Can't say that I do, Detective.'

'I see.' Having ascertained where Charlotte Glasson was currently working and that it was within walking distance, the detectives departed with their thanks.

'There was no love lost there for the ex-fiancé,' Harland said as they made their way to Bonbon's Confectionary Shop.

'No, Sir,' Gilbert agreed as the store came into sight. 'I confess, Sir, I have a sweet tooth. I may not resist departing with a box of fruit drops for Miss Yalden, some toffees for my mother and Jujubes for me.'

'You have guilted me into buying sweets for Miss Astin now,' Harland said with a smile.

'Do you know her favourites, Sir?'

'I have no idea and feel quite remiss for not knowing, Gilbert,' Harland said as they entered a quaint confectionary store decorated in black and white with red ribbons on the counter.

'Good morning, Sirs. May I help you?' a petite young lady with ginger hair, bright green eyes, and a starched white uniform with a red apron asked. A sound from the back of the office indicated another staff member was working in another room.

'Yes, please, we are looking for Miss Charlotte Glasson,' Harland said.

'That's me,' she said and stepped back towards the door.

'Fear not, Miss Glasson. Detectives Harland Stone and Gilbert Payne concerning your missing engagement ring,' Gilbert said.

She slumped with relief, her hand going to her heart. 'Thank goodness, I thought my ex-fiancé sent you. He has been particularly nasty of late.'

'A bitter break-up?' Harland asked.

'To say the least, Detective.' Her eyes narrowed. 'Has he told you I have done something wrong?'

'No, no,' Harland assured her. 'I believe you visited the police station to register a stolen or lost engagement ring. Can you describe it to us, please?'

'Yes, it was stolen,' she said. 'It's a large ring with a ruby in the centre because the idiot said it matched my hair, a diamond on either side and a gold band.'

Harland did his best not to smile at her description and, with a nod to Gilbert, watched as it was retrieved and presented.

'That is it! Oh wonderful, wherever did you find it, Detectives?'

'Well, that is the odd thing, Miss Glasson,' Harland said. 'We found it in strange circumstances; thus, we cannot return it to you now.'

'But it's mine!'

He held up his hand. 'Then it will be returned to you. But it is part of an ongoing investigation. Do you know anyone with the initials E.R.?'

She repeated the initials, and then the gentlemen moved aside as an elderly pair of ladies entered the store, and Miss Glasson served them. Both men window-shopped the products on display, and one of the elderly ladies patted Gilbert's arm.

'A gift for your sweetheart?' she asked with a smile.

'Yes, Ma'am. She likes the jelly and fruit drops.'

'Ooh, so do I, but sister likes the toffees,' she said with a nod toward the other elderly lady, adding in a low voice, 'She doesn't have the teeth for them anymore.'

Gilbert nodded knowledgeably. 'I could say the same about my mother, but she persists.'

Charlotte Glasson was a most competent sales assistant, and the ladies left with more than they intended to buy. She returned her attention to the detectives.

'I am sorry, but I cannot think of anyone I know with those initials.'

'Do you know of a young lady named Elizabeth Rowe?' Harland continued.

'Ah, that is the person with the initials E.R. then,' Charlotte Glasson surmised.

'She is a victim. Her husband is Mr Ernest Rowe,' Harland said.

'Well, I don't know a Mr E. Rowe or a Mrs E. Rowe. What is she a victim of? Did she find my ring?'

'In a manner of speaking. Can you remember when or where you lost your ring, Miss Glasson?' Harland persisted.

'I don't believe I lost it; I think it was stolen. I always kept it in my dresser. I don't wear it now that we have broken up, but I am sure it went missing from my room. My ex-fiancé, Donahue Marsh, no doubt took it. He believes I should have returned it, but he was cheating on me, kissing another girl, so I earned that ring.' She narrowed her eyes. 'Did he give my ring to this other woman, Elizabeth Rowe?'

'We can't say as yet, Miss Glasson. But could we have Mr Marsh's address, please?' Gilbert asked and took down the details.

'How soon can I have it back? You won't give it back to Donahue, will you?' she asked.

Harland refrained from sighing. 'Soon, hopefully, Miss Glasson, and as you reported it missing, the ring will be returned to you.'

'Good,' she smiled. 'Can I interest you in some confectionary?'

Chapter 11

JULIUS OBSERVED THAT THE viewing of the beautiful Mrs Elizabeth Rowe was an odd affair. He attended the session while his grandfather met with another client, and Ambrose and Will managed a funeral. Downstairs, Phoebe prepared Miss Ida Neilsen for her viewing, and next door at the mourning wear store, Mrs Nellie Shaw repaired the late Miss Neilsen's hat for her burial.

It was a small gathering, and very few friends of Mrs Rowe's age were in attendance. Her mother did not appear to weep or wail at the loss of her daughter; the kin present mourned in a dignified manner, and the only truly distraught person was Mr Ernest Rowe, the widower.

Julius looked up to see Harland lingering near the door and went to meet him, sharing his observations. 'It is only a small gathering, and the only family member to show genuine emotion is the husband; he has been quite overwhelmed.'

'That is interesting,' Harland said. 'Gilbert and I spoke with the family this morning. Her mother said Elizabeth was a selfish girl with few friends; a harsh recommendation. But I am convinced that this man did not kill his wife. So, if she did not die in the sinking of the ferry, who killed her and why?'

'Have you shared your suspicions with the family?'

'No, only the husband, but he was not able to cope this morning.'

'So it seems. Will you go to the funeral?' Julius asked.

'Yes, Gilbert will meet me there. Sometimes, who attends can be very telling. Thank you for your insight. May I come in and observe on the pretence of paying my respects?'

'Of course,' Julius said, moving to allow Harland entrance.

On seeing the detective again, the husband flopped into a chair as if expecting an interrogation. Harland did not approach him. In a short time, the family stood and passed Julius, offering thanks. Elizabeth's parents, her parents-in-law, brother-in-law Leslie, and a small number of family friends and colleagues of her husband departed, and most would make their way to the funeral in two hours at South Brisbane Cemetery. Elizabeth's husband, Ernest, waited until last.

'With your permission, Mr Rowe, we will remove Elizabeth's body now and prepare her for burial,' Julius said.

'Yes, thank you, Mr Astin. Thank you for this dignified farewell. She looks most beautiful.'

Julius closed the lid on Elizabeth's coffin, and with a nod to Claude waiting outside, the pair carefully moved the coffin out of the room, leaving Harland with the bereaved husband.

'Detective, if you believe my wife was not on that ferry, then I imagine you suspect me,' Ernest said, his voice wavering. The widower was handsome, but Harland found his nature weak and foppish and never felt comfortable with the dandy type during his schooling years. They, in return, avoided the boxing, sporty Harland Stone.

'Why would I suspect you, Mr Rowe?'

'My wife is dead, and I will inherit a great deal of wealth as a result.'

'That is grounds for suspicion, but most people prefer their loved ones alive rather than improved financial circumstances. Were you both insured?'

'No. Her wealth goes back to her first husband. You see, Elizabeth and I loved each other from the moment we met,' he said and paused to control his emotions. 'But her parents wanted her to marry the son of a family friend. He was ten years older than Elizabeth and extremely wealthy. He made his money in the building industry. Elizabeth did what she was told; she was a dutiful daughter.'

'How long were they married?'

'Only a few years and he died. It was an accident, and I assure you, I had nothing to do with it. Then, after her mourning period, we were free to marry. Her parents still didn't favour me with their approval, but she was of age and independently wealthy. We were a love match.'

'Was she on the ferry that day?' Harland asked.

'I have no reason to believe she wasn't, Detective. I was at work; I'm a stock manager at Burton's Stationery Supplies. My wife did not work,' he said as if that were a matter of pride. 'She often shopped or met a friend in the city and was always home to greet me after work.'

'Are you missing any money, Mr Rowe? A roll of pound notes?' Harland asked.

'I have never had a roll of notes in my possession,' Ernest said, frowning and confused by the odd question.

'Do you know who might own an engagement ring with a large red ruby in the centre, bordered by two diamonds on a gold band?'

'No,' he huffed, sounding somewhat bemused. 'Not my wife, that much I know.'

Randolph Astin appeared at the doorway, saw the two men, and nodded to Harland before departing.

'May I ask, have you always smoked the same brand of tobacco?' Harland continued with his questions.

'I don't partake of tobacco, Sir.'

'But you have a tobacco tin in your pocket with your wife's rings and a lock of her hair.'

Ernest Rowe's eyes widened with alarm. He patted his jacket, feeling the tin there, and looked relieved again.

'I do.' He pulled it out and looked at the maker – *Old Judge Tobacco*. 'We have a collection of these tins at home. Elizabeth's late husband smoked this brand. She collected the tins.'

'Why?' Harland asked.

Ernest gave a small shrug. 'She uses them for coins and sewing buttons. Elizabeth is, I mean, she was, quite frugal despite her wealth. I think it was drummed into her by her parents.'

Harland exhaled with frustration. He was going around in circles. If Mr Rowe was telling the truth, the tin, cash and ring did not belong to the widower.

'Thank you, Mr Rowe. I wish you the best getting through today's funeral and hope you get stronger as the days pass,' Harland said sincerely.

Ernest Rowe looked surprised. 'Thank you, Detective. So, was my wife a ferry victim? Do you think I had something to do with her death?'

'I cannot say as yet if your wife was on that ferry, but I don't believe you played a part in her demise.'

Ernest Rowe visibly slumped, and then he began to cry afresh. Harland rose and excused himself, leaving Mrs Dobbs and her offered cup of tea to console the bereaved.

With the mourning party gone and Phoebe yet to return from the post office, Randolph took the opportunity to deliver the clean shrouds and freshly washed work towels to Phoebe's storage cupboard. He enjoyed briefly stepping away from the desk and knew Mrs Dobbs would keep an ear out for the bell.

The walk-in, large storage cupboard in Phoebe's room was crammed as space became increasingly limited at *The Economic Undertaker*. The overflow of fabric from the mourning wear store next door was also stored there. Randolph liked Julius's idea, although he doubted his eldest grandson had time to act on it yet – but should the mourning wear dress store become a bridal store and move to another location, they could convert the dress wear store next door to additional viewing rooms, and even a room where a small funeral could be conducted in-house, which was becoming a requested item for small gatherings of under ten or so. He mused about the convenience of that and the changing industry.

While packing the shelves, he heard someone coming down Phoebe's stairs, a male by the sound of the tread, and then he heard Julius's voice. Was he looking for Phoebe? Randolph was just about to leave the storage area to advise that Phoebe was not present when he realised Julius was speaking with someone, but Randolph could not hear a response. A spirit. His grandson was talking with a spirit!

My brother, Reggie?

Julius can see him. He can see spirits, like Phoebe.

Randolph held his breath. To step out of the storage room now would embarrass Julius, who had refused to admit he shared Phoebe's visions from their mother's side of the family. But to stay hidden was dishonourable. He was frozen with indecision.

Panicked, a hundred thoughts ran through Randolph's mind... should he pretend to have not heard him? Should he walk out and admit his presence? What if he were discovered? He desperately wanted to talk with his brother, Reggie, whose life was cut short.

He listened as Julius's voice drifted to him, a one-sided conversation. He could not hear what the spirit had to contribute or see Reggie's handsome and dashing form as Julius greeted his uncle.

'Have you encountered Mrs Elizabeth Rowe yet, Uncle?' Julius asked.

'No, I have not seen her as yet. Phoebe is keen to speak with her, though,' Reggie answered for Julius's ears only.

'Mrs Rowe may not return, given she was buried today,' Julius mused.

'Perhaps. I wish Phoebe would not take it upon herself to try to grant everyone's last wishes.'

'As do I, Uncle. She feels something is not right about this young woman; I would prefer Phoebe did not deal with her at all.'

'I do have some interesting information. Would you like to relay it to Phoebe on my behalf, or should I wait to tell her directly?'

'Please tell me.'

'I have met Mrs Rowe's first husband. He claims to have died by foul play.'

'That worries me.'

Randolph heard Julius pause as someone came down the stairs – a lighter footstep. Phoebe was back, and Randolph heard her confirm the name of the spirit present, his beloved brother.

'Hello, Uncle Reggie! And here you are, Julius. Mrs Dobbs said Grandpa was down here,' she said.

Randolph stepped out of the storage area.

Julius's reaction was visceral as he spun around to look at his grandfather and then his uncle. 'You have succeeded, Uncle.' His voice was icy, and the distrust on his face was quickly replaced by hurt.

Reggie held up his hands but did not deny it.

'Julius, I assure you, it was not my intention to trap you,' Randolph said, seeing his grandson's seething anger. 'I was storing

Phoebe's towels when I heard you talking, and then it was too late to declare that I was here. But Reggie, he is here? How I would long to see him.'

Reggie's hand went to his heart, and he groaned softly.

'Well, there he is, Grandpa.' Julius pointed in the direction of Randolph's younger brother. 'I wish I could not see him.'

'Oh, Julius!' Phoebe cried.

'I'm sure Phoebe can translate between the two of you. Are you happy now, Uncle Reggie? Who else do you intend to expose me to?' Julius turned and stormed up the stairs, leaving Phoebe staring after him and Randolph staring toward his brother's spirit.

'That was very bad form, Uncle Reggie,' Phoebe said and then threw her hands up in the air. 'He is gone, Grandpa.'

'But why?' Randolph asked.

Phoebe shook her head. 'We don't know why he has not moved on. I have asked him several times if I could be of assistance, but he has not revealed his reasons. I can only assume it is something he must admit to you and cannot face you yet.'

'I can't imagine what he could say that would change my feelings for him. And now I have offended Julius.'

'Well, you haven't; Uncle Reggie has done that all by himself.'

'No. I could have declared I was here when I heard his footsteps on the stairs, but I didn't, and then it was too late.'

'He is very private about his visions.'

'But he told you,' Randolph said, pained by that fact given his closeness to Julius.

'Only recently, Grandpa, when Father Damien Horan caught him out and asked for help. He told Violet too, against his better judgment because she asked him directly.'

'It is a shame he could not trust me,' Randolph said softly.

'Oh no, Grandpa, it is not that. Not for a moment. He doesn't want this gift; he knows it is from our mother's side of the family, not your line. He has been denying it for so long, hoping it would leave him.'

Randolph sighed. 'I have not seen Julius so angry in a long time. He has done so much for this family; he deserves his privacy. I have tried not to push him to tell me, even though I suspected he had the gift and his grandmother is sure of it.'

'Is she?' Phoebe asked, surprised.

'She has always said so. I shall go and try to make amends.' Resigned, Randolph took to the stairs to seek his eldest grandson.

Chapter 12

DETECTIVE GILBERT PAYNE WAS assigned several jobs while his superior, Harland Stone, was at *The Economic Undertaker's* place of business. Gilbert would normally have attended with the senior detective, but given their workload and the number of people traipsing through the funeral home, they decided it was best if just one of them slipped in.

His last task, just accomplished, was to find the address of Donahue Marsh, the ex-fiancé of the lolly shop assistant, Miss Charlotte Glasson. He certainly had good taste in jewellery. Gilbert updated the board on their progress and was happily interrupted by the sergeant, who announced that Miss Lilly Lewis had arrived.

'Ah, Detective, thank goodness you are in and making progress,' she said, looking at the board. She looked around.

'Good morning, Miss Lewis. Detective Stone is at the viewing for Mrs Elizabeth Rowe at *The Economic Undertaker*; he will be here shortly,' Gilbert said. 'Are you well?' he asked with a smile.

'Never better, as my father would say, thank you, Detective. And you?'

'The same.'

The young people exchanged smiles, guessing their source of happiness – both enjoyed job success and happy romances.

'I had dinner with the *Vexed Vixens* last evening, and if you do not already know, I am pleased to report that your orchid is doing well,' Lilly said, and Gilbert laughed. 'Emily was so concerned she might kill it.'

Gilbert said, 'I should not have put her under that pressure, but I thought she might like the challenge. My mother says they are a difficult plant. Are you on a deadline?'

'Always,' Lilly said. 'Is there anything you can share that Detective Stone would approve of you doing so?'

'No need, I am here,' Harland said, striding into the office and removing his hat. 'Good afternoon to you, Miss Lewis.'

'Detective! What good timing. You have escaped my interrogation, Detective Payne,' she said in jest, and Gilbert mopped his brow in relief, amusing Lilly and Harland. 'So, do we have a murder case?' Lilly asked and read the detective's expression. 'Oh, I guess that is no.'

'We may have,' Harland said, running his hand through his hair and looking at the board, 'but at the moment, we are chasing our tails.'

'Can I help then?' Lilly asked. 'Could I ask the public to come forward with any observations or to identify something for you?'

'Thank you, and while that has worked in the past, I'm afraid it will not on this occasion,' Harland said. 'Do you know of the tin and its contents found on Mrs Rowe's body?'

'Yes, Phoebe told me at our *Vexed Vixens* dinner.'

'Good. Well, we have found the owner of the engagement ring, Miss Charlotte Glasson, but she does not know the victim, Mrs Rowe, or how it came to be in her possession with a roll of pound notes. We also have no way of proving Mrs Rowe wasn't on the ferry, and in the panic that ensued that day, unless someone saw her or conversed with her, I doubt anyone would remember Mrs Rowe.'

'Perhaps after we visit Miss Glasson's ex-fiancé, we may have a clearer direction,' Gilbert said, subtly not naming him in case Detective Stone did not wish to do so yet.

'Do you know who that man is?' Lilly asked.

'Yes, Donahue Marsh, and we shall call on him soon.' Harland requested Mr Marsh's name not be published and continued, 'Afterwards, we will decide whether to give up the case or if there are grounds to continue investigating.'

'I do hope there is,' Lilly sighed.

'If you wish, you can write of finding a tin with an engagement ring and a roll of pound notes within it on the body of a deceased woman, and that investigators hold grave suspicions she was not on board but was made to appear as such. Please do not identify Mrs Rowe as yet. We have only shared our suspicions with her husband, not her parents.'

'Is he a likely suspect?' Lilly asked.

'Having met him, I would say he's very unlikely,' Harland said with a small smile.

Lilly grimaced. 'It's a sad news day then, but that is a titillating start to a story. Thank you, Detective. I will report that, and in the interim, I shall tread water.' Lilly looked repentant. 'Goodness, that was an inappropriate saying given the watery case we are dealing with, but you know what I mean.'

'Indeed, Miss Lewis,' Gilbert said with a smile. 'Are you reporting on the inquest?'

'Yes, it starts tomorrow, and both Fergus and I will be at the court, as will Bennet on behalf of his client. I shall see if he has an angle for me from his insurance investigation. Hopefully, after the inquest, I might report on Mrs Elizabeth Rowe, or earlier if...' Lilly sought more diplomatic words than discovering Mrs Rowe was murdered.

'Anything washes up?' Gilbert offered, and Lilly laughed.

'Precisely so, Detective.'

'Very well then,' Harland said. 'Gilbert, let us speak with the ex-fiancé and see if he knows why the engagement ring that he purchased was in the pocket of a deceased woman who was not his ex-fiancée.'

'Yes, Sir, I have the address. Miss Lewis, we are going past Mr Martin's private investigator premises. If you are heading that way, would you like a lift with us?' Gilbert asked.

'Most definitely, thank you, Detective,' she said, pleased.

And the party of three departed.

Randolph found his grandson alone, drinking a cup of tea, most likely forced upon him by a caring Mrs Dobbs. He warily sat beside him.

'Julius—' and before he could discuss what happened, Mrs Dobbs re-entered the room with Ambrose.

'Tea and cake, gentlemen?' she asked, smiling at the gathered group.

'No, but thank you, Mrs Dobbs,' Randolph answered, wishing the pair would depart.

'Yes, please, Mrs Dobbs. I have a funeral this afternoon and need to keep up my strength,' Ambrose joked. Noticing that neither of his relatives reacted, Ambrose looked from his grandfather's frowning disposition to his brother's intense focus on his teacup.

'What is wrong with you two?' he asked, sitting opposite Julius and thanking Mrs Dobbs as his cup was filled.

'Nothing,' they both answered in unison, and Ambrose raised an eyebrow in Mrs Dobb's direction. She gave a small shrug.

'Well, it is very frosty here, and it is not the weather,' Ambrose persisted.

Phoebe entered, keen for a cup of tea and a slice of cake while the business was momentarily quiet. She looked from her grandfather to her brother, and her lips thinned nervously.

'We have Mrs Elizabeth Rowe's funeral soon,' she said, making light conversation.

'Yes,' Julius said.

'She has not reappeared to you, Phoebe?' Randolph asked.

'No, Grandpa, and I know Harland was here earlier but could not stay, so I don't know if there has been any progress on her case.'

Julius rose.

'Where are you going?' Phoebe asked.

'To check on the hearse and horses. We should go shortly, Ambrose,' he said and, thanking Mrs Dobbs, strode from the room.

'Do you know what is going on between Grandpa and Julius, Phoebe? Neither will tell me,' Ambrose said.

'There is nothing to tell,' Randolph said before Phoebe could speak. 'All is well.'

Ambrose continued to stare at Phoebe, and she reddened.

'All will be well,' she said, giving her grandfather a sympathetic look.

'You are not resigning, Grandpa?' Ambrose said, alarmed, then realised Julius would not be cranky about that.

'Of course not,' he answered. 'A small misunderstanding related to Julius's ability to see the spirits as his sister does. You know he doesn't like to talk about it and thus did not take it well.'

'I am sure he sees them,' Ambrose said. 'Fear not, I will endeavour to improve his mood at the funeral this afternoon.'

'An oxymoron if ever there was one,' Mrs Dobbs piped up, placing a slice of cake before Ambrose. 'Who has ever been cheered up at a funeral?'

'Oh, Mrs Dobbs, we could tell you some stories,' Ambrose said, grinning. Then he heard Julius bellow his name from the back door and rolled his eyes. 'I see this will be a greater challenge than I thought.'

Randolph rose. 'Ambrose, please give me ten minutes with your brother; finish your tea.'

Ambrose dropped back down into his seat. 'Happily.'

Randolph strode down the hallway; he would end this here and now, as he used to do when tension arose with his son, Montague

– Julius's father. Coming down the backstairs, Julius looked up expecting Ambrose, and his eyes narrowed.

The stable staff of Will, Claude and Charlie respectfully greeted the senior Astin, who reciprocated and excused himself as he pulled Julius aside.

'This will not do, Julius; let us talk for a moment.'

'What is there to say?' Julius asked, removing his hat and running his hand through his dark hair. 'You have asked me a thousand times, Grandpa, and now, thanks to your brother, you have your answer.'

'And yet I have never forced you to tell me or coerced you. Today, I was trapped. I could have declared I was there, but you started speaking before you arrived at the bottom of the staircase, and I knew no one else was in the room. What would you have me do? Had I not been discovered, I would have remained until you left and still not mentioned it until you chose to share your secret with me.'

Julius looked away, and Randolph did not speak as he watched his grandson—his favourite child—consider what was said.

Randolph lowered his voice. 'Forgive me, Julius. I assure you I can be trusted with this.'

Julius slumped and looked at his grandfather. 'I know that. I never doubted that. You have been my father, grandfather, mentor, and business partner; I trust you implicitly. But now you will tell Grandma, and as Ambrose is the only family member not to know,

I will have to tell him, and he will tell his girlfriend, Miss Kirby, and swear her to secrecy, and on it goes.' He looked away, fiddling with the hatband on his hat.

'Even if that eventuated, do we regard Phoebe as different? Has it changed our relationship with her? I suggest not, so why would it change how we see you? And should it get out, who would believe such rot? Funeral directors who talk to the dead! If that were the case, would we not make a fortune by finding out who the next deceased might be and be on hand to provide our services?'

Julius chuckled at the thought. 'That would be good for business.' He sobered and looked towards young Charlie, who was brushing down one of the horses, the action calming. 'Grandpa, this is not from your side of the family; I don't expect you to be tolerant of it.'

'What nonsense,' Randolph said as if Julius were a child. 'There are no sides of the family. You are my flesh and blood. We will not speak of this again, and I will not tell your grandmother. It is not my secret to share, but you may do so when you see fit.'

Julius gave a brief nod.

'I envy you, your skill,' Randolph said, and Julius stared at him, eyes wide.

'But why?'

'Imagine if Ambrose passed away and you could have one more moment with him.'

Julius shook his head. 'But it doesn't work like that. I have never seen Mum or Dad, and I am not sure I want to do so.'

'You have never encouraged the gift either,' Randolph pointed out. 'So perhaps in some small way, you control what you see.'

Julius thought about this. 'Perhaps,' he conceded.

'Am I forgiven?' Randolph asked with a small smile.

Julius could not help but smile in return. 'We have overcome this hurdle.'

'Good Lord, let us hope there are no more. Any other secrets you wish to share then?'

'No,' Julius huffed.

'Good. I love you, my boy,' Randolph said and, with relief ebbing through him, retreated before Julius could reply. All was well in the world again, except that his grandson was a portal to the spirit world. Working at a funeral home, that would have its challenges.

Chapter 13

Private Detective Bennet Martin had thrown himself into the work required for his new insurance client—to prove negligence by the captain of the *River Lady* ferry—much to the surprise of his clerk, Daniel Dutton.

'And here you were telling me no more insurance cases, and yet I have never seen you so dedicated,' Daniel said, looking over at his boss through his thin, steel-rimmed glasses.

'There's a reason for that, my good man, two reasons actually,' Bennet said, looking up from his desk as Daniel's aunt—Bennet's housekeeper—entered with tea and a platter of sandwiches.

'Ah, Mrs Clarke, your timing, as always, is perfect. I need to replenish after doing such a thorough report for tomorrow's inquest, even if I say so myself.'

'Well, I knew that, Mr Martin,' Mrs Clarke joked. 'I could see the steam coming from the engine room.'

Bennet laughed at her description and happily tucked into a sandwich while she poured tea.

'You were saying?' Daniel asked, accepting the same and thanking his aunt.

'Yes, two reasons. First, as you know, the inquest was scheduled for a week after the accident, which is tomorrow. So, I have not had time to dilly-dally. And second, the love of my life may wish to attend with me, and I do want to appear at my best if I'm called to the stand.'

'Wear your grey suit and red tie then,' Daniel said with a mouthful of sandwich.

'Do you think? Righto, I will. But I wasn't referring to my sartorial elegance, but rather my impressive digging up of facts.'

'Our finding of facts,' Daniel said.

'Yes, precisely.'

A carriage pulled up in front of Bennet's office, and looking through the glass windows, he recognised Lilly amongst the passengers. Leaping to his feet, he hurriedly wiped his mouth on a serviette, ran a hand through his hair, and rushed outside to Daniel's amusement.

'Miss Lewis, detectives!' Bennet added the latter, surprised at seeing them in the hansom cab.

'Hello, Bennet, we cannot stop as we are off to interview a suspect, hopefully,' Harland said.

'But we have a special delivery for you,' Gilbert said.

'A most charming one,' Bennet agreed, offering his hand to Lilly as she alighted. 'Thank you, gentlemen, for delivering Miss Lewis.'

'Yes, thank you, kindly detectives. I shall call again tomorrow, but I am at your disposal, of course.'

Bennet saw Harland's grimace and imagined he barely refrained from rolling his eyes, but Gilbert gave Lilly a reassuring nod and a smile. With a wave, they were gone, and Lilly turned to Bennet.

'Hello to you,' she said.

'Well, hello to you, Miss Lilly Lewis, best reporter from *The Courier*. And why do I have the pleasure?' Bennet asked, leading her inside as she laughed at the title he afforded her.

When her eyes adjusted to the light, she saw Daniel Dutton standing.

'Mr Dutton, good afternoon to you. Oh, please sit; do not let me interrupt your lunch.'

'Hello Miss Lewis, you are just in time for a sandwich and cup of tea; there are plenty,' Daniel said, clearing the visitors' table and hurrying out to get another plate and cup for Miss Lewis.

'I won't say no if you have enough. I have been going all morning,' Lilly said as Bennet grabbed his cup and plate and directed her to sit, joining her at the table. 'It is hard work writing articles about this case when there are so many loose ends.'

'Most frustrating for you, but I know you love the unfurling of a good story,' Bennet said.

'I do,' she smiled. 'And what of you?'

'I have just finished my summary for the insurance agency and have been asked to attend the inquest, should I be required.'

Daniel rejoined them with Mrs Clarke, and Lilly greeted her and thanked her for the cup, saucer, and plate. 'Forgive the intrusion, Mrs Clarke.'

'Not at all, Miss Lewis. It is lovely to have a civilising presence in the office,' Mrs Clarke said with a wink and departed with the good-humoured howls of false offence behind her.

'I am struggling, Bennet, to write something today unless Fergus has come up with a new angle. Have you anything of interest you can share?' she asked and selected an egg sandwich. After a bite, Lilly stopped. 'Ooh, delicious. Cream and seasoning!'

'Aunty makes a good sandwich,' Daniel agreed.

'Lilly dear,' Bennet started, 'I cannot share any of my inquest findings with you, but you can report on them as soon as they are delivered at the inquest. Would you care to attend with me tomorrow then? I have been allocated two seats, and Daniel won't want to come.'

'Won't I?' Daniel said, surprised, and then hurriedly added, 'No, of course not, how dull.'

'He will be having a day off, as will Mrs Clarke, on full pay, of course,' Bennet said to appease him.

'Will I? Well, that is exciting,' Daniel buoyed, and Lilly laughed. 'How kind, thank you, Mr Dutton.'

Bennet sulked. 'All he has done is give up a seat; I must do all the hard work.'

'Poor you,' Lilly said. 'My editor wants Fergus and me to cover it, but to have a seat in the middle of the action is wonderful. I shall go tell him now and file what I have from the detectives before my deadline. Thank you both.'

'You are leaving? So soon?' Bennet said, disappointed.

'I must. It was a visit in the hope that you might have a story, but time is of the essence.'

To her delight, Mrs Clarke appeared with a small linen towel and wrapped several sandwiches for Lilly.

'I shall hail a hansom and accompany you. Please put more sandwiches in that bundle, Mrs Clarke. Miss Lewis and I shall have a picnic on the way. Daniel, I have finished this report. If you make those few changes, I will return promptly.'

'Yes, Sir,' Daniel snapped with a grin. 'Could you get the mail on the way back?'

Bennet sighed. 'The cheek. But if it will save you going out and another hansom fare, I will play administrator.'

He departed with a delighted Lilly, who effused about securing a ride with lunch included. The day was looking up.

Detective Harland Stone was surprised to find Donahue Marsh in residence when he and Gilbert arrived at the boarding house in Fortitude Valley. The man in question was tall and cocky, muscly of build, with dark hair and a square jaw. Harland imagined him winning over the petite red-haired confectionary sales assistant, Miss Charlotte Glasson.

'It's fine, thank you, Ma'am,' Donahue said to his landlady, who was pegging sheets on the clothesline at the side of the house and came around the corner to see who was knocking. 'The men are here to see me.' She eyed the two detectives suspiciously, but given their good-quality suits, she accepted his word and resumed her work.

'Come on in,' Donahue said and led them to the first room near the entranceway. Three bedsit flats were on each side of the hallway, and a small sign indicated that the landlady's quarters were on the floor above.

He closed the door behind them, adding, 'It's not much, but it's comfortable, and my meals and washing are included in the board.'

'Perfect for a bachelor, Sir,' Gilbert said, fishing to see if Donahue Marsh was still single.

'Exactly. I was engaged, but... well, have a seat.'

The three sat around a small wooden kitchen table, and Donahue offered tea or water. Both were declined, given the state of the crockery that neither detective could fail to notice.

'We didn't expect to find you at home, Mr Marsh. Do you not work?' Harland asked.

'I sure do. I'm a labourer for hire. I just finished a job two days ago and start another tomorrow. I work for myself,' he said proudly.

'Your own master,' Gilbert said.

'Exactly. Although every job has a foreman, and he thinks he is the top dog, so I've just got more bosses,' he sighed.

'Have you always worked independently, Mr Marsh?' Harland asked.

'No. When I started work, I toed the line for years for slave drivers, and then I thought I'd go out on my own, go where labour was needed, and ask my price. So, what's this about?'

'Your fiancée's diamond ring,' Harland said, and Donahue looked skyward and shook his head.

'She's been bleating on about that for months. I said she should give it back, and she refused, blaming me because she said I called it off. I didn't, but she did catch me kissing another dame... just one of those things. Anyway, then the bloody thing gets stolen, and she blames me. I ain't got it, but you can look around if you don't believe me,' he said, finally drawing a breath.

'We don't need to search, thank you, Sir,' Gilbert said, 'but we have a few questions.'

'Do you know anyone with the initials E.R.?' Harland asked.

He looked at the ceiling and thought before saying, 'Edward, Edgar, Elwood, Eddie, Everett, no, I can't say I do.'

Harland gave him a less-than-impressed look. 'We're very busy, Mr Marsh, and if you prefer to come to the station to answer questions, that would be more convenient for us.'

'No, no, carry on, detectives. But truly, I don't know an E.R. Should I?'

Harland ignored this. 'Do you smoke?'

'Yep. You'd be hard-pressed to find a labourer who didn't.'

'What brand of cigarette or tobacco do you smoke, please, Sir?' Gilbert asked.

Donahue Marsh pulled a crushed packet from his top pocket and threw it on the table. Gilbert noted they were Cameo and not Old Judge.

'What's this about then? Search the place if you like; I don't have the ring,' he said.

'We know, Mr Marsh, as we have found it,' Harland said.

'You found it? Where?' Donahue Marsh leaned forward, his face lit up like he had hit payday.

'Well, that is why we are here, Mr Marsh,' Harland continued calmly.

'Can I have it back? It's rightfully mine since I bought it for my bride, and she won't be it. You would think I had committed a mortal sin; it was a bloody kiss.'

Harland held up his hand to calm the man. 'The ring is now part of an investigation and will remain in our possession for now.'

'Why?' Donahue asked, throwing his hands up in a display of frustration.

'Because it was found on a deceased woman's body. A woman believed to have been in the ferry disaster. Do you know Elizabeth or Ernest Rowe?' Harland continued.

'Ah, that's the E.R. you were talking about. Can't say I do, sorry detectives, but there's something fishy about that ferry disaster.'

'Why do you say that, Mr Marsh?' Gilbert asked.

'If you give me the ring back, I'll tell you.'

'If you tell us, we won't arrest you for obstructing the police,' Harland countered.

'Well, that's hardly fair. Can't you lose it again, here, now, and no one will be the wiser?' He gave the detectives a grin that would charm many women and make him a larrikin amongst his mates; it did nothing more than frustrate Harland Stone.

'Mr Marsh, that's two crimes you have suggested we participate in. You do realise we are from the Roma Street Police Headquarters?'

Donahue chuckled. 'Yeah, keep your hair on. It was worth a try.'

Harland gave him a small smile. He knew the type – lads who always pushed their luck and won over the unsuspecting to get what they needed.

'Give us a break then, Mr Marsh, tell us why you think the ferry sinking was fishy?' Harland prompted him.

'I'll throw you a bone, detective, but you never heard it from me. Deal?'

'Deal!' Harland agreed.

'The captain of that ferry, Gordon Crouch, owes a bit of money to the wrong people and can't pay. All I'm saying is that its sinking might not have been an accident. Crouch might have done it to get the insurance money so he could pay off his debts, or someone came looking for him.'

Harland rose, and Gilbert followed. 'Thank you, Mr Marsh. That information is very useful and appreciated.'

'So where is the ring going?'

'Back to the station. As your ex-fiancée filed a report of it being stolen, it will likely be returned to her, but you can take it up with your legal person.'

'Legal person,' Donahue scoffed, 'who can afford one of those.' He got to his feet and saw the detectives out, saying, 'Remember, I didn't say anything to you about Gordon Crouch.'

'Agreed,' Harland assured him.

As the detectives strode to the corner to await an omnibus back to the city, Harland said, 'What did you make of Donahue Marsh, Gilbert?'

'I think he is a shifty character, Sir,' Gilbert said, and Harland smiled at his description. 'He comes across as your best mate, but I think he'd sell his mother for a pound or two.'

'My impression exactly. We already know he is a womaniser; hence Miss Glasson calling off their engagement. But given his tip-off, we need to make some enquiries about the captain. Perhaps this is a bigger murder investigation than we thought. Or, attempted murder, given the captain is still alive.'

'Something might come out at the inquest tomorrow about his debts,' Gilbert said.

'That's something Miss Lewis can help us with since she will no doubt be at the court. We should be able to interview the captain now if he is out of hospital. We will try to get an audience with him and learn more about his character.'

'Sir, just a thought...'

'Go ahead,' Harland encouraged him.

'I recall that Mrs Elizabeth Rowe's first husband made his money in the building industry. That's what her second husband, the widower Mr Ernest Rowe, said.'

'Yes,' Harland said, understanding where Gilbert was going with his train of thought.

'So, I wonder if Donahue Marsh was ever a labourer for the Rowe family and if he ever met Mrs Elizabeth Rowe even though he denies knowing the name.'

'An excellent thought, Gilbert. The second husband might not know, but let us try Elizabeth's parents and, failing that, her first husband's parents. Someone might recall Mr Marsh, or there may even be a book of jobs and hired employees. An excellent thought,' he said again, to Gilbert's great delight. 'Let's see what Donahue Marsh isn't telling us.'

Chapter 14

THE COURIER – *LATE afternoon edition*

RIVER LADY FERRY TRAGEDY
MAGISTERIAL INQUIRY BEGINS
SENSATIONAL ACCUSATION AGAINST CAPTAIN

An exclusive report by Lilly Lewis and Fergus Griffiths

An inquiry was commenced at the South Brisbane Police Court this morning into the sinking of the *River Lady* ferry and the circumstances surrounding the death of passengers onboard on Thursday afternoon, the 13th, while on their way over the

Brisbane River between North and South Brisbane. The inquiry was presided over by Mr. W. Younger, P.M., of South Brisbane.

The first witness called was James Wilson, a carpenter residing at Russell Street, South Brisbane, who boarded the *River Lady* ferry in company with his wife and possibly ninety passengers on board, but he could not say for certain. Mr Wilson thought he was the last person to get on the ferry, and he and Mrs Wilson remained on the boat's bridge, where the captain was at the wheel. The gangway was pulled in, and the boat started on her journey over the river, heading up the stream, where two boats were already anchored.

Mr Wilson said, 'When the ferry was about half the length of the other boat, Captain Gordon Crouch ordered the engines to stop.

'The *River Lady* ferry then dropped downstream and passed so close to the other boat's stern that I could have jumped on board,' Mr Wilson said. 'As soon as we passed the stern, the captain gave the order, "Full speed ahead," and as I stood beside him and saw our approach to the second boat, I asked him, "Do you want to drown all hands?" He made no reply to me, and within moments, we were swept toward the second boat.'

Mr Wilson said he heard the captain give the order, "Stop!" In the witness's opinion, there was no room for the *River Lady* ferry to get past. Instead, she came up on the chains of the other boat, which caused her to turn completely over.

'My wife and I went into the water together, and I wrapped my arms around her waist. She said to me, "I will stick to you, Jim; I know you cannot swim," and we went under the water together.'

Mr Wilson broke down when recounting how she slipped away from him in the rough water, and he kept himself afloat, clinging onto a piece of timber until a boat picked him up. He never saw his wife again.

The witness said he had known Captain Crouch for some years, off and on, and had seen him in charge of boats before the 13th instant. Based on the captain's behaviour and demeanour, he thought the captain was under the influence of drinking.

'He did not appear to be standing at the wheel as a man in charge of a boat should do,' Mr Wilson concluded.

Private investigator Mr Bennet Martin, hired by the ferry's insurance company, also testified that surviving passengers who had contact with the captain agreed with the witness, Mr Wilson, that Captain Gordon Crouch was drunk on duty.

Phoebe squeezed in between Ambrose and Will, her pink dress a startling contrast to their black suits as the men headed off in the hearse to collect a body from a private residence for an afternoon funeral. Phoebe was comfortable travelling in the sombre funeral vehicle and enjoyed being out in the afternoon light in the company of two of her favourite people.

'Tell Kate I am most jealous you should get to visit, and I must drive on,' Ambrose grumbled.

'No doubt she would rather see me,' Phoebe teased, and Will laughed beside her. Phoebe sobered, 'I have been worried about her.'

'She assured me she is fine. Kate is no stranger to photographing death scenes for the police, and she has done some death portraits,' Ambrose said.

'True. But to view people in the throes of death...' Phoebe's voice trailed off.

'Awful,' Will agreed and shuddered. 'I saw a man hit by a horse and cart once; he rolled underneath it. I heard later that he had died. It was so violent, and the image will always stay with me.'

'That is how our parents died,' Ambrose said, and Will inhaled sharply.

'I didn't know. I am sorry to speak of that,' he said, glancing at Phoebe. 'I wondered how you came to be raised by your grandparents.'

'Do not fret, Will; it was a long time ago now, and I can only think of them with love, not pain,' Phoebe said.

'As do I,' Ambrose agreed. 'How will you get back to the office, Phoebe?'

'I will take the omnibus. Grandpa wants me to check in at the post office, so you may beat me back. Any messages for Kate?'

'None that I want you repeating,' Ambrose said, nudging his sister. He pulled the trap to the edge of the road on Roma Street and glanced over at the second floor of the white building, hoping in vain that Kate might be at the window. She was not, but a young couple exited the building.

Will jumped down, offering his hand to Phoebe as she alighted.

'Thank you both. I hope the funeral goes smoothly.'

'My parents met at a funeral,' Will said, getting back into the seat beside Ambrose.

'See, good things do happen there,' Phoebe grinned, and with a wave, she carefully crossed the street to Kate's photographic studio. Phoebe nodded to the tailor on the ground floor as she neared. She went up the stairs and was pleased to find Kate alone.

'Phoebe! What perfect timing.' Kate wiped her hands on a cloth and pushed down the sleeves of her pale green dress. 'Two clients have just left—an engagement portrait—and I was cleaning up,' Kate exclaimed. 'I shall make us both a cup of tea. Do sit by the window. Is everything all right?'

'Very much so, but that is why I am here. Ambrose and Will dropped me off on their way to a funeral, and he was most cranky that he couldn't visit.'

Kate laughed as she prepared the tea. 'He is so petulant at times, like a spoilt child.'

'Grandma did spoil him. He can get anything past her. But how are you? I was worried you still might not be sleeping.'

Kate slumped slightly. 'It is kind of you to worry, and I am glad to have the opportunity to speak with you.' She brought the teapot to the table and, on a separate tray, the cups, saucers, and some shortbread biscuits. 'I am in turmoil.'

'Oh, Kate, I am so very sorry.'

'Not about the photographs. Even though that was very traumatic, my mind has settled somewhat over the past week.'

'So what ails you?' Phoebe accepted the small milk jug, adding a dash to her cup of tea.

Kate sighed, looking out the window in the direction she imagined her beau was travelling. 'It is Ambrose. I think we are not suited. If we are no longer together, will you remain my friend?'

Phoebe dropped the spoon and jumped at the clatter it made. 'Forgive me; you took me by surprise. Of course, Kate, and I hope you will remain my friend. We are *Vexed Vixens*! We knew each other long before your interest in Ambrose. May I ask what is prompting your decision?'

'I don't think he is ready for me, that is, for a serious relationship. He enjoys his time with Lucian and his friends, and I think he might be more interested in settling in a few years from now. But I am ready to find a husband, and I am sure the thought would frighten him away.' Her voice hitched, and she looked down at her teacup.

'May I ask you a personal question?'

Kate nodded.

'Do you love him as a wife would love a husband?'

'Oh, Phoebe, without a doubt. I love him. I would marry him in a heartbeat; we have such fun together. My heart skips a beat every time I see him. Our temperaments are very similar,' she smiled. 'My father said we are both silly creatures who will always be chasing adventure.'

Phoebe laughed. 'I can see that too.'

'But I don't want him feeling trapped or resenting me.'

'Kate, I will be in trouble for telling you this, so you must not let Ambrose know I told you. In fact, do pretend not to know at all,' Phoebe said, studying her friend.

'I promise. Do tell? What is it?'

'I think Ambrose might not be very adept at expressing his feelings, but he is definitely planning a future with you and soon. He has spoken with Julius about buying a house; Julius has given him a promotion with a higher wage, and Lucian has gone with him to look at several houses. I believe he intends to move out, have a home and be established very soon, and then he can provide for his wife.'

Kate's eyes grew larger as Phoebe spoke. 'Truly? I had no idea. He never speaks of the future.'

'Perhaps his childhood has something to do with that. No one knows better than Julius, Ambrose and me how quickly life can change. But I assure you, my dear friend, Ambrose is busily preparing for the next stage of his life, and hopefully yours.'

Kate clapped her hands together. 'Oh, Phoebe, I am so happy you came by. I was so morose after taking the ferry disaster photographs, followed by today's happy engagement picture. I kept thinking about how short life is and how I must move ahead with my life in matters of love and children, too. Oh, this is such happy news!'

'Perhaps you might subtly speak to him of the future,' Phoebe suggested. 'Perhaps Ambrose is trying to read your feelings.'

'I will then. I will find a way to do so.' Kate blinked back tears. 'You cannot imagine my relief.'

'Oh, Kate, I am sorry you were so upset. We must lean on each other more. Let's agree to do so,' Phoebe said, offering her hand, which Kate squeezed.

'Agreed. You will not mention our discussion?'

'Of course not,' Phoebe said. They spoke of other matters briefly, and then, having finished her tea, Phoebe rose. 'I'd best be off and thank you for the afternoon tea.' She moved to the counter and saw several photos of the ferry tragedy laid out. 'Oh, you have more.'

'Yes, these were taken from the bank, capturing people watching with the ferry in the distance,' Kate said. 'It was a beautiful sunset.'

Phoebe gasped. 'Kate!'

'What is it?' Kate rushed to her side. 'Do not look if they are too distressing.'

'No, look! It is Mrs Elizabeth Rowe standing on the bank with a man. You can clearly see her face.'

'This is the spirit you are trying to help?' Kate realised the significance of her photograph.

'Yes. She was alive and not on the ferry when it sank. That man must be her husband.'

'It is a shame we cannot see his face,' Kate said, reaching for a magnifying glass and studying the man. She handed it to Phoebe, who did the same.

'I believe I saw him at the funeral; he was tall and dark-haired, like this man in the photograph, and he was mourning so sincerely. Kate, we must show this to the detectives,' Phoebe said.

'Take it with you, Phoebe, and do what you must. What a visit it has been,' Kate said, hurriedly wrapping the photograph.

Phoebe laughed and kissed her goodbye. 'Indeed, romance and justice. A good day's work.'

Now, the challenge was to get this photo to Harland. Julius would not have time to go to the Roma Street Police Headquarters with their current workload. Although Phoebe was not keen on going there, especially since the detectives may not be present, she would have to brave the police corridors and the looks of men and deliver it herself.

Chapter 15

SITTING NEXT TO THE private investigator, Bennet Martin, was a far better location than those seats allocated to the press, Lilly thought as she caught Fergus's eye below in the press row. He indicated he was going to question one of the witnesses. She nodded and turned back, awaiting the next person to be called to the stand.

'Is everything all right?' Bennet asked, seeing her fidgeting.

'I believe so, but I shall leave shortly. We have plenty for tomorrow's piece, and I want to see if the detectives or Phoebe have unearthed anything new,' Lilly said in a hushed voice.

'Is that a funeral pun?' Bennet asked, and Lilly grinned.

'Yes, a tried and true one. May I say that you looked most handsome and very clever on the stand,' she said and nudged him.

'You may. Were you madly in love with me when you saw me there?' he teased her.

'Madly,' she agreed, and he delightedly squeezed her hand. 'Oh, who is this now?' she asked, easily distracted.

The court was back in session, and as the judge reappeared, everyone quietened down and returned to their seats.

'State your name and address, please?' a small, thin, nervous-looking man was asked once his hand was on the Bible. He vowed to tell the truth.

'Bert Rowbotham,' he said, clutching his hat and looking in need of a good feed as he rattled off his address.

'Mr Rowbotham,' the lawyer began, 'tell us what you claimed to have overhead at the hotel which you frequent.'

'I didn't just overhear it, Sir, and I had not yet had a drink, so I was sober and alert.'

'Carry on, please.'

'Well, I was asked if I was interested in some work and that a captain owed a lot of money and since he couldn't pay, he and his boat would be taught a lesson.'

'And that captain was?'

'Captain Gordon Crouch, who owns or did own the ferry boat, *River Lady*.'

There were gasps from the galleries, and when silence prevailed, Mr Bert Rowbotham continued. 'You see, the *River Lady* wasn't normally a ferry boat, but she was pressed into service because the flood took the bridge out, and many people needed to cross the river.'

'Yes, we have already established that, thank you, Mr Rowbotham. However, Sir, I cannot believe any man would avenge the captain when he had a boat full of passengers.'

'I can't say, Sir. I can only tell you what I know, and I was approached to sink that boat, but I don't do that kind of work. I only do honest work.'

'How much were you offered, Mr Rowbotham?'

'We didn't get to talking money because, like I said, I declined. But plenty of men there that night needed the money and might have stepped up to do the job.'

'Do you know of any who did?'

'No, Sir, I couldn't say.'

'I'm sure you can't,' the Judge agreed drily.

Mr Rowbotham was dismissed, and the Inspector of Shipping, Mr Dern, was called to the stand.

'Inspector, you arranged for a diver to view the *River Lady* near Hancock Bros. wharf. Is that correct?'

'It is, Sir. Our diver was able to identify that the wreck was undoubtedly the *River Lady*. I then sent a second diver to inspect the damage, and they reported that no bodies were on board.'

'Could you detail the state of the damage?'

'I can speak on that, Sir,' Inspector Dern said, enjoying his moment in the spotlight as attendees hung on his every word, especially Miss Lilly Lewis and the rest of the press gallery. 'My divers described the decks as being all torn up and smashed to pieces, as well as the sides. The wreck is lying with her bows facing the upstream and canted a little on her port side. The bulwarks were also broken in, the awning was gone, and there was no trace of the funnel. The boilers were missing and believed to have fallen out. There is a large hole on the port side, and the deck has been swept clean.'

'Thank you, Inspector, and in your expert opinion from the reports you received, could the *River Lady* have been deliberately damaged?'

'We saw no evidence of any damage inconsistent with the event described by witnesses and surviving passengers. I can also confirm that the vessel was in good working order before the accident, and I do not consider the *River Lady's* course dangerous for a capable captain.'

'What if the captain were incapable and under the influence of alcohol?' Bennet muttered.

'My thoughts exactly. I must go, Bennet,' Lilly whispered. 'I need to speak with the detectives and, if possible, get an interview with the captain.'

'My, that is ambitious. He has not appeared at the inquest as yet,' Bennet said.

'No, but I overheard one of the solicitors claiming he had been discharged from the hospital and was home. I can only try. I bet the detectives will be doing the same.'

'If anyone will get an interview, it will be you, Lilly,' Bennet said loyally. 'What if I get called up again, and you miss seeing me?'

'Then do not look too attractive, please,' she teased. 'I do not want ladies trying to ensnare you.'

'Impossible,' he declared. 'Hurry then, or you will implode,' he joked. Lilly sidled past him with a quick smile and slipped out to seek the detectives.

Violet could not help but smile every time she caught the eye of her young seamstress, Miss Mary Pollard, who had been beaming on and off throughout the day.

'So, are you happy with the change in our business, Mary, even if it does mean changing premises?' Nellie teased.

'It is hard to tell; I don't think she is,' Violet agreed, joining in the teasing, and Mary laughed.

'I cannot believe it, Mrs Astin... Violet. I am sure I will never get used to that,' she said with a frown. 'To think we will be making bridal wear. It is very exciting. And to think I helped inspire that with your wedding dress. I cannot believe I have had these opportunities; I am so blessed.' She stopped and drew a breath as the ladies chuckled.

'Not to mention you have worked hard and are talented,' Violet said.

'And proven yourself,' Nellie added. 'You are a young slip of a thing; imagine what you will achieve in your lifetime.'

'Anyway, we are not moving too far – only a few shops down the road if Julius can lease the premises. The fact that it is already a haberdashery store will be helpful with its existing shelves and tables,' Violet said.

'And we will be close enough to still indulge in Mrs Dobbs's cooking,' Nellie said with a small smile.

'Oh! Something is going on,' Mary proclaimed, looking out the large window near her desk and narrating the events as they unfolded for her fellow seamstresses. 'The hearse has just pulled up out the front, and Mr Astin, that is, Mr Ambrose Astin, just hurried into the office like he was on fire. Will is holding the reins.'

'Goodness, I can't imagine, and through the front door of all things,' Nellie said.

'I hope they have not buried the wrong body,' Violet said.

Mary gasped, her eyes wide with shock, until she realised Violet was teasing. 'Has that ever happened?'

'I could not say, but I'm sure it has never happened to the men of *The Economic Undertaker*. Or at least I hope not,' Violet said with a grimace.

'Oh, no, another hearse has stopped behind them, and your Mr Astin has also jumped off and run into the store. He never hurries through the front door,' Mary said. 'Claude is waiting in the carriage.'

'I would love to know what is going on, but it's best we stay out of the way,' Violet said. 'Mary, keep us informed.'

'I will Miss, uh, Mrs,' she shook her head, 'Violet.'

The back door burst open, and Ambrose hurried in. 'Forgive the intrusion, ladies; I need the hat for Miss Ida Nielsen.'

Violet leapt to her feet. 'It is repaired and ready,' she said, handing over the small black hat with yellow and black feathers. 'Is it too late to put it on her?'

'No, I will pry open the coffin now and do so. Thank you,' he said, rushing out the back door only to be replaced by Julius rushing in.

'So sorry, ladies,' he said, glancing around in fear of distressing customers.

'No one is here. Heavens, what is the matter, Julius?' Violet asked, still standing from attending Ambrose.

'The widowed bride insists on wearing her wedding dress to the funeral, and the deceased's parents refuse to release the body from the house where we were to collect it if she does not change into mourning wear.' He drew a breath.

'Good Lord, on such a day,' Nellie said, shocked.

'My sentiments exactly, Mrs Shaw,' Julius said. 'Have you a black cape I could offer as a compromise? They were open to it, and the widow can drape it around her so everyone is satisfied.'

'I have just the thing, Miss..., Violet,' Mary said, leaping to her feet and rummaging in the cupboard behind her. 'It was a design I was making in my spare time,' she said, reddening and pulling out a cape with a hood in black.

'Oh, look! Most fashionable indeed,' Nellie exclaimed.

'Perfect, Mary, we will compensate you,' Violet assured her, rushing the garment to Julius.

'You are a lifesaver, Miss Pollard,' Julius said, accepting it from his wife with a quick touch of her hand and thanking them all. He then departed just as quickly.

'What will become of us all?' Nellie said with a shake of her head.

'They are off again,' Mary reported, her face still flushed from Julius's compliment. 'The two hearses have left in different directions.'

'Goodness, what will they do in the future if such a thing arises and we are making bridal wear?' Violet said.

'Perhaps we should make both,' Mary said.

'Or add christening clothes as well and call ourselves "Hatch, Match and Dispatch", what do you think?' Nellie joked, and the ladies laughed, but Violet did not dismiss the idea out of hand.

Chapter 16

THE ROMA STREET POLICE Headquarters was not far from Kate's photographic studio, so Phoebe hurried there on foot. She always felt uneasy entering the police station. No sooner had she started climbing up the stairs than several police officers offered assistance or stared blatantly at the pretty blonde in the pale pink dress. Would that change if they knew she was Detective Harland Stone's belle?

Phoebe slowed to wait for an elderly lady who was also entering the premises and offered to help with the several bags she was carrying. She hoped they could walk in together, then most men would assume they were related and might not be so quick to approach her.

'Oh, you are too kind, dear. Thank you,' the small, hunched lady said, handing over one of her string bags to Phoebe, who tucked the photograph under one arm to take it. The elderly woman hurriedly wrapped her stole around her to ward off the autumn breeze.

'My pleasure. I am Miss Phoebe Astin. It is brisk today.'

'I feel the cold so much more now that I'm heading into middle-aged, Miss Astin,' she said with a small smile as if denying she was already old, and Phoebe laughed at her teasing.

As they approached the entrance, a departing police officer held the door for the two ladies and doffed his cap.

'Lovely to see you, Mrs Turner,' the young man said, and she greeted him by his rank and name.

The pair entered, and as they walked down the hallway, everyone passing greeted Mrs Turner, who seemed to know them all.

'Goodness, you are popular, Mrs Turner,' Phoebe said. 'Are you a regular visitor then?'

'No. I'm a hardened criminal,' she answered, then winked.

'Mrs Turner! You have a wicked sense of humour,' Phoebe laughed and placed the bag on the counter as requested.

'Oh, Mrs Turner, you spoil us, please don't stop,' John, the desk sergeant, said, and Mrs Turner laughed with pleasure. 'And you have Miss Astin in your thrall. Here to see the detectives? I am afraid they are out.'

'I feared as much. May I please leave a message on Detective Stone's desk, Sergeant?'

'Of course. This way, Miss Astin.'

The ladies farewelled each other, and the sergeant left Mrs Turner surrounded by other police officers who helped her unpack her bags.

'How is it you all know Mrs Turner?' Phoebe asked as she walked down the hallway with the tall, middle-aged sergeant by her side.

'The lovely old dear is a police widow, and since her husband died five years ago, once a week, she will bring in home-baked cakes and biscuits for our morning tea, enough to last a few days. We all love her.'

'How lovely for you both. I won't keep you a minute, Sergeant,' Phoebe said and hurriedly entered the office, put the wrapped photograph on Harland's desk and quickly left a note advising it was from her.

'No hurry, Miss,' he said, waiting before walking Phoebe back. Seeing Mrs Turner had gone, she hurriedly departed as well. Mrs Turner had not stayed around for the glory, but by the looks of the police officers tucking into her treats, she had made an impression.

Phoebe hoped her photograph would have the same effect on Harland. But that is not what dominated her thoughts on the way home; she wondered if, one day, she might be a police widow like Mrs Turner.

Detective Harland Stone did not know whether to be annoyed or relieved to see Miss Lilly Lewis arriving as they knocked on the door of Captain Gordon Crouch's small cottage. He may allow them to enter with a lady present or reject them all out of hand.

'I had no idea you would be here,' she said, hurrying up the path and greeting both detectives. 'I was hoping to get an interview with the captain; I've just come from the inquest,' she said, panting slightly. Lilly stopped, brushed back her hair with one hand and hurriedly looked at her attire to ensure she was respectable.

'Was anything said about the captain at the inquest, Miss Lewis?' Gilbert asked as Harland stood poised to knock.

'Yes, his financial situation was discussed,' Lilly updated them. 'But the court was not convinced that retribution was made on him and his passengers, and the inspector thought the damage was consistent with a boat collision as a result of mismanagement by the captain.'

'What were Bennet's findings for the insurance company? Is that not his client?' Harland asked.

'That is correct, Detective. He also believed the captain's skills were to blame and, possibly, his state of intoxication. May I come with you and seek an interview?'

'I think that is a question for the captain, but you may enter with us,' Harland said and knocked. The three waited, and soon, footsteps could be heard approaching the door.

It opened a few inches, and the man who peered out looked like he had been to war – bedraggled, tired and wretched.

'I knew you would come,' he said after the detectives made the introduction. 'And you are not the first to come from the newspaper,' he said to Lilly, 'but you might as well enter.'

The smell of alcohol was evident on his breath, and the room was in a state of dishevelment, but he waved the three towards vacant lounge chairs and sunk into one with a knitted blanket thrown over the back, groaning as he did so.

Harland began, 'Captain Crouch, you have a heavy load to carry.'

'More than I can bear,' he agreed. 'All those people...'

'Will you appear at the inquest?' Gilbert asked, and the captain nodded.

'I have been summonsed and will say my piece.'

'Sir, we have been reliably informed that you are in significant debt, and your boat might have been sabotaged, given you could not repay your debt,' Harland said.

The captain visibly brightened momentarily as if there may have been a reason for the accident, and the deaths were not at or by his hand.

'We do not believe that,' Harland finished, and the captain's shoulders slumped. 'Please, Captain Crouch, tell us in your words, as you will tell the inquest, what happened that day.'

'May I tell your story to the people of Brisbane as you relay it to the detectives? It will be a fair report and may help people understand the turmoil on the river at the time,' Lilly said quietly, and Harland saw how her gentle charm might persuade him to allow it. The captain gave a brief nod, and Harland thought Lilly Lewis was most restrained in not looking excited but instead adopting an empathetic look. She was very good at what she did, he concluded.

As the captain cleared his throat, it was obvious from the narrowing of his eyes that he was thinking, and Detective Gilbert Payne leant forward.

'Sir, this is not the time for denial or justification. So much is lost, and to honour those souls in your hands that afternoon, please tell us the truth.'

The captain closed his mouth, blinked away tears and nodded. He began.

'I started on my last trip with the *River Lady* a little before 5 o'clock when I reckon we had about seventy passengers on board. The steamer was barely half-loaded, being licensed to carry 120 passengers.' He stopped, gathered his thoughts and continued. 'After leaving the Queen's Wharf, I had to steer between two boats to get to the other side. The river was crowded with vessels, and the water was flowing and full of debris.

'I steered towards the stern of one of the boats and went so close to her that the *River Lady* touched it slightly. Everyone on board remarked that it was a close shave,' he shuddered, took a sip from a cup that held a substance stronger than water and admitted, 'It gave me quite a start.'

'I imagine so, Sir, but still, you went forward,' Harland said, and the captain nodded, continuing.

'Just as we got to this point, one of those whirls that come in flood times caught the bones of the *River Lady* and threw her violently towards the other boat, the *Lucille*, that I had to steer past.

'As soon as I realised we were going to collide with it, I ordered the engines to go astern, thinking to get clear of her, but we drifted toward the boat, striking it, and the *River Lady* started going up the chains of the *Lucille*. One fellow near me called, "Grip onto something", as she startled to tilt, but I replied, "I am going down with her".

'Almost immediately afterwards, she sank, and I went down. I could feel the bridge breaking under my feet. Then, as the vessel turned over, I was thrown against the *Lucille's* anchor chain and sunk again. When I next came up, the *River Lady* was below the water level, and I was astern of the *Lucille.* Close by, I could see two women struggling in the water. I don't know who they were, but I looked around and saw a lifebuoy close to me. I seized it and got the two women to hold on to it. The three of us, supported in this way, drifted down the stream towards the Dry Dock.' He shook his head, then sighed. The only sound in the room was the scratching of Lilly's pencil on her pad as the detectives listened attentively.

'The lifebuoy was not quite sufficient to support the three of us, and I wanted to let go and leave them to cling to it, but by this time, one of the women was half-senseless, and I had to support her weight. We rose and sank, and I had to keep kicking; I had little strength left before we were picked up.

'When I was assisted onto the dock, I saw my clothes were torn from the woman clutching me, so I went home to get changed. It was all over when I came down to the wharf again.'

The captain stopped, his story told, but Harland asked, 'What do you attribute to causing the accident, Sir?'

Captain Crouch straightened and appeared most indignant to be asked such an obvious question. 'The accident most certainly is due to those boats being there. They were right on the track of the ferry boats, and if I had gone astern of these steamers instead of between them, I would have had everyone grumbling and asking, "Why are you not taking us the short way?" The eddy of the flood swung us round against the wind and caused the accident.'

Lilly asked the captain, 'Had you been drinking, Sir?'

'Most definitely not.'

'Best prepare yourself, Captain,' Harland said, rising to depart. 'Some survivors would beg to differ.'

Chapter 17

JULIUS AND CLAUDE ARRIVED at *The Economic Undertaker* shortly after Ambrose and Will returned from their funeral duties. The day was nearly done, and the afternoon was cool and pleasant. Julius privately gave thanks that the ferry tragedy had happened in autumn and not summer, but of course, it would have been preferable had it not happened at all. He never liked the profits to come from tragedy; unavoidable in the funeral industry. The men headed inside after handing over the reins and thanking Charlie and the young workers hired to assist him, who would finish up today.

'That is the last of it, lads,' Randolph told them as they entered through the back door. 'The rush is over. We have a reprieve tomorrow morning and back to normal numbers from now on.'

'Praise the Lord,' Ambrose said, coming out of the kitchen with a piece of cake in his hand. 'I have had enough of the dead this week.'

'Thank you, Claude and Will, for stepping up,' Julius said as the young men went to change, leaving their suits to be cleaned. Claude was keen to return to the stable, where he felt most at home.

'My pleasure, Julius,' he said. Like Julius, he was a man of few words.

'Do grab a cup of tea and a piece of cake before you return to the stables, Will and Claude,' Randolph said, and the young men thanked him.

'It's apple tea cake,' Mrs Dobbs called out.

'And it's good,' Ambrose assured everyone present.

'It was good of you to leave us some then, Brother.' Julius slapped him on the back. 'It will be you and me working together again as of tomorrow.'

'I am very much looking forward to that,' Ambrose said, and Julius looked surprised when no joke or retort followed.

'As am I,' he agreed, slightly taken aback, and departed to wash, as was his routine. He was more thorough than Ambrose, who gave himself a brush down and shook out his jacket. Julius scrubbed his hands and face to wash off the cemetery dust and dirt for fear it would accumulate and he would find himself dead and buried.

After washing, he did not return to his family but headed downstairs to seek Phoebe, not knowing she was absent and on the way back from the Roma Street Police Headquarters. He found the room empty and, for just a moment, lowered himself onto her couch where he could rest without company. Julius sighed and closed his eyes, enjoying the reprieve after a frantic week. Tall, dark and handsome, no one was present to admire him, but he cut a striking figure in his dark suit in the basement of his most successful business. When he opened his eyes, Uncle Reggie stood nearby, watching him.

Julius jumped to his feet.

'Please, nephew, a moment of your time,' Reggie asked, his hands raised in a pacifying gesture.

'What more do you want of me, Uncle?' Julius said, displeased.

'I did not want to expose you as such, Julius; you must believe me. Lord knows I have waited and waited for you to reveal you had the gift.'

'I had no intention of doing so, and it is not a gift.'

'Nevertheless, these things have a way of revealing themselves despite our best intentions, and this is a significant part of your character, Julius, even if you choose to deny it.'

'What do you want, Uncle? The game is up. Grandpa knows now. Did you want me to reveal my news to Ambrose and Grandma, too? Will you be happy then?' he asked less than graciously, still fuelled with anger.

Reggie sighed and sat on the edge of Phoebe's desk. 'I do not want that. Might you sit and give me a few minutes of your time, Nephew? I know time is precious to the living.'

Julius's eyes narrowed, but he lowered himself back onto the couch and nodded at his uncle to begin.

'I cannot rest until you get a message to my brother.'

'To Grandpa? Phoebe could have done that for you a thousand times,' Julius scoffed.

'It is not a message for a young lady to relay, although I am sure she would have done so capably and graciously,' he said the latter with a dig at his nephew. 'It is a message that must be delivered man to man. I hoped you might think of yourself delivering it to Ambrose if the situation were reversed and treat it with the same respect.'

'Is Grandpa expecting to hear from you? Is it something that will hurt him?' Julius asked.

'Ah, your loyalty and love are admirable,' Reggie said, his hand going to his heart as he studied his great nephew. 'But rest assured, Julius, no one loves your grandpa as I do. We were the closest of brothers, and to this day, he does not understand why coldness settled between us or why I was so reckless in the end. I want him to know so I can be at peace.'

Julius could hear the emotion in his uncle's voice.

'And then, I hope once you deliver my message, you will see fit to forgive me,' Reggie added.

'Do you want Grandpa here while you relay this message so I can deliver it word for word?'

'I have thought about that, but no. I could not bear to see his reaction. Maybe a day or two later, when he has time to process my thoughts and feelings, he might have a message for me, but I trust you will sensitively handle this, Julius. That is why I waited for you. You are his favourite grandchild.'

Julius huffed. 'I doubt that.'

'You are. How could you not know that? He is closer to you and worries about you more than anyone else, as he used to do for your father, Montague.'

Julius leaned forward, rested an elbow on each knee, his hands clasped, and studied his handsome uncle. 'I will do it, Uncle Reggie, but that does not mean you are forgiven, or I condone your methods.'

Reggie beamed, 'That is a great relief. Let's not talk today; you are weary. Perhaps another time when I can get you alone. Thank you, Julius, thank you.' With that, Reggie disappeared, and Phoebe hurried down the stairs.

'Here you are, escaping the noise above!' she exclaimed. 'Grandpa and Mrs Dobbs wondered what became of you. Are you all right, Julius?'

'I'm very well and relieved we have buried the last of the flood victims, well, unless any more bodies are found,' he said. 'And how are you?'

'Good. I just delivered a photograph to the police station. You will not believe it,' Phoebe said excitedly, telling him of her find at Kate's photographic studio.

'Well then, your spirit was telling the truth. She was murdered. But why has she not tried to assist you more?'

'It is a mystery to me,' Phoebe agreed. 'Come, let us finish the day with tea and apple tea cake. Grandpa is guarding a piece for both of us, but Ambrose is circling.'

Julius laughed and followed his little sister up the stairs, relieved to be on good terms with Uncle Reggie again and intrigued by what this delicate message might be.

Detective Stone had not been in a good mood since leaving Captain Gordon Crouch's cottage.

'Despicable,' he muttered for the second time, shaking his head as the detective pair entered the premises of the Roma Street Police Headquarters, striding down the hall like men with a purpose. Harland was accustomed to the looks they got from fellow offices. At first, it was ridicule – the youngest detective with the sidekick he was saddled with. After successfully closing several high-profile and complex cases, they were now regarded with curiosity.

'The man has no shame,' Harland said as they entered their office. He placed his hat on the stand in the entranceway.

'Was it the part where he went home to change while the tragedy was happening around him, or his lack of culpability, Sir, that has you so astounded?' Gilbert asked.

'Both. I thought he would be bereft, but it appears he is only concerned for his own state of misery. I doubt he has spared a thought for the anguish he has caused.' Harland shrugged off his jacket, placing it over the back of the chair. 'From what Miss Lewis said, the inquest is likely to find the ferry sinking his responsibility and not an act of sabotage. I hope his punishment will allow him plenty of time to consider his culpability. Let's assume that outcome to focus on the other case at hand.'

He saw the wrapped document and note on the desk and recognised Phoebe's handwriting. Grabbing it, Harland read her note, opened the paper wrapping and exhaled at the image before him. 'Gilbert, come and see this.'

His protégé hurried over from his nearby desk as Harland placed the photograph of the blazing red sunset over the water on the table and explained, 'Miss Astin dropped this in. She found it among Miss Kirby's photographs this morning. Look if you will, who is upon the hill.'

Gilbert leant over and gasped. 'Is that not Mrs Elizabeth Rowe? Alive and well as the *River Lady* sinks behind her. Oh, that is dastardly. She was murdered, as Miss Astin said, and it was made to look as if she were a victim.'

'I imagine it happened not long after this photograph was taken; she did not go home that evening,' Harland said, subdued at the thought of this life they viewed finishing so abruptly. He had plans for his future, which now centred around Phoebe, and he could not imagine if that ended because Phoebe had taken the wrong ferry, omnibus, or train that day.

'How very sad. And how amazing the art of photography is, Sir,' Gilbert said practically. 'To think we can capture the last moments of someone's life forever. It almost seems unholy.'

'It does, Gilbert; I was thinking the very same. Imagine in history if all the famous paintings that depict events were replaced by photographs – the Napoleonic wars, the sinking of the Dunbar, the assassination of Lincoln,' Harland shook his head.

'The beheading of John the Baptist and the Crucifixion of Jesus Christ,' Gilbert added and shuddered. 'Too graphic. I can only imagine what photography will mean for the future.'

'Yes, sobering,' Harland said. 'Well, thanks to the ladies—Miss Astin and Miss Kirby—we now have a confirmed murder on our hands. I want to see the husband's reaction when we show him this.'

'Is that him with Mrs Rowe, do you think, Sir?' Gilbert squinted, then returned to his desk to get his magnifying glass, offering to his superior on his return. Harland gestured for Gilbert to go ahead. 'Hmm, it looks very much like him from the back, but I cannot be sure without seeing his face.'

'We will study his reaction then,' Harland said, accepting the magnifying glass and looking for himself. Straightening, he said, 'We shall call it a day, Gilbert. Tomorrow, first thing in the morning, we will call on the parents of Mrs Elizabeth Rowe's first husband and see if, by any chance, they have his employee records. Let's determine if there is a connection between Donahue Marsh and Elizabeth's first husband. If there is, then there is a chance he knew Mrs Rowe despite his denial. Then we will visit her second husband, Ernest, and show him this photograph and study his reaction.'

'Yes, Sir,' Gilbert muttered absent-mindedly as he looked at the blackboard in thought.

'What puzzles you, Gilbert?'

'Idle thoughts, Sir. We determined that the tobacco tin did not belong to Mr Ernest Rowe, who claimed he did not smoke but that his wife, Mrs Rowe, collected her father's tins for her sewing and coins. So, might someone have paid her for doing a deed if the tin was hers and in her possession?'

Harland thought about this, moving to sit on his desk and study the board. 'It is a good thought, Gilbert, and the initials E.R. could just as easily be Elizabeth, not Ernest Rowe. But she did not need money, as we have learnt, and the note makes little sense. Why did she still have it confirming the deed was done if she was paid? Surely she would have given that to the payee?'

'Yes, it is an annoying clue.' Gilbert shook his head. 'And why did she have Miss Charlotte Glasson's ruby engagement ring upon her? Perhaps she had intended to give the note and the money to someone she was meeting. But what of the deed?'

'And who was she meeting? If that man in the photograph is not her husband, was the tin meant for him and why did he not take it if that was the case?' Harland mused. 'We cannot rule out her husband. Mrs Rowe might have been delivering the tin on his behalf.'

'He did not mention her doing so, but he was in shock, and I doubt the thought would have occurred to him in his grief.'

Harland glanced at the large clock on the wall. 'I hope to walk Miss Astin home, so let's sleep on it, Gilbert. Something brilliant might occur to us overnight and give us a fresh perspective,' he said in jest.

'Very true, Sir. We will look at everything differently in the morning,' Gilbert agreed and started to pack up. 'As the philosopher Heraclitus said, "No man ever steps in the same river twice"—'

'— "for it's not the same river, and he's not the same man",' Harland finished, noticing the surprised look on his protégé's face.

'Very good, Sir,' Gilbert grinned. 'I thought I was the one who loved philosophy and poetry.'

'You are. But I had a teacher who loved to drum such quotes into our heads at school. He would be smiling now if he knew I remembered that,' Harland chuckled as the pair closed their office door for the evening and departed, going their separate ways.

Chapter 18

THE STRIKINGLY HANDSOME, TALL, dark-haired man and the beautiful woman accompanying him often drew looks as they took their weekly walk through the Botanic Gardens. Both smiled and greeted other young couples, the elderly and families, but Julius Astin's greetings were curt when it came to men smiling at his wife, Mrs Violet Astin. She looked fetching in a new pale blue dress with lace trimming, which he insisted she order, along with several other dresses, since observing her spartan wardrobe. While Violet might be an extremely capable dressmaker, she rarely spent the time or money producing her own clothing.

Julius looked back to glare at one man, and Violet, smiling, turned his attention back to herself.

'He is just being friendly.'

'Friendly!' Julius huffed. 'If he thinks I am too handsome to box his ears, he will be in for a rude shock.'

Violet laughed out loud as Julius pretended to be serious but could not help but smile at her reaction.

'You are ridiculous,' she teased her husband. 'I only have eyes for you, oh handsome one.'

Julius chuckled, and they continued their walk.

'I thought once we were married, you would wish to stop our weekly walk as you see me all the time now,' Violet said.

'But I don't always see you, and this is our time. Perhaps as we move into winter, we might trade it for a cosy night before the fire, but for now, I enjoy the break between work and home.'

'I love escaping into nature,' Violet said, breathing deeply. Everything around them was rich and green with a few tinges of autumn colours. Brisbane could not boast the autumn of the southern states, but there was a chill in the air and the promise of change.

They passed the lake and duck pond, where neither would ever forget the day Julius jumped in to save five-year-old Alfie, who had slipped in chasing adventure. Julius continued his planned proposal, all soggy and flustered, as Alfie encouraged Violet to say "yes".

'We should have invited Alfie to the wedding,' Violet laughed.

'I was just remembering him too,' Julius said. 'He would have caused havoc in Lady Palmer's gardens; I'd be fishing him out of the duck pond,' he joked with a shake of his head. Changing the subject, he asked, 'What do the ladies think about the change in business plans?'

'They are excited and cautious.'

'Why cautious?' he asked, frowning.

'Well, I don't think Mary is one for change and is nervous about our new location. Should you get the lease on the haberdashery store, I will have to seat her near the window so she can continue to see the comings and goings at *The Economic Undertaker* and report to us.'

'Well, that is manageable. I have secured it; Grandpa and I are signing it tomorrow morning.'

'Oh, congratulations!' Violet said, smiling up at him. 'Why did you not tell me such good news?'

'I intended to, of course. I forgot,' he admitted sheepishly.

'Do not worry. We were both very independent before our marriage; it may take us a while to think as two,' she said with understanding.

'What else are you all feeling cautious about?' Julius asked, his tone relaying concern.

'Nothing to worry about; we are all excited about the change. However, we have been so frantically busy these past weeks that we wondered if there was still a market for mourning wear and—I know this probably sounds silly as we are not business owners—but if there were a way to incorporate the mourning and the bridal wear, somehow.'

Julius frowned and looked out over the lake.

Violet added, 'It's silly, ignore me.' She gave a small laugh and waved her hand as if expecting Julius to dismiss the idea.

Julius indicated a seat protected from the breeze and perfectly placed in the afternoon sun. As always, he reached for his handkerchief and put it on Violet's side of the bench. The pair sat, admiring the view of the rose gardens before them.

'Don't be cranky; I did not mean to overstep,' Violet said, and Julius turned to face her.

'I am not at all cranky. Why would I be upset when you are trying to improve our business? Besides, I might manage the figures, but you, Mrs Shaw and Miss Pollard, are immersed in the day-to-day activities. I would be a fool to ignore your counsel.'

Violet smiled, delighted. 'Thank you, Julius. Not all men think as you do.'

'There are some stupid people around,' he agreed, making Violet laugh. 'You tapped into something I was thinking about as well, after this week of high demand. I know the mourning market is declining, and *Finney and Isles* department store has taken a chunk; while it might not sustain us long-term, there's still life in it, so to speak. I confess I have an idea I am considering.'

'I bet you do,' Violet said. 'We have been most industrious since we married.'

'You must inspire me,' he teased.

'Tell me then,' she prodded him, 'what have you been plotting, or is it a secret until you have refined it?'

'No, I will tell you so you can laugh and redirect me if you think my idea is fanciful. I was thinking about what mourning wear and wedding dresses have in common.'

Violet mused. 'I cannot imagine. They are such different cycles of life – different fabrics, colourings, and one spends considerably more on their bridal wear and undergarments than mourning wear.' She blushed at the thought of her lace undergarments made especially for their first night together.

Julius, ever the gentleman, said, 'And your designs and garments were most beautiful.'

'I thought you looked pleased by them,' she teased. 'So, did you come up with anything they had in common?'

'Yes. A veil.' He watched her for a reaction.

'A veil,' she whispered and gave a small nod.

Julius continued. 'What if we called the store "*Beyond the Veil*" and made wedding and mourning wear?'

Violet's eyes widened, and her mouth opened slightly as she stared at him.

'Now I am being ridiculous,' he said, looking away and sitting back, trying to make light of the situation to defuse his embarrassment. 'It was just a thought. I am glad I ran it past you, given your reaction.'

'Julius, that is brilliant, and why not? *Finney and Isles* sell both, why can't we?' she asked, and he turned to see if his wife was sincere. 'It truly is brilliant. What a clever play on words – "Beyond the Pale" and "Beyond the Veil", we could easily continue to make both.'

'You are serious? Do you really think that the name and producing the garments side by side might work?'

'Absolutely, and I am very serious. I would never joke with a businessman about his business,' she assured him. 'Given our proximity to *The Economic Undertaker*, would we continue to produce economic wear?'

'Yes, I believe that would continue to be our best market, but we can offer economical to high-priced garments depending on the fabric and workmanship involved. Do you not agree?'

'I do,' she said, and he could see her mind ticking over. 'I think the name is the cleverest, and it will give us plenty of variety. For example, if our business grows, beyond the veil might mean maternity wear after the wedding or light mourning wear for those moving into grey and mauve gowns.' Realising she was most excited and full of ideas, she flushed a little with embarrassment and gave a small shrug.

'I love that idea,' Julius said sincerely, admiring his wife.

'You know, the haberdashery building has two large display windows. If we model my wedding dress in one window and our most successful mourning dress in the other, both with beautiful veils of lace on display, I think it will be most tasteful.'

Julius smiled as he thought about the display. 'Then I shall leave that aspect to you.'

'How exciting,' Violet said. 'Can Nellie, Mary and I see inside the store once you sign the lease? If I tell them your idea, they will be excited and keen to help me plan.'

'Absolutely, tomorrow lunchtime then. I will sign the lease mid-morning, and Grandpa will witness it.' A breeze chilled the pair, and Julius rose to his feet, offering his hand to his wife and collecting his handkerchief from the chair. 'I have one concern.'

'What is it?'

'What if brides are superstitious and fear buying their dress where mourning wear is being made and sold?'

Violet nodded. 'Yes, I can imagine that. Hmm, let me ponder that.'

The pair began their walk back to the main road to hail a hansom home. Violet was lost in thought, and Julius smiled occasionally as he observed her, not saying a word for fear of interrupting her thought process.

'I have it!' she said.

'My, that was quick.'

'Well, I have a suggestion,' she said. 'As there are two large windows at that store, can we not have two doors opening inside to the business – one white for bridal and the other grey or black for mourning? Once inside, we could divide the room with greenery or a large display of flowers in the centre. It is an open room like we have now, so you could go left for bridal or right for mourning. Mary could work in the bridal store, and Nellie and I will work between both as needed.'

'Yes!' Julius said and smiled. 'Yes, that might work. Cousin Lucian could look at that for us. Thank you, Violet.'

'Whatever for?' she asked, snuggling closer to him as they departed through the park gates.

'For the inspiration and support,' he said.

'I hope you still feel that way when Nellie, Mary and I come back to you with all our ideas,' she joked, and Julius laughed.

'I am sure I will. I hope I can afford them and don't have to let one of you go. I'd hate to lose you,' he teased, and she playfully hit his arm.

'You are stuck with me now, for better or worse.'

'Just as I like it,' he said, and arriving at the street entrance, Julius hailed a hansom to take them home.

Chapter 19

DESPITE THE EARLY MORNING visit, the parents of the late Richard Tyson—first husband of the deceased Mrs Elizabeth Rowe—were well into their day and pleased to have the opportunity to talk about their beloved son. His portrait adorned their lounge room wall, and he looked remarkably like the pair: robust, intelligent and pleasant, which was surprising given most portraits portrayed the subject as austere. The Tyson home was large and well-appointed but did not boast extravagant furnishings. Harland believed them to be successful and sensible people, not unlike his own parents.

'Work has always been our family ethic, Detectives,' Walter Tyson said proudly after Harland mentioned they had come to discuss the family business.

Having served the detectives tea and sat beside her husband, his wife, Agnes, nodded in agreement. 'The Scottish philosopher Thomas Carlyle first spoke of the dignity of labour,' she said.

'Very true, my dear,' Walter said. 'It does not matter what your profession might be; labour is life, and God gives life.'

Harland feared they would not escape without a sermon, but Gilbert seemed to be very much in agreement and quite at home, adding his learnings to the discussion.

'Very true, Mr and Mrs Tyson. I try to live by the words of the apostle Paul: "There is joy when you work, and see the results of your efforts. There is dignity in labour." So very true.'

Agnes sighed happily. 'A young man quoting from the Thessalonians. Most heartening.'

'Most heartening,' Walter agreed with a smile. Sensing the senior detective's impatience, he addressed Harland. 'How might we help you today, Detective? A matter of business, you said?'

'Yes, thank you, Mr Tyson. It is a request you might find odd, but we understand your son, Richard, was wed to the late Mrs Elizabeth Rowe.'

'Yes, and both gone now, so young. God moves in a mysterious way,' Agnes said, her face falling with an expression relaying familiarity with grieving. 'It was a happy union. You see, we are family friends of her parents, and both families encouraged it. Richard was ten years older than Elizabeth, a good age to provide for her. She was bereft when he died. That is probably why she married again so soon.' The latter, she said with a trace of displeasure.

'And Richard was a very successful businessman; Elizabeth wanted for nothing,' Walter said.

'Could you tell us about his line of work, Mr Tyson?' Gilbert asked.

'Richard purchased business and domestic properties, restored and resold them,' Walter said. 'He was the type of man who was in boots and all – did the negotiation, the legal work and the hard labour, whatever was required of him.' Walter Tyson's pride was evident. 'He always gave a desperate seller a good price, too; he was not the type of man to take advantage of anyone.'

'That was Richard, through and through, a good man,' Agnes said with a smile. She returned her attention to Harland. 'I believe we glimpsed you at Elizabeth's viewing and both of you at the funeral.'

'Yes, I was present that day at *The Economic Undertaker,* and Detective Payne and I paid our respects at the funeral,' Harland confirmed but did not elaborate on his reasons for being in attendance.

'Did you know Elizabeth?' Walter asked.

'No, but we have been assigned to investigate her death,' Harland informed them, and before they could ask why, he said, 'May we ask how your son met his death?'

'At work,' Walter said, shaking his head. 'The floor collapsed in one of the buildings he was repairing. He was gone in moments, gone.' His voice trailed off.

Agnes Tyson's breath hitched. She closed her eyes and gathered herself. 'Forgive me,' she said, opening her eyes and drawing a deep breath, masking her pain.

'No, please forgive us, Mr and Mrs Tyson,' Harland said quietly. 'I know our questioning must be painful for you, but we believe that Elizabeth was murdered.'

Agnes made the sign of the cross, and Walter's gasp relayed their shock.

'That is why you were there at the viewing and funeral,' Walter said. 'I have heard that sometimes a murderer might still be amongst us, wearing a face that appears as normal as the rest of us.'

Harland nodded and waited until the elderly pair had gathered themselves.

'And you think Richard might have been murdered as well?' Walter asked suddenly, putting two and two together.

'No, we do not believe that, Mr Tyson,' Harland assured him. 'However, we would like to rule that out completely.'

'God preserve us,' Walter Tyson said as his wife clutched his arm. 'Then you must seek answers, Detective, please. If it were foul play, justice must be done for our boy.'

'We will, but do not be concerned yet, Mr and Mrs Tyson. We have nothing that indicates he was, but we would like to eliminate that as part of our investigation,' Gilbert calmed them.

'Thank you,' Agnes said to the younger detective.

'If you could cast your mind back,' Harland said, 'Mrs Elizabeth Rowe was found with a large wad of money on her person and an engagement ring that wasn't hers. We have found the gentleman owner, and now we need to establish if that man has a connection to Mrs Rowe, despite his claims that he does not know her.'

Gilbert continued. 'It is a long shot, but given he said he worked as a hired labourer, we wondered if he might have worked for your son's company and come in contact with Mrs Rowe when she was Mrs Tyson.'

'Walter did the books for Richard's business; he will know,' Agnes said, looking to her husband, and Harland brightened upon hearing that news.

'What was his name, Detective?' Walter asked, adopting a business mode.

'Donahue Marsh,' Harland said.

'Donahue Marsh!' He looked at his wife, Agnes, whose lips thinned, and she shook her head slightly as if in disbelief.

Walter straightened. 'He most certainly did work for Richard, detectives, and Richard was quick to let him go from his employ. That scoundrel!'

EXTRACT from The Courier *– Morning edition*
RIVER LADY CAPTAIN FOUND AT FAULT
CAPTAIN'S LICENCE CANCELLED
By reporter Lilly Lewis

The evidence taken at the late enquiry into the *River Lady* ferry disaster was considered at a meeting of the Marine Board late yesterday afternoon. The Board stated it was of the opinion that the master of the *River Lady*, Captain Gordon Crouch, displayed a lack of skill in navigating the vessel and that the steamer was lost through his default. His licence to take charge of steamers within the limits of any port was cancelled.

The two young ladies in the basement of *The Economic Undertaker* were as pretty as a picture in the morning light streaming through the window that was too high to see through unless you stood on the couch or were Julius, Ambrose, or Randolph. Mortician Phoebe Astin looked most elegant in a long silver-grey skirt with a swirling print around the hem and a delicate, long-sleeve, pale matching blouse. Beside her, reporter Lilly Lewis looked very fashionable in a fitted mint green dress with white cuffs and a collar.

Phoebe placed the newspaper on her desk and gave Lilly a sympathetic look.

'So well written, Lilly, as always, and while I feel sorry for the Captain, I reserve my deepest sympathy for the victims.'

'I feel sorry for me,' Lilly joked. 'That's the end of that story, and the detectives have nothing exciting to share. I am going to have to seek another story shortly and keep Mrs Elizabeth Rowe's murder on the boil if she was, in fact, murdered.'

Phoebe's eyes widened. 'You have not caught up with the detectives this morning, then?'

'No. But I shall attempt to. Why do you ask?'

'They had an exciting breakthrough, courtesy of our Kate.' Phoebe told of the photograph showing Mrs Elizabeth Rowe on the slope of the riverbank as the *River Lady* sank behind her.

'Oh, Phoebe, that is wonderful,' Lilly clapped her hands in delight. 'I shall go and get Fergus, and we shall find the detectives with haste. I wonder if Kate might have another copy of the photograph. This is very exciting,' Lilly said, now full of energy.

Phoebe turned. 'Good morning.' A large lady with abundant freckles, red hair and an equally loud dress in a geometric pattern of green and gold appeared. A straw hat with a green band was perched on her head.

Lilly snapped to look in the same direction, but no one was there.

'Yes, I am the mortician, Phoebe Astin, and this is my friend, Miss Lilly Lewis. Lilly is a reporter. May we help you?' Phoebe asked.

'Who is there? Who are you speaking with?' Lilly asked, fascinated, following Phoebe's eyes in the direction they moved. Phoebe listened and nodded, her expression relaying her surprise.

She turned to Lilly. 'A lady of our age is with me, named Miss Frannie Firth. She is, or rather, Miss Firth was, a friend of Mrs Elizabeth Rowe when she was alive.'

'But now she and Mrs Rowe are both dead, most unfortunate,' Lilly said. 'Has she seen Mrs Rowe?'

'I shall ask,' Phoebe said and then addressed the spirit, 'Miss Firth, Elizabeth told me she was murdered but has not returned since. Might you have seen her? Could you tell her I must speak with her, please?'

The lady responded. 'Call me Frannie, and I have indeed seen Elizabeth.' As Frannie spoke, Phoebe stopped to relay the conversation to Lilly in snatches.

'Frannie said that Elizabeth does not want to return for fear we will think the worst of her.'

'But why would we?' Lilly asked.

'Frannie said because she did not love her first husband, who was ten years older, and she was in love with Ernest Rowe and wanted to marry him.'

'Well, she got her wish,' Lilly said, looking at the light streaming through the window but not seeing Frannie Firth in it as Phoebe did.

'Yes, but Frannie said all is not as it seems. Elizabeth was very happy when her first husband, Richard Tyson, died, and her mourning was not genuine.'

'She would not be the first lady to feel that way,' Lilly said with a shrug, impatient to get going.

'But Frannie says... oh goodness,' Phoebe exclaimed.

'What? What does Frannie say?' Lilly asked, tugging on her friend's arm.

'Frannie says Elizabeth Rowe played a part in her first husband's death, and now she will pay for it in the hereafter. Frannie says Richard Tyson did not die by accident, and we must do something about it.'

'Does she know how he died or who had a hand in it?' Lilly asked.

Phoebe listened, then shook her head. 'No. It was an accident at a worksite, Frannie believes. But she said Elizabeth was most knowledgeable about it, and we should start the investigation there.'

'But how? Elizabeth is dead?' Lilly frowned. 'I supposed we could see if the coroner did an autopsy or still has the first husband's file.'

'Richard Tyson,' Phoebe said, providing his name again. 'Perhaps there is a site manager who might know something. Is there anything else you can think of to help us, Frannie?'

'Deed done,' Phoebe repeated, and with that, she turned to Lilly. 'Frannie is gone but wishes us well. She said Elizabeth boasted the deed would be done concerning her first husband, and Frannie hoped that might help. That was the wording on the note in the tin retrieved from Elizabeth's body. Remember?'

'I do, but there were several years between her first husband's death and the tin being found recently. This is getting sinister. How exciting!' Lilly grinned. 'I shall find the detectives immediately. May I relay this discussion, Phoebe?'

'Of course, Lilly, with haste,' she said, hugging her friend goodbye. After Lilly's departure, she gathered her powdered goods and headed to the body in the corner, determined to make Mrs Evans look her best for the last time her family would see her earthly form.

Chapter 20

FOR THE FIRST TIME since the dreadful sinking tragedy two weeks past, *The Economic Undertaker* did not have an afternoon funeral scheduled. The senior Astin, Randolph, welcomed the break to catch up with his paperwork and order new stock as needed. There were no bodies to collect, and downstairs, Phoebe finished her preparation on a lady who would be buried after her viewing in the morning. Randolph found his serenity interrupted by his grandson, Ambrose, who appeared to be at leisure.

'Where is Julius?' Ambrose asked, having finished raiding Mrs Dobbs's kitchen and pestering Phoebe.

'He is a few doors down showing the ladies the haberdashery store for which we just signed a lease,' Randolph announced triumphantly.

'Excellent. Which ladies?' Ambrose asked, his interest piqued.

'Mrs Shaw, Miss Pollard and Violet, that is, Mrs Astin,' Randolph said with a smile. 'In a month or so, the mourning wear store will be converted to additional viewing rooms for us once Lucian opens up the adjoining wall.'

'That will be handy. Where's Mrs Dobbs?'

'She is next door minding the mourning wear store for a moment. She is handy with a tape measure and will take measurements if needed while the ladies are momentarily absent.'

'Well, that is all very boring. We have no more collections to do today?'

Randolph chuckled. 'No, you are up to date. Claude, Will and Charlie are doing inventory and cleaning the stables, hearses and horses. Would you like to help them?'

'No, I don't think so,' Ambrose said, making his grandfather laugh again.

'You could visit Lucian and enquire how he is progressing with the dumb waiter to bring bodies from Phoebe's room directly to the viewing room, although we will now need a door from that viewing room to the new ones,' Randolph mused, realising more changes would need to be made.

'No, I'll see Lucian tonight. Can you not find a reason for me to visit Kate?' Ambrose asked.

Randolph smiled at his middle grandchild. 'Ah, let me think... no, I can't imagine one,' he said drily. 'But if you wish to shirk work,

I suggest you do so before Julius returns.' He mused, 'I do need to check if there is anything for us at the post office.'

'Done. I will do that for you and be off then,' Ambrose said, happy with a reason to depart.

'Don't forget to bring the mail on your return,' Randolph said in jest as Ambrose departed with a wave, and Randolph Astin found himself alone again, enjoying the quiet to continue his work.

Less than fifteen minutes later, Julius entered and removed his hat. 'I have left Violet and Miss Pollard in the store; Mrs Shaw will return shortly to release Mrs Dobbs from her duty. The ladies are designing their space and are quite excited about its potential. I would value your input too, Grandpa. Where is Ambrose?'

'Collecting the mail via the long way,' Randolph said with a smile, and Julius chuckled.

'He has earned it this week.' Julius sat on a chair in the reception area, ran a hand through his dark hair, and cleared his throat, a frown appearing on his countenance.

'Do you wish to tell me something?' Randolph asked, well familiar with his grandchildren's mannerisms.

'Yes,' Julius said. 'Are we alone?'

'Phoebe is downstairs, and the boys are in the stables. What is it, lad?' Randolph saw the look of mistrust cross Julius's face as he leaned forward to check that the rooms within his view were empty. It saddened Randolph to think that existed between them now.

'I do not want to shock or distress you...'

'I am of hearty stock,' Randolph assured him. 'Is it Reggie? Do you have a message for me from my brother?'

Julius grimaced, and his grandfather added, 'I know you do not want to play this role, lad.'

'I am all in now, regardless. And yes,' Julius sighed, 'Reggie wants me to relay a message to you – he insists it is delivered man to man but has not yet revealed it. He feels he cannot rest until you know this, whatever it might be, but I said I didn't want you hurt or to risk your health if you were shocked by his news.'

Randolph exhaled, studying his grandson, and gave a small nod. 'Thank you, Julius, but I always knew he remained for some reason, and I want him to rest. I assure you I am quite prepared to handle it. Is he here now?'

'No,' Julius said. 'He does not want to be present at the time of the telling. He wants me to relay it and allow you time to think about his words. I can't imagine what it might be that would put a wedge between you both.'

'Nor I. He lost his way for a while, and I begged him to come home and resume his life with the family, but he was determined to play the adventurer. Perhaps it is related to that.'

'Perhaps. He gave me no indication.'

'Please speak with him soon, Julius; I wish to know.'

Julius rose. 'I shall seek him, Grandpa.'

'Will you tell me even if you don't like the message?'

'Of course, if that is what you wish.'

'Thank you, Julius.'

The door swung open; a middle-aged couple entered, and both men went into business mode again. Mrs Dobbs appeared behind them just in time to offer the bereaved couple a cup of tea.

Kate Kirby looked up as the bell rang over the door of her photographic studio. She was about to close the shop to take a late lunch, but Ambrose Astin entered, smiling and bearing flowers.

'I am here for my portrait,' he said in jest, and Kate laughed.

'I would very much like to take that, but I doubt you could stand still long enough or be serious enough for me to capture you.'

'You have already captured me,' Ambrose assured her with a quick kiss on the cheek and the presentation of his flowers. 'We have no one to bury this afternoon, unbelievably, so I escaped on the pretence of collecting the mail, which I must remember to do.'

'Goodness, no one to put underground. There's a turn-up for the books,' Kate teased him.

'The books, that is, the accounts, look very good after those few weeks of demand. Let's hope there are no more tragedies for a while. We prefer the steady flow of people turning up their toes.'

'Understandable. There is so much to consider when dying; I never realised until I met you. I promise I will endeavour to pass away during business hours and in winter.'

'Most considerate, my dear. Did you get any requests for death portraits after the ferry accident?'

'Several, but I don't do them.' Kate inhaled the mixed bunch of colourful flowers and smiled. She sought a vase. 'They are beautiful, Ambrose. Thank you.'

'A pleasure. Why don't you do death portraits?' he persisted.

'It is too distressing, and I find it a little frightening. While the dead make good subjects—they stay very still—I prefer to photograph the living, even if they are impatient subjects,' she said with a smile in his direction.

'You are right,' he agreed. 'I was tested even in the photographs you took out the front of our premises; the horses were restless too,' he said in jest. 'If not for your taking the photographs, I would have bolted along with the horses before the photograph was captured.'

'Is that so? I don't know whether to be grateful or impressed,' she said. 'On the other hand, your brother and grandfather were the perfect subjects, most restrained.'

Ambrose rolled his eyes. 'Of course they were. Julius can stand still for hours. I watch him during the funerals and sometimes poke him to make sure he is still alive.'

Kate laughed. 'It is a discipline, not one I profess to have.'

'I often wonder what is going on in his head.'

'Probably business ideas, from what I hear from Violet. Their honeymoon produced quite a few,' she said, arranging the flowers.

'I wonder what we would produce on our honeymoon,' he teased her.

'The start of a family, hopefully,' Kate boldly said. Having had encouragement from Phoebe, she determined not to hide her feelings. She would have her answer if she shocked Ambrose or caused him to pull away. But he did not flinch or appear shocked; quite the opposite.

'They would be beautiful children without a doubt,' he agreed with a grin, making her laugh.

Kate sobered. 'I do hope and pray...' she hesitated.

'What?' he prodded, now looking concerned.

'That they might take after me.'

Ambrose laughed and waggled a finger at her. 'You have tempted fate now. They will all take after the Astin side of the family.'

'All?' she said, surprised. 'How many children would you like?'

'The same number that you want,' he said. 'But we need to talk about a betrothal first, and a wedding, your father's permission, how good I will look in my wedding suit, a house for our future which I am seeking...'

Kate's heart pounded with excitement as she watched him walk around the studio, looking at the images she had on display, including those waiting for customers to collect. The door burst open, startling them both, and reporter Lilly Lewis rushed in.

'Oh, you have a customer. No, you don't! Hello Ambrose,' she exclaimed. 'Dear me, am I interrupting something?'

'No, do come in,' Kate assured her, secretly cursing the timing of Lilly's visit.

'Yes, you are interrupting our dreaming,' Ambrose said, crossing his arms across his chest, 'but come in anyway'. He delivered it with a smile that said he was not serious, but Kate suspected he was. Given Ambrose's rare business-hours visits, it was bad timing, especially when they were discussing matters of the heart.

'I promise I won't keep you both,' Lilly continued, a little breathless from rushing up the stairs. 'Kate, I cannot find the detectives, and Phoebe told me of the photograph of Mrs Elizabeth Rowe on the rise of the river.'

'Yes, amazing! I have several photographs that she appears in. Would you like to take one?' Kate said, moving to her sunset images of the ferry sinking and the local people watching in distress.

'Desperately, please. May *The Courier* publish it and attribute it to you, like last time?'

'Yes, of course, if it will help your story.'

'Thank you, Kate,' Lilly said, hurriedly kissing her cheek. 'I need it for the late edition, and I have nothing else.' She brightened. 'What an unexpected twist! But I must find the detective first to seek his permission. I don't wish to stand on Detective Stone's toes less he breaks our arrangement. I will hail a cab and seek him, but where? He was not at Roma Street headquarters when I called.' She stopped and took a deep breath.

'I have the trap with me,' Ambrose said. 'Where can I take you?'

'Oh, Ambrose, that would be so helpful. I am sorry, Kate, to break up your meeting.'

'Not at all. It's best to rush then, Lilly,' Kate said, handing her the photograph wrapped in paper for protection.

She watched her dear friend and the man she loved leaving together. As much as she trusted in Ambrose's feelings for her after their romantic discussion this very day, she felt a pang of jealousy that he had departed with the woman he was sweet on before her. Kate could not help but think it was made worse because they looked so good together.

Chapter 21

GIVEN HIS STATE OF grief, the detectives were surprised to find Mr Ernest Rowe in the office of Burton's Stationery Supplies. The sales assistant at the front desk led them to the supply room at the back of the building, where they found the slumped Mr Rowe looking over a ledger.

'I could not bear to be at home without Elizabeth,' he said to the detectives, looking like a man who had lost his will to live. As Harland's first impression of him was that he was a dandy, his appearance was dramatically different. His hair looked unwashed, his skin sallow, and he had lost weight. 'At least at work, I can stay busy filling orders and managing supplies.'

'Of course, Mr Rowe, totally understandable,' Gilbert said sympathetically.

'What I don't understand,' Ernest said as if speaking to himself, 'is why after all those years that we waited and longed to be together, then with the death of her first husband we could finally marry... why was she taken from me?'

'It is one of life's great mysteries, Mr Rowe,' Harland said. 'We know from working in crime that many a good soul has lost their life early while those with no moral compass live on.'

'How could God do that to us?' Ernest wailed.

Harland quickly shook his head at Gilbert, preventing his protégé from starting a theological discussion that would take time and offer little comfort to a despairing man.

'Mr Rowe, may we show you a photograph?' Harland asked.

'Of what?' Ernest said, looking up at the detective with interest.

Gilbert moved forward with the photograph and took the paper from it. He placed it on the desk before Ernest Rowe.

'It is Elizabeth! My darling wife. When was this taken? Oh my, is that the *River Lady* sinking behind her? Oh, the anguish of some of these people watching.' The realisation of the situation dawned on Ernest Rowe. 'What is this, Detective?' he asked, his voice almost a whisper.

'It is evidence that your wife was not on the *River Lady*, Mr Rowe.'

'And that you are beside her, Sir,' Gilbert said.

'She's not on the ferry,' he said, as if the detective's words were catching up with him. 'That's not me!'

'Could you please stand and turn around, Mr Rowe?' Harland asked.

He stood, his movement somewhat shaky, protesting, 'I assure you, that is not me. That is Donahue.' He turned, as requested, not seeing the glances the detectives exchanged. But Ernest Rowe was correct. His hairline and shoulder width differed from the man photographed with Mrs Elizabeth Rowe.

'Thank you. Please sit, Mr Rowe,' Harland said. 'You believe this to be Donahue. Would you be referring to Donahue Marsh?'

'Indeed, I would. Elizabeth's cousin,' Ernest said. 'But why is he with her, and if she was not on that ferry, how did she end up drowning in the river? Perhaps they ran to help the ferry victims? But then, why would Donahue leave her and not tell me?'

Harland held up his hand to halt Ernest's ramblings. 'You believe Donahue is Mrs Rowe's cousin?'

'Yes. They were close, and he was always around. He is good fun and—' he stopped seeing the expression on the detectives' faces. 'Are you saying they are not cousins?'

'I doubt they are, Sir,' Gilbert said. 'We have just discovered that Mr Donahue Marsh was employed as a labourer by your wife's first husband in his business. He was dismissed when he was found kissing Mrs Rowe.'

'Forcing himself upon her, we were told,' Harland painted the full picture.

Harland watched Ernest Rowe process the information. As expected, the previously devastated Ernest Rowe suddenly did not look so bereaved. His back straightened, his eyes narrowed, and the widower realised he had been played.

Lilly desperately wanted to make *The Courier's* late edition, but the clock was working against her as it was nearly mid-afternoon. She thanked Ambrose profusely as she leapt from his trap, ignoring his attempt to assist her, and rushed into *The Courier's* offices, carefully clutching the photograph.

Her editor, Mr Cowan, would need to approve the art department's preparation of the image for copying and use, and their job would take some time. She and Fergus would have to drum up some accompanying words, but Lilly needed to find the detectives to seek permission to use the image. It was a breakthrough and would make a riveting headline story.

Rushing to her desk, she threw her bag and hat on the chair, startling her partner.

'Come, Fergus. We have a breakthrough. Time is of the essence, so as I brief Mr Cowan, pretend you have known all along,' she said, bumping him to his feet and insisting he follow her to the editor's office.

A quick knock on the door and a grunt from the editor was enough, and Lilly and Fergus barged in.

'Mr Cowan, we have a breakthrough in our murder case. I am trying to find the detectives for permission to print this image, but we must get the art department started on it.' She unveiled it before him.

'It's a good photograph, but we've already printed these shots of the ferry sinking,' Mr Cowan said dismissively.

'No, Sir, look here,' Lilly said. 'That's Mrs Elizabeth Rowe, alive and well on the shoreline with a man as the *River Lady* sinks behind her.'

Fergus gasped, and Lilly elbowed him. He hurriedly made it appear as a cough, adding, 'As she was not on the ferry and could not have drowned in that accident, it is proof she was murdered,' he summed up, and Lilly nodded encouragingly.

'Very well done, young ones,' Mr Cowan said with a sly grin as he looked at the photograph with fresh interest. He chuckled and muttered, 'Got you, whoever you are. Get it to the art department right now. It's a headliner.'

'Sir, what if I can't find the detectives before the deadline?' Lilly asked.

'Where did you get the photograph?' Mr Cowan asked.

'From the photographer, Miss Kate Kirby. The same lady who gave us the other shots, Sir.'

'Well, there's your answer. You didn't get it from the detectives, so they weren't your source; you don't need their approval to run it.'

'I know, Sir, but we have a beneficial working relationship, and I don't want to jeopardise their case by going early with the photograph. I heard they had it, so I sourced a copy from Miss Kate Kirby.'

Alex Cowan nodded and turned his attention to Fergus Griffiths. 'What would you do, Griffiths?'

'The same as Lilly, Sir. They have been an invaluable source for us, not one we want to lose.'

The editor momentarily looked disappointed before his expression was replaced with anger and impatience. 'You two aren't hungry enough. You'll never be a real journalist if you don't have that edge. You need to be cut throat to break a story.' He passed it to Lilly and waved her off. 'Take it to the art department, and as your editor, I'll be running with it. That's how you should be thinking.'

'Yes, Sir,' they agreed and departed, their moment of glory diminished by the editor's displeasure. Behind them, they heard Mr Cowan bellowing to the sub-editor, 'Hold the front page.'

'Thanks for agreeing with me,' Lilly said when they were far enough away not to be heard by Mr Cowan. 'Do you really believe as I do?'

'Yes. We don't want to anger the best source we have. Do we know who the man is with her?' Fergus asked.

'Not yet. The detectives might. I'll take this to the art room, then let us write our copy, and I will leave you to clean it up while I race out and try to track them down.'

'No, I'll take it to the art room and draft the copy. You go and find the detectives.' Fergus shook his head. 'A dreadful predicament.'

'Thank you, Fergus,' Lilly said gratefully. 'But to play safe, don't just focus on it being a murder investigation; perhaps add an appeal for information to appease the detectives in case I can't find them.'

'Excellent idea,' Fergus agreed. 'Hurry then.'

'Yes, I will be back as soon as I can.' She felt ill with stress, thinking that she might lose the trust of her best contacts and Phoebe.

Bennet Martin was disappointed to have finished the inquest, as it afforded no more opportunities to see Miss Lilly Lewis in action. As it was lunchtime—for those who ate late—he gambled and took a hansom to her place of work instead of his own office abode. His driver had just pulled up when Lilly raced out of the building.

'Lilly,' he called and waved, and she raced towards him.

'Bennet, what brings you here?' she asked, slightly panting.

'I just finished at the inquest and hoped to have a very late lunch or afternoon tea with you,' Bennet said.

'Bennet, forgive me, but Fergus and I have a most pressing deadline. I need to find the detectives with post haste.'

'I just saw them leaving Burton's Stationery Supplies on my way here. I offered them a ride, but they were going the opposite way, back to Police Headquarters. Get in,' he said and leaned up to the driver. 'The Roma Street Police Headquarters as fast as you can, my good man. I'll pay you double to make haste.'

The driver grinned. Lilly squeezed Bennet's arm as she pushed in beside him into the cosy cabin. 'You have come to my rescue again!'

'It is my primary goal in life,' he joked. 'My, this is exciting,' but on seeing Lilly's face, added, 'and most serious of course.'

She laughed at his enthusiasm. 'It would be exciting if so much weren't at stake.'

'What is at stake?' Bennet asked, gripping onto an arm piece as the hansom hurried along.

'My working relationship with the detectives,' Lilly said and explained, finishing with, 'It may already be too late. Mr Cowan intends to publish it regardless of Detective Stone's approval.'

'But the detectives don't know that and need never,' Bennet said, enjoying Lilly's admiring glance for the second time since he offered her a speedy ride.

'Thank you, Bennet,' she said. 'But what if they say no?'

'Then you must present it in the most persuasive way to assist their enquiry,' Bennet said.

'Great minds think alike,' she agreed.

'Let me hear your plea then,' Bennet said. Lilly drew a deep breath and explained that they would publish the photograph and ask anyone who recalled seeing Mrs Elizabeth Rowe or speaking with her that day to contact the detectives. She would downplay how they might dramatise the murder aspect a little.

'I am convinced you must publish it,' Bennet said, and she smiled with delight.

'Now, let's hope I convince the detectives, and they are not worried that the person in the photograph with Mrs Rowe might flee if we feature it.'

They reared back as the hansom suddenly stopped, and Bennet jumped out to assist Lilly from the cab. She kissed Bennet on the cheek and rushed into the station. Bennet was still grinning as the driver cleared his throat, waiting for instructions.

Bennet hurriedly paid him, adding, 'If you might rest the horses, I'll pay you to wait for a return trip.'

The driver smiled. 'Happily, Sir' and moved the horses to the shade and water trough while Bennet relocated to a bench outside the police station. He had no desire or need to be in the meeting and preferred to wait to see the face of his love as she emerged. He hoped it would go to her advantage.

Chapter 22

IN A MANNER MOST unbecoming for a lady, Lilly Lewis raced down the hallway of the Roma Street Police Headquarters. The desk sergeant, John, was in discussion with a difficult man and uncustomarily waved her through. Lilly shot him a grateful smile.

Rushing into the detectives' room, she was overwhelmed with relief at seeing them, and it appeared they had only recently returned. Detective Stone shrugged off his jacket but reinstated it on seeing Miss Lewis.

'Forgive the intrusion, Detectives, but Fergus and I have a pending deadline and seek your approval on a story.' She added, 'I also have information.'

'Miss Lewis,' both detectives greeted her. 'Fortunately, we have just returned,' Gilbert said.

'I know, Detective, I feel as if I have been chasing you around town. Bennet dropped me here, having sighted you both.' Lilly continued without invitation. 'We have a similar version of Kate's photograph of Mrs Elizabeth Rowe on the hill next to a man as the *River Lady* sinks behind her,' she hurried on. 'We have drafted a story saying it is proof she was alive, and if anyone spoke with Mrs Rowe or remembers seeing her or her companion that afternoon, please get in touch with you both here at the Roma Street Police Headquarters. She is bound to have commiserated with someone who can remember her face; she was a beautiful, memorable lady,' Lilly said, selling the advantage as best she could and as rehearsed with Bennet on the hurried journey. 'May we publish that, Detective?'

Harland thought for a moment, as he often did. It was an agonising moment when Lilly's heart stopped beating, and she was sure the colour drained from her face.

'Yes, I think that would be most helpful,' he said, and Lilly sagged with relief.

'Thank you, Detective.' Lilly drew a deep breath and relaxed for the first time in hours, the tension leaving her body. They did not need to know that the story and photograph were running with or without their permission, but thankfully, all remained intact with their arrangement. 'I need not rush back for fifteen minutes. Do you wish me to tell you what I have learned from Phoebe?'

'I shall make us all a terrible cup of tea from the police tearoom,' Gilbert said, rising with a smile. 'I don't want to get your expectations up, Miss Lewis, that it will be to your usual standards.'

'I am parched, Detective, and would welcome it regardless of the taste, thank you,' she said. 'I won't speak of Phoebe's news until your return.'

Detective Payne hurried away, keen to return for the update, and Harland invited Lilly to sit. His calm manner allowed her to relax a little.

'Do you know who is in the photograph with Mrs Rowe? I imagine that is her husband?' Lilly asked.

'As did we, but as it turns out, it is not,' Harland said, telling of Donahue Marsh's involvement and deception. 'Even though we believe it to be Mr Marsh, please do not name him yet.'

'Of course,' she said and thanked Detective Payne for the washy-coloured cup of tea he placed before her. 'Might Elizabeth Rowe have had the tin and money for him? If the ring belonged to his ex-fiancée, did she procure it somehow, and was that the deed done? But what was the money for? Should he not be paying her?'

Harland shook his head. 'That is our dilemma; it does not fit the scenario. We will ask Donahue Marsh, but we are not expecting a straight answer.'

'He will be alarmed when he sees the photograph in tomorrow's newspaper,' Gilbert said. 'It might loosen his tongue unless he thinks no one will recognise the back of his head.'

Lilly offered a theory. 'What if the three of them worked together in the past? If Elizabeth was in love with Ernest and wanted her husband dead, could they have conspired to kill Richard Tyson and hired the labourer, Donahue Marsh, to do so?'

'That is a very real possibility and plausible, especially if Ernest Rowe thought Donahue was his wife's cousin,' Harland said. 'But why take so long to pay Donahue Marsh? Richard Tyson has been dead for nearly two years.'

'True,' Lilly mused and sighed.

'We must consolidate our facts and be prepared when we see him. He is involved; of that there is no doubt, but in what capacity?' Harland mused.

'If he was attracted to Elizabeth Rowe, and her first husband sacked him for his advances, why claim to be her cousin, fooling her second husband? Why did he not offer for her when the first husband died?' Lilly speculated, speaking quickly as she had not fully unwound from the hours of tension.

'Perhaps he was not wealthy enough or of sufficient standing in the community for Elizabeth Rowe,' Gilbert suggested. 'Although she was a wealthy widow, and did not need his money.'

'No,' Harland agreed. 'Ernest Rowe said he and Elizabeth loved each other and were not permitted to marry due to a family promise. But when Richard Tyson died, he was able to wed her. There seems no place in that scenario for Donahue Marsh.'

'And we know Donahue is a dreadful womaniser,' Gilbert said. 'Miss Charlotte Glasson called off their engagement when she caught him kissing the barmaid.'

'Deed done,' Harland muttered.

'Oh, let me tell you my news from Phoebe before I must rush off,' Lilly said and, lowering her voice, began. 'A spirit visited her... a lady of my age named Frannie Firth. She claimed to be a friend of Elizabeth Rowe when they were both alive. She said Elizabeth pretended to mourn when her first husband died and is not of the sweet disposition she portrayed.'

The detectives exchanged looks.

'It appears that way,' Gilbert nodded.

'Let me get my notes so I can relay this correctly,' Lilly said seriously. 'I wrote it down on my journey back to the newspaper.'

They waited as Lilly hurriedly collected a small notebook from her bag and thumbed to the page she sought. She looked at the detectives and then read: 'Frannie said Richard Tyson did not die by accident, and we must do something about it. She claimed Elizabeth was pleased with herself after his death and had said, "Deed done".' Lilly looked up from her notes.

'*Deed done*. Those words again,' Harland said, mulling over it as Gilbert added the information to the board.

Lilly continued, 'Now, with your permission, I must hurry back to the editor and tell him we are good to go to print and help Fergus finish our copy.'

'Of course, thank you, Miss Lewis. Please let us know if any witnesses approach you directly as a result of your article. Tomorrow, I shall see the coroner and find out if he did an autopsy on Richard Tyson, and Gilbert will find the worksite where Richard Tyson died and seek Mr Tyson's construction supervisor. Let us discover exactly what the accident was that caused Mr Tyson's death.'

'May I meet you at the coroner's rooms, Detective Stone?' Lilly asked.

He nodded. 'Nine o'clock, Miss Lewis.'

Lilly rose, relieved, and thanking the detectives, hurriedly took her leave.

Bennet waved his hand as Lilly came down the external stairs of the large police station; her eyes widened in delight at seeing him waiting. He raised his hand to the hansom driver, who gathered the reins and brought the cab toward them.

'Oh, you waited,' Lilly exclaimed, relieved.

'Of course. I shall take you back to *The Courier* post-haste.' He handed her up and gave the driver the return address. Once inside and settled, he asked, 'The verdict?'

'Approved,' she grinned. 'I am not in such a hurry now, but I will check with Fergus to see if he has finished our copy and let him know all is well. Why are you not at work?'

'I decided to participate in your adventure instead.'

'What timing, I am truly grateful, Bennet.'

'The pleasure is mine, Lilly,' he said, bringing her hand to his lips.

'Oh, do say you can take me out for a drink and dinner later,' she pleaded. 'I would so like to celebrate tonight.'

'It would be my absolute pleasure,' Bennet said. 'What are we celebrating?'

'All being well in the world again,' she laughed. Lilly took his arm and pressed herself against him in a hug before releasing Bennet.

'Thank you,' she said, smiling up at him.

'What for? A ride? That was nothing.' He brushed off her thanks but never took his eyes off Lilly's expressive face.

'It was everything. I have never loved you more than I did when you paid double to get me to the police station quickly and promised to keep my secret that we would go to press with or without the detectives' approval. Thank you for supporting me so.'

'Loved me?' he asked, only hearing the words of affection.

Lilly smiled. 'Yes, Mr Martin, love. I love you.'

'What a wonderful coincidence,' he said, grinning, and with that encouragement, he took the liberty of kissing her.

Late afternoon, with several deliveries to make, Kate was preparing to close the business for the day when she heard footsteps hurrying up the stairs. A little alarmed, she paused by her desk and then relief washed over her; Ambrose had returned.

He entered, removing his hat, and gave her a small bow and a large smile.

'Forgive me for rushing off earlier, Kate, and I could not return before now. What a day!' he proclaimed.

'What a day indeed. I did not expect you back, so do not be concerned,' she assured him. 'Do tell, did Lilly find the detectives and make her deadline?'

'I cannot say, but she got the photograph to her editor in ample time. I swear she almost leapt out of my trap when *The Courier* came into view. What a grand girl she is,' he said with a laugh.

Kate smiled and agreed graciously. 'If she were not with Bennet, would you court her, Ambrose?'

'Is she not?' he asked, mishearing her, and his eyes widened with interest. Then Ambrose realised Kate was speaking rhetorically; she was supposed to be his focus, his love interest.

'Yes, she is still with him.'

'Oh, of course,' he said, his expression scrambling to remain neutral and mask his error. 'Believe me, I am not interested in Miss Lewis. I am taken with this beauty before me.' Ambrose moved toward Kate, but she held up her hand to stop him.

'Oh, Ambrose.' She touched her heart. 'I fear you have wounded me.'

His expression relayed a sense of panic. 'Come now, Kate, don't be silly. We have such fun together, and I am planning many more occasions.'

She shook her head. 'No, Ambrose. You see, I love you more than you love me.'

He opened his mouth to protest, but she stopped him again. 'I trusted in your love and indulged in daydreams of a home and family. I was a fool. I should have realised how soon you turned to me after learning your love was unrequited with Lilly.'

'No, Kate. I saw only you, a lovely, talented and beautiful woman. I just misheard you before; it was curiosity asking, nothing more.' His nervous shuffling of his hat from hand to hand told a different story.

'But I am not your great love, and I know that shouldn't matter, especially for a woman not in her youth. I know I should accept a handsome man's hand without question, but you see, Ambrose, I don't have to do so.' She looked around. 'I have this business to support me, so I don't have to marry for anything but love. I am sometimes silly and not the strongest person, but I made myself that promise.'

'But you do love me,' he proclaimed like a petulant child, keenly aware now that he would lose Kate as he did Lilly and have no one.

'I do love you, but I am not your love.' She choked on the words, swallowing a small cry of pain and gathered herself. 'It would be so easy to pretend that didn't matter and carry on so my heart didn't ache, but I want a man who thinks of me and wants me as you do, Lilly.'

Ambrose groaned, swallowed and looked away, but he had no words to save the situation.

'I want to be someone's great love, not their second choice. I am sorry, Ambrose. I am more sorry than I can say,' she finished in a whisper.

Ambrose moved closer, taking her hand. 'Don't do this, Kate,' he pleaded. 'Do not throw us away.'

'Please, Ambrose, leave while I can still stand and speak because my resolve is fading. Please go.'

She felt him studying her, but Kate could not raise her eyes and look at him. She withdrew her hand from his.

'Kate, I do love you.'

She shook her head. 'Go, dear Ambrose, please,' she pleaded, but he did not move. Kate closed her eyes. 'Please,' she pleaded before hearing him turn and leave. Then, opening her eyes, she found herself alone and stumbled to the door, locking it. Kate collapsed to the floor, clutching her chest and crying, breathing in huge gulps of air. Yesterday, everything seemed so perfect; today, it was all gone.

An hour or so later, when she had cried out her pain and managed to control her emotions, Kate rose from the floor and went to her desk. She took out the framed photograph of herself and Ambrose. She cried as she looked at his handsome face and herself wearing his hat as he held the umbrella over her. Kate thought her heart might tear in two.

She took the image from the frame and, with a shaky hand, wrote on the back, '*Mr Ambrose Astin, 1891*.' Going to a white box in the corner, she opened it and added the image to her mementos.

In time, she would look back on that photograph with a smile and no pain. But not for a very long time.

Chapter 23

It was one of the few mornings of the week when Mr and Mrs Astin did not come to work together. Violet had her breakfast catch-up with Aunt Viv, who was not her aunt but a dear friend in the old neighbourhood, so Julius sent her off in a hansom. As Rufus, the hound, was going to work with Tom for the day, where he was quite a favourite and made an appearance twice a week, Julius made his way to the office on an omnibus. Being socially taciturn, Julius avoided the mode of transport where possible as people often recognised him – his wedding had featured in the newspaper, as had the story of his rescue of young Alfie, and he was one of the city's most successful sons.

Despite his introverted nature, Julius was polite and a businessman, so he acknowledged fellow travellers and did his best to look amused at their banter despite having heard it all many times.

'No grave mistakes of late, Mr Astin?'

'I am not surprised you are a mourning person, Mr Astin.'

'Heard any good plots lately, Mr Astin?'

'I must say, I made a grave mistake recently but was able to dig myself out. What say you, Mr Astin?'

'I thought you would be on the graveyard shift, Mr Astin.'

But occasionally, he encountered a like-minded traveller who was happy to sit in quiet contemplation or to make sensible conversation, like the young lady who sat beside him on this morning's journey.

'It's a frantic time for you, I imagine, Mr Astin. Is the demand from the ferry tragedy easing up now?' she asked, and Julius could see several faces turning their way and listening to the conversation.

'Thankfully, yes. We are not ungrateful for the work, but nobody wishes to gain from such a tragedy.'

'Of course not. Our company benefited as well,' she said, and Julius studied her with renewed interest, offering his full name as an introduction and requesting hers in return.

'Miss Billie Prout,' the attractive young blonde beside him said. She offered her hand most forwardly, reminding him very much of Miss Lilly Lewis. He shook her hand and observed that she was around Phoebe's age but with the full figure of a young woman, whereas Phoebe was slender and boyish.

'Billie?'

'Willamina, but I refuse to answer to that,' she warned him.

'Duly noticed,' Julius said with a smile. 'May I enquire about your business?' And then it occurred to him... 'Prout! Prout Monumental Masons?'

'The very same,' she smiled. 'It would be Prout & Daughter, but while my father is quite modern in his outlook, he has his limits and would not be swayed. And why don't you do business with us, Mr Astin?' she asked boldly but with a smile. She was not flirting, which he thought was refreshing, but rather, it was two business minds engaged in a discussion about their industry. He had momentarily forgotten the other passengers around him.

'Why indeed,' he said. 'Habit, perhaps, that we have stayed with the same supplier who has served us well.'

'I would not wish to usurp them, but we have some creative new designs.'

'Of your making?'

'Now I will seem boastful if I say yes,' she laughed. 'But I like to work with beautiful stone and offer interesting alternatives. My father works in the traditional stones and designs.'

'There is little room for variation for us in pricing, which limits the type of monuments we can offer,' Julius said.

'As *The Economic Undertaker,* that must take precedence.'

'Exactly,' Julius said, finding her understanding refreshing.

'If I have some modern, economical designs, perhaps I could impose on your time to show you a sample of my monuments, and you might consider adding them to your catalogue for customers to have a wider selection.'

Julius smiled. 'Miss Prout, I am open to that idea.'

'Excellent,' she said. 'This is my stop. I will be in touch, Mr Astin. Good day.' She rose as did he and doffed his hat as the very astute and confident Miss Billie Prout exited the omnibus.

Two stops later, Julius alighted and strode to work, wondering just how modern Miss Prout's designs were. On arrival, Julius greeted young Charlie, who always arrived early to care for the horses, unlocked the back door to the business premises and entered. He enjoyed the solitude of the business he created before the staff arrived and the workday began. It had provided for his family, and he was proud that it looked after the people of Brisbane with honesty and integrity. If only something similar had existed when his poor grandparents had to bury his mother and father and went into debt to pay off their funeral and graves. The thought still made him angry to this day.

He removed his hat, opened the blinds and curtains and moved throughout the business, settling and straightening items as he went. Descending into Phoebe's room, he saw Uncle Reggie standing by the window.

'It's a peaceful time of the morning before the day's trade begins,' Reggie said.

'It is. One of my favourite times of the day,' Julius agreed.

'I used to ride at sunrise; there is something magic about the quiet of the world then. Are you busy now?'

'Now is a good time for us to speak,' Julius said and sat on the couch. 'I spoke to Grandpa last night. He is keen to hear what you say and can't imagine anything that would make him think less of you.'

Reggie's smile was one of sadness, but he exhaled with relief. 'I hope that is true. Relay what you think is best then, Julius.'

'I will, but he does not want me to censor your words,' Julius said, encouraging his uncle to begin. It had been a long time coming, and he was pleased to be of assistance, even if Uncle Reggie's manner of outing him still smarted.

Reggie began, unaccustomed to being so serious with his nephew. 'This story began before I reached my majority. I met the woman I wanted to marry when I was seventeen, Rone was twenty.'

'Rone?' Julius interrupted.

'Sorry, Randolph, my brother, your grandfather,' Reggie chuckled. 'Because we were Randolph and Reginald, our mother—your great-grandmother—called us R-one and R-two. R-one merged as Rone. It's funny; I had not thought of that nickname for years, and it came to me with great familiarity then.'

'I have never heard that before,' Julius said.

'No, no one is left to call your grandfather by that name. So, this charming woman was my age, and I was madly in love with her. Even at a young age, I had always had success with the ladies, but she was my match. Funny, beautiful, and much smarter than me. She had confidence. Other girls preened and flirted, but not Miss Hubner. I adored her for months before I mustered the courage to seek permission to court her.'

'What became of her?' Julius asked hesitantly, expecting his uncle to speak of her death and the tragedy of her young passing.

'I introduced Miss Maria Hubner to my brother.'

Julius's eyes widened in surprise. 'Grandma?'

Reggie gave a brief nod and continued. 'Randolph did not know I had been flirting and dancing around my intentions for a while. Maria and I were both so young, and she was not short of suitors. Now, when I think back on it, I am sure I appeared quite young and silly to her compared to some of her mature suitors.'

'How could Grandpa not know?' Julius asked.

'He had been studying bookkeeping and was quite unsocial. I was working in sales and was always out and about. While we were close, like you and Ambrose, I did not always move in his circles or reveal my feelings. But I intended to ask Maria if I might court her and ask her father, too, of course. It all came to a head at church on Christmas Eve. The extended families were present, and Maria was there with her family and visiting relatives. I made it my business to catch up with her once mass was finished, and naturally, we introduced each other to our relatives. I keenly watched for my parents' reaction to her.' He shook his head as if remembering that day in great detail.

'Was that the first time she met Grandpa?' Julius asked.

'Yes. He was three years her senior and a lot like you, my nephew. Tall, handsome, conservative. I swear I saw her change the moment they were introduced. It was as if they were drawn to each other. She never looked at me that way. I confess I was devastated.'

'Why didn't you say something?'

'What would be the point? I could not make her have feelings for me, so why would I attempt to separate them? They were engaged within six months, and her father insisted on a two-year engagement so Randolph could get his qualification and support his daughter.'

'And what became of you?'

'I went away. I travelled, worked in different places, and stayed away from my brother and the family I loved. A year after their marriage, your father, Montague, was born. Maria nearly died in childbirth, and thus Montague was their only child, and how they doted on your father. Then, Randolph asked me to be his son's godfather.'

Julius groaned, and Reggie shook his head. 'It was an honour; he did not know that would pain me. Maria's close friend, Miss Palmer, was to be his godmother.'

'So she was not Lady Palmer then?' Julius asked after the godmother he shared with his father.

'No, she was young and beautiful, but we were not interested in each other, and she married well. So, I came home for the christening, and my feelings for Maria had not changed; I still loved her. And him. Straight after, I left again. I was a very absent godfather to your father.'

'But you must have met other ladies and fallen in love, surely?'

'I did, of course, over the years. But imagine if Ambrose had married Violet. How easily could you mask that pain?'

Julius shook his head. 'I would hopefully learn to do so to be with my family.'

'Yes, I was sure it would be easier each time I visited, but it was not. I fell in love and asked a lady to marry me, but my love grew cold. I was dishonourable and called it off. So I enjoyed my bachelor life until you were born.'

'Me?' Julius said, surprised. 'What part did I play in this?'

'I came home late autumn, twenty years after the marriage of my brother and Maria. I barely knew them anymore and felt like a stranger amongst my family.' He shook his head. 'My godson, your father Montague, was expecting his first child with your mother, and Randolph begged me to come to the christening. He never stopped asking me home, writing, worrying about me as you do for Ambrose and Phoebe. A boy was born. A very handsome boy, whom they named Julius,' Reggie teased.

'I think I know him,' Julius said with a smile.

'I held that boy in my arms and looked at Randolph's beautiful family, and I was filled with despair, anger and jealousy. I am sorry to admit it. To know that she might have been my wife, her son could have been mine, and you, my grandson.' Reggie looked away as he spoke of his lost dreams. 'That day, I took to my horse and rode recklessly without a care for my welfare. And here I am. I cannot say that I am not happier here.'

'Uncle Reggie, I will not tell Grandpa that part; it would devastate him.'

Reggie nodded. 'Of course, you are right; it was indulgent and selfish to say that. Forgive me. When Montague died, I did not know how Randolph and Maria would survive his loss. I think having you three to care for saved them.'

'They were the worst of times,' Julius agreed, not asking after his parents on the other side.

'Please, Julius, you must tell my brother of my weakness and that I am deeply sorrowful for the pain I have caused him because I am a petty man.'

'You are not that, Uncle. You are human.'

'No, I should have put my feelings for him above all else. Recently, I feared that if you were attracted to that young reporter, it might have been history repeating, given Ambrose's feelings for her.'

'Miss Lewis? No, she was never for me. It is a relief that Ambrose showed no romantic interest in Violet, given we met her at the same time.'

'It's a great relief,' Reggie said. He sighed and added sincerely, 'Thank you, Julius.'

'I shall tell Grandpa all you have said, and I am sorry, Uncle, for your torment.'

'It is all of my own making, Julius.'

'No, fate can play us all.'

With that, they heard the door upstairs opening and the staff arriving for the day. Reggie gave a low bow and disappeared as Julius gathered himself, rose to his feet, and headed upstairs to start his morning's work.

Chapter 24

THE CONSTRUCTION SUPERVISOR LOOKED very much the part as he made notes and shook his head at the slightest issue that proved unsatisfactory, including the two men approaching him at such an early hour of the morning when he liked to get organised for the day.

'Mr Stenner, a detective to speak with you,' the guide said, giving Detective Gilbert Payne a nod and leaving him in the hands of Mr Stenner.

Gilbert introduced himself and added, 'A minute of your time, Mr Stenner, if you will?'

'Yes, Detective. What is this about then? You seem very young to be a detective,' the supervisor said, putting his small notebook into his pocket and appraising Gilbert.

'Perhaps, Sir, but nonetheless, I am one.' Gilbert stood taller, trying to look a little more authoritative. As always, he was well-groomed in his dark suit and highly polished shoes. His hair was neatly cut, and his hat was of good quality. 'I wish to speak with you about the death of Mr Richard Tyson. Were you the construction supervisor on this site then?'

'Richard Tyson! Good Lord, why would a detective be asking questions about his death now? That has to be nearly two years ago.'

'Yes, Sir, you are correct; it has been nearly two years. In fact, I am surprised to find you here and the building still under construction.' Gilbert looked around. 'I understand Mr Tyson purchased this property intending to repair and upgrade it when he had a most unfortunate accident. Were you here then?' he asked again.

'I was in the role then but not present when he fell, Detective, and no one was more shocked than I was when he met his death. Sadly, the building sat on the market for some time after his death; it was purchased recently. People can be superstitious, and as you can see, work has recommenced.' He lowered his voice and added, 'I was lucky to be reinstated, although I had a very good construction record before Mr Tyson's death.'

'Is that why you were so shocked by his death, Sir?' Gilbert asked. 'You have not encountered a worksite accident before?'

'Oh, they happen often enough as workers lack discipline and budgets dictate skill and material shortcuts; it is the way of the world. But the small stairway and bridge Mr Tyson fell from had just been completed. It was new, not old, and rickety. It was also built from the best timber.'

'May I see it, Sir?'

'Of course. This way.'

Gilbert followed Mr Stenner, avoiding areas as directed, ducking his head when told, and excusing himself as they passed workers.

'Just here,' Mr Stenner pointed to the bridge and railing above him. 'He fell from that ledge; the timber gave way. Quite a fall.'

'What repairs have you done since to this bridge?' Gilbert asked, looking at the overhead landing.

'Not a great deal. It's good timber and sturdy. We just replaced the four boards that were snapped. I don't know how that happened, but I told the police that at the time.'

Gilbert took to the stairs and the landing, studying the area and the fall. He knelt to touch the timber and study the boards surrounding the replaced wood.

'The broken boards were the same timber as that surrounding them?'

'They were, Detective. Mr Tyson didn't scrimp when it came to quality. That's why I enjoyed working on his projects.'

'Thank you, Mr Stenner. One last question: do you recall an employee named Donahue Marsh, a labourer?'

Mr Stenner scowled. 'I do indeed. He approached me about work recently with grand notions that he'll set his own price for his work and that he is above the other boys because he's working for himself. He was on this job originally, but I wouldn't have him back.'

'Thank you, Mr Stenner, you have been most helpful.'

'Well, that's good to hear. I am always happy to help the constabulary. My nephew is a policeman up north. Seems to like his work well enough.'

'They do a fine job up there. My superior recently spent several years in the North Queensland office,' Gilbert said, thanking Mr Stenner again. He departed for the police headquarters, very pleased with his morning findings.

With his rugged, reddish appearance and welcoming smile, the Scottish coroner clapped his hands at the sight of Detective Harland Stone and reporter Lilly Lewis.

'I have been feeling neglected,' he said. 'Only the dead have been visiting, making for poor company.'

'It has been a tumultuous time with all the ferry victims, Dr McGregor,' Lilly agreed. 'We have hardly had time to come up for air, although that might not be the best analogy given the recent drownings,' she said with a frown.

'No, but most accurate,' Harland said. 'May we talk of an older post mortem, Tavish?'

'By all means, Harland. I was gathering my thoughts before starting the day and an autopsy. What brings you here then?'

'A challenge,' Harland said with a smile. 'Can you think back almost two years ago and recall a gentleman by the name of Richard Tyson, a developer, who died in an accident at his building site?'

'Richard Tyson,' Tavish said and shook his head. 'What else can you tell me?'

'He had a beautiful young widow, Elizabeth, and she was about ten years younger than him,' Lilly offered.

Again, he shook his head. 'No, I cannot recall either of them, but fear not; I have seen many deceased in the past two years, and my forgetfulness does not mean they did not grace my table. Allow me to check my files.' He wandered over to the large filing cabinet in the corner of the room and, reaching down, opened the drawer of surnames beginning with T. 'What has Mr Tyson done?'

'We think he might have been murdered and not accidentally fallen to his death,' Harland said. 'If you did an autopsy, you might have something supporting that on file.'

'Oh, please do, Dr McGregor,' Lilly said. 'It would be lovely for my story.'

Tavish laughed. 'I have missed you, Miss Lewis. Do come by more.' He drew out a file and waved it at them, returning to their side. 'Well, you are in luck; he came through my rooms.'

He opened the folder and looked at the notes. 'Oddly, the building supervisor requested an autopsy, most likely to protect his reputation or at the insistence of his insurer.'

'It is strange that the family would allow it,' Harland said.

'Perhaps they wanted to understand more about his death,' Tavish said, reading his notes. 'His injuries were consistent with falling from a reasonable height onto a hard surface.'

Harland sighed. 'It was a long shot.'

'This could be ambiguous,' Tavish said, tapping his chin, and both the detective and Lilly leaned forward. 'Mr Tyson was found lying on his front, hence significant damage to his face, forehead, and nose. But there was evidence of a significant blow to the back of his head as well.'

'Like he was struck and pushed off the ledge?' Lilly asked with hope.

'And the police did not act on this?' Harland asked.

'I imagine they inspected the crime scene and determined it was an accident. Someone might argue he hit his head on the way down, perhaps on a rail or similar. I cannot say without seeing the area.'

'Still, that is something, thank you, Tavish,' Harland said. 'We shall leave you to your dead.'

'How dreary. Until next time, then,' he said and could not help but smile as he heard Miss Lewis's voice on her way down the hallway asking. 'What do you make of that, Detective? It is suspicious, is it not?'

Julius entered *The Economic Undertaker's* kitchen with his grandfather to find Ambrose nursing a cup of tea and looking slightly worse for wear.

'Lad, could you not find a razor this morning?' Randolph asked of his youngest grandson.

'No, Grandpa. I could barely get to my feet, let alone check my grooming,' he muttered, declining all offers of food from Mrs Dobbs.

'Are you ill?' Julius asked, concerned.

Randolph sat and leaned across the table, placing a hand on Ambrose's forehead as he did when they were children. 'You are not feverish,' he said.

'Oh, Ambrose,' Phoebe said, entering the kitchen and seeing him. 'I just received a note from Kate.'

At the sound of her name, Ambrose looked up and winced. Phoebe continued. 'There is an urgent meeting of the *Vexed Vixens* this evening. What has happened? What have you done?'

'Me! Why should I have done anything? She has cast me aside, and I am miserable.'

Julius groaned at the drama unfolding, and Randolph and Mrs Dobbs fussed over Ambrose, offering tea and sympathy.

'Why did she cast you aside?' Phoebe persisted. 'You must have said something untoward.'

'Why are you taking her side?' Ambrose asked, offended. He sat back and glared at his little sister.

'Because,' Phoebe softened her tone, 'only two days ago, Kate spoke of wanting to marry and have a family with you. Did she tell you this, and you rejected her?'

'Quite the opposite,' Ambrose said, looking utterly dejected. 'I made one small mistake.'

They all looked at him expectantly, and Ambrose rolled his eyes and sighed. 'I admired Miss Lewis, and I thought Kate said that Miss Lewis and Bennet were no longer an item. I showed an interest.'

'Oh, Ambrose, you are a proper ninny,' his sister exclaimed, and Julius did his best to hide his smile at her proclamation.

'I am a miserable ninny, and she won't have me back even though I pleaded.'

'You have broken her heart, poor dear Kate,' Phoebe said. 'I'm sorry if your heart is now pained, too.' She touched his arm sympathetically. 'But I strictly forbid you from courting any more of my friends. I would include you too, Julius, but as you are married, you are exempt.'

'Thank goodness for that,' Julius said. 'Come, brother, finish your tea. I will do my best to distract you with work and to keep your spirits high. Perhaps we should see about a shave first unless you want to work in the stables for the day or with Lucian, and I will partner with Claude.'

'No.' Ambrose rose to his feet. 'Let us be off then. At least my mood will reflect the solemnity of the funeral.' He departed for his hat and jacket, and Julius finished his tea before rising.

Randolph shook his head. 'And just when I thought I had you all happily partnered.'

'A parent's work, or in your case, Mr Astin, a grandparent's work is never done,' Mrs Dobbs agreed.

'Poor Ambrose,' Phoebe said, 'but poor Kate. She truly loved him, but not enough to turn a blind eye to his fascination with Lilly.'

Julius rose. 'It will be a most awkward meeting tonight,' he said to his sister.

'Yes, I am not looking forward to the gathering for the first time.'

Julius thanked Mrs Dobbs, and as Ambrose strode past, Julius indicated to his grandfather that he needed a word.

'What is it, lad?' Randolph asked as they moved into the reception area.

'I have spoken with Uncle Reggie,' Julius said in a low voice. 'Can we speak later today?'

'Yes. Should I be concerned?' Randolph appeared anxious

'No. It is a matter of love and loss but not something that will stain your memories or that you can fix now.' Julius stopped talking as Ambrose returned.

'Could you take me home to shave before the funeral?' he asked.

'As long as the dead don't mind being parked outside while you groom,' Julius said drily, heading down the hallway towards the waiting hearse.

Chapter 25

Detective Gilbert Payne arrived at the Roma Street Police Headquarters not ten minutes after his superior, Detective Harland Stone, had returned with Miss Lilly Lewis. He was surprised to find the pair discussing the case with the sergeant at the front desk and Harland accepting several slips of paper from him.

'It is the names of people who read my article and recall seeing Mrs Elizabeth Rowe the day the *River Lady* sank, Detective,' Lilly said to Gilbert as the three walked up the hallway to the detectives' office.

'Oh, that could be very helpful,' Gilbert said as both detectives stood back to allow Miss Lewis entry into the room first.

'You have made good time, Gilbert,' Harland said, surprised. 'I had not expected you back for another hour.'

'Yes, Sir, a bit of good luck.' Gilbert removed his hat and went straight to the large board, where he kept the case details recorded. 'I was pleased to find the site under construction and the very same construction manager present.'

'After all this time?' Lilly asked and took the offered seat at the meeting table.

'Yes, very lucky,' Gilbert said. 'The construction manager, Mr Stenner, said buyers were scarce on the ground after the accident, and it had only recently been sold and the work commissioned. He was pleased to be back on the job.'

'Do tell, Gilbert, what of Mr Tyson's death then?' Harland asked as he went to remove his jacket. Remembering Miss Lewis was present, he left it on. He sat at his desk, giving Gilbert his full attention.

'Mr Stenner had no opinion about whether it was an accident; however, the area where the fall occurred had already been repaired before the accident. It was new timber, and yet the boards gave way.'

'Well, that is odd,' Lilly said, her notebook always at the ready.

'And most unlikely,' Harland said. 'Unless the boards were not secured and came loose?'

'I asked that same question, Sir, but no. They were snapped as if they had shattered from the weight on them. I am confident they were deliberately broken, maybe even after Richard Tyson had fallen, so it would appear as if they had given way underneath him.'

'I would very much like to have a solid lead, but how can you be convinced of such, Gilbert?' Harland asked.

'Because, Sir, it is ironbark timber. I confirmed the surrounding boards were the same then and now, and they were. Ironbark is one of the strongest timbers in Australia and would not shatter in the middle when one man walked upon it, especially as it was a new deck.'

Harland's eyes widened with interest. 'How do you know of Ironbark, Gilbert?'

'Sir, when I was a school lad, my best friend's father owned a sawmill. Mr Bailey taught us a great deal about timber and would give us off-cuts to build our sleds. It was always ironbark because he said it had to be the strongest timber for two lads to use safely.'

'You are a wealth of knowledge, Detective Payne,' Lilly said with a grin.

'Thank you, Miss Lewis, but my knowledge is often abstract; I am pleased it is useful in this instance.' He turned to his superior. 'Sir, I think we can safely say that Richard Tyson's death was suspicious.'

'The coroner also allowed us room for doubt,' Harland said, informing Gilbert of their findings as the young detective summarised it on the board.

'Will you speak with Donahue Marsh now and see how he reacts to your discovery?' Lilly asked keenly.

'Not yet,' Harland said, fishing out the pieces of paper from his pocket and looking at the notes from the sergeant. 'We will follow up on the leads from your story first since several people spoke with Mrs Elizabeth Rowe that day. Gilbert and I will get a description of the man she was with, and if it is a match, that will place Donahue Marsh at the scene. He might be the last person to see Mrs Rowe alive.'

'Maybe she refused to give him his ex-fiancée's engagement ring and the money, and he killed her,' Gilbert mused.

'You are assuming the "Deed done" was stealing the engagement ring?' Lilly asked the younger detective.

'But when we spoke with Miss Charlotte Glasson at the confectionary store, she claimed not to know Mrs Rowe. So how did the ring come into Mrs Rowe's possession?' Harland said. 'Perhaps we should talk with Miss Glasson again and see if she has recalled anything.'

Lilly sighed. 'The cash still does not make sense. Why would she be paying him? I could understand if it were just the ring and the note in the tin. Was she paying him for a deed done in return?'

'That is the great mystery,' Harland agreed. Frustrated, he ran his hand through his dark hair; a trip to the barber was overdue.

All three of the room's occupants glanced at the door as the desk sergeant entered. 'The inspector is requesting your company,

Detective,' he said to Harland, who thanked him and nodded briskly.

'He has another case for us, Gilbert, and wants this one concluded. Having a second murder to dangle before him will buy us more time.'

'Plus, we have Donahue Marsh on the hook now, Sir.'

'True, and I do not want to risk losing him. When we speak to Mr Marsh, I want him to feel like he has no room to manoeuvre.'

'You are hoping he will confess to killing Elizabeth Rowe and her first husband, Richard Tyson? But what is his motive?' Lilly asked.

'Love, greed, jealousy, hatred... who is to say. But we must tread carefully,' Harland said.

'Can I report you are both now revisiting the death of Elizabeth Rowe's first husband, Mr Richard Tyson?' Lilly asked. 'I would like to include Dr McGregor's report that Mr Tyson sustained injuries that could be suspicious.'

Harland thought about the consequences of this, as he always did, before answering. 'Yes, I have forewarned his aged parents, so that should be fine. But please do not mention the ironbark floor or any detail of Mr Tyson's death other than what Tavish has said, Miss Lewis. I do not want Donahue Marsh to know what we know if he is guilty.'

'Understood, Detective,' Lilly said. 'We don't wish to give him time to make excuses. May I also speak to those witnesses who saw

Elizabeth Rowe? Their quotes would make for good reading.' She nodded at the pieces of paper on his desk.

'As they came forward because of your story, I don't see why not, Miss Lewis,' Harland said, offering the small notes for her to copy. Lilly hurriedly wrote their details. 'If you or Mr Griffiths sees them before we do, please let them know we are coming to call.'

'I will. Thank you, detectives,' Lilly said, rising. She returned the slips of paper to Harland. 'It is so exciting when we are on the cusp of a case being solved. Thank you again, and good day.'

She hurried from the room, and Harland exhaled. 'I have no idea who might have killed Mrs Rowe, and it might well have been Donahue Marsh – the man she flirted with and called cousin, but it is encouraging that Miss Lewis feels we are on the cusp of it.'

Gilbert grinned. 'I agree with Miss Lewis, Sir. I feel we are very close to revealing all.'

'Well, I shall be inspired by your infectious optimism. Let me see the inspector, and we will be off. We will call on Miss Charlotte Glasson first as she is near several of the witnesses and then work our way through the list.'

Detective Stone hurriedly groomed himself and headed out into the hallway and up the stairs to update the inspector.

Julius declined politely. 'Thank you, Grandma, but I've already had two cups of tea from Mrs Dobbs and her endless teapot. Besides, we are on the clock.' He shifted impatiently, willing his brother to appear.

'Is Ambrose all right?' Maria asked, looking toward where her youngest grandson had disappeared to groom himself.

'He will be. Miss Kirby, however, is no doubt devastated. Phoebe said she hoped to marry Ambrose, but he inadvertently revealed he still held a flame for Miss Lilly Lewis.' Julius sighed as he moved to the window to look out at the hearse and keep his eye on the horses.

'The poor dear. She's such a lovely girl, but there is nothing worse than not being truly loved. I understand her actions; it is a credit to her.'

Julius studied his grandmother for a moment. She was graceful and delicate but strong of will, and he could imagine how both Astin brothers had loved her in their youth. After revealing his ability to see spirits to his grandfather, he felt he should share the confidence with his grandmother, given her love and support. Also, with the message he would soon convey to the senior Astin, it would be better if his grandparents could discuss it and support each other. He glanced at the stairwell, ensuring they were alone, and said, 'Grandma, I need to tell you something in confidence, but it truly must be kept so.'

'I am the keeper of secrets, my boy,' she said. 'I have secrets that your mother and father told me that I will never reveal, as well as my own secrets.' She gave him a smile.

'But if they are dead, can we not know?' he asked curiously.

'Definitely not,' she said. 'They did not say I could tell everyone when they passed. Besides, it might make you see your parents in a manner that they would not wish. I promise you will meet no one more discrete than me.'

'That is comforting,' Julius said. 'I recently told Grandpa my secret, and now I must tell him something more. I hope you will support him, but you can only do so if you know my truth,' he said awkwardly, adding, 'I wish it would go away.'

'You do not need to declare it, Julius. I have always known you and Phoebe have the gift,' she said, unsurprised.

'But how?' he asked, equally annoyed and flabbergasted.

'Your dear mother told me. You often communicated with the other side when you and Phoebe were children. Phoebe never stopped, but you did when you realised that not everyone saw what you saw. I assure you, I will say nothing; I never have.'

Julius gave a surprised huff, and Maria chuckled.

'I have rendered you speechless, my dear. What is the message you must relay to Randolph?'

'It is from Reggie. Since we were speaking of Miss Kirby and unrequited love...'

Maria nodded. 'It reminded you of Reggie and his love loss.'

'Did you know he loved you?'

'Of course,' she said, 'but I never encouraged him, and I can say that with all sincerity. I would not lead a young man on, and we were young.' She smiled. 'He was so much like Ambrose – fun, lively, so charming, but the moment I set eyes on your grandfather, and he kissed my hand on introduction, I was a fool for him.' She gave a small laugh. 'Nothing has changed. I am so very sorry for the pain it caused my brother-in-law, and I have tortured myself, wondering if I should have declined Randolph's advances so I did not come between the brothers. It was too late when I realised the depth of Reggie's love for me; I was engaged and could not imagine a life without Randolph. I love him as much today as I did then, if not more.'

Julius smiled. 'I hope I can say that about Violet and me in the coming decades.'

'As do I.'

'Reggie called Grandpa "Rone",' Julius said.

Maria gave a small gasp. 'Only Reggie would know that name; I haven't heard it for years and years.'

'Did Grandpa know Uncle Reggie loved you?' Julius asked.

'No. The brothers were close but did not speak of such things, and once Randolph started courting me, Reggie stayed away; he had very little to do with us, which truly hurt Randolph.'

They heard Ambrose's footsteps above as he started down the hallway.

'I will be here for him,' Maria said, and Julius thanked her.

'That is more presentable for the dead,' Julius looked up and inspected Ambrose as his brother descended the staircase.

'I hope the dead appreciate it,' he mumbled.

'I am sure their living family will, dear,' Maria said. 'Don't nurse a broken heart; talk with your brother. It will do you a world of good.'

Julius could not resist putting his arm around his brother as they exited the house, mussing up his hair for old time's sake.

Miss Charlotte Glasson smiled as the two detectives entered the sweet store, BonBon's Confectionary, and Harland was relieved to find they were the only customers there.

'Are you back for more sweets for your lady friends?' she teased, and Gilbert laughed.

'No, Miss Glasson, but as we are here, it would be remiss of us not to purchase some.'

'It would indeed, especially should you mention the visit and not present some of our offerings,' she joked, and Harland berated himself again. He had not thought to purchase any and would have left empty-handed. He realised he needed considerable work in the romance department.

'Let me see,' Miss Glasson continued tapping her chin, looking endearing with her ginger hair and bright green eyes. 'It was fruit drops for your girlfriend and toffee for your mother,' she said to Gilbert, 'and I think it was a box of chocolates for your lady,' she said to Harland.

'You are an excellent saleswoman, Miss Glasson, and you have a good memory for faces,' Harland complimented her, hoping that her recall of faces would work to his advantage.

'I never forget a face and a sweet,' she agreed, delighted with their compliment.

'What is your favourite, Miss Glasson?' Gilbert asked, his curiosity getting the better of him.

'Turkish delight,' she said and sighed as if the thought was heavenly. 'But before sweets, business first, I imagine.'

'Yes, thank you, Miss Glasson. We asked you previously if you knew Mr Ernest Rowe or Mrs Elizabeth Rowe, and you did not.'

She shook her head again.

'Might you know a lady named Elizabeth Jenkins?' Harland asked.

'French bon-bons,' she answered and smiled. 'She came in several times for them and was such a friendly lady. I complimented her on her bonnet, and she insisted on gifting me a hat that she said would suit me better than herself. It was a gift from her former mother-in-law, but she had never worn it.'

Harland's eyes narrowed with suspicion. 'Did she bring it to your workplace?'

'Oh no. She said it came with a hatbox and that it would be best to leave it at my home. I gave her my address; my mother was home and on hand to greet her.' She added under her breath, 'The hat was very expensive and beautiful.'

'Did she have access to your bedroom by any chance, Miss Glasson?' Gilbert asked.

The young lady paused, surprised by the question. 'Yes. She asked my mother if she could place it there while Mum made tea. She is very kind. I have not seen her for some time, though.'

'Miss Glasson, I am sorry to tell you she passed away at the time of the *River Lady* ferry accident.' Harland ignored her distress and continued, knowing she would soon recover when she heard his theory. 'Elizabeth Jenkins was married to Mr Richard Tyson, widowed, remarried and is now known as Mrs Elizabeth Rowe. I believe she claimed your engagement ring that day of her visit and returned it to your ex-fiancé, Mr Donahue Marsh.'

Charlotte Glasson sputtered, 'My ring... she knew Donahue? Oh, I have been such a fool!'

'No, Miss Glasson, you have been trusting, and there is nothing wrong with that,' Gilbert assured her. 'It is a sad state of affairs when people take advantage of the good-hearted.'

Harland was pleased Gilbert was on hand to offer the perfect words of comfort when needed. Given the nature of the news they just delivered, the detectives bought up most generously before departing.

Chapter 26

REPORTERS LILLY LEWIS AND Fergus Griffith were pleased to discover that the addresses of the witnesses who had come forward claiming to have seen Mrs Elizabeth Rowe that fateful afternoon as the *River Lady* sank were near each other. A combination of shop owners and workers who had hurried out to the banks of the river to see if they could assist or to watch the horror unfolding, as was human nature.

'I've never been interviewed by a reporter before,' Miss Daniher said, adopting an expression of importance. She was of medium height, appeared to be in her late forties and dressed brightly in a gold fabric that matched her slightly unnatural hair colour. 'My sister and I have owned this fabric store for a decade, but I have never seen anything like I did that afternoon. Dreadful.'

'May I take notes and quote you, Miss Daniher?' Fergus asked, flipping open his notepad and leaning on the counter that housed ribbons, laces and trims of every kind.

'Of course you may, young man,' she said. 'It's Jean Daniher. My sister is Jane. I believe the newspaper has an important role to play in our community. Doesn't it, Jane?' she asked the woman who appeared from the back of the shop and had Lilly and Fergus looking twice.

The similarity was uncanny, and they also wore the same dress.

'We're twins,' Jane explained with a small laugh. 'We always get that reaction. And yes, I agree wholeheartedly with Jean; we read the newspaper daily. It's very important.'

'This is Miss Lewis and Mr Griffiths,' Jean said. 'We love their crime pieces.'

'Goodness, in the flesh, well I never! We love your writing,' Jane agreed. 'So our names might be in the paper tomorrow. How exciting, Jean.'

'It is. We'll clip the story, Jane, and keep it,' Jean said. Returning her attention to Lilly, she said, 'Now, you asked if we recalled seeing this young lady on the hill.' Jean put on her glasses and considered the photograph before her. Jane came to look over her shoulder.

'It was a dreadful afternoon,' Jane shook her head.

'I just said the same thing to the reporters, dear,' Jean nodded.

'We felt so helpless watching people struggling in the water, and we couldn't do a thing to help. We had no life raft, and neither of us can swim,' Jane said. 'The young lady said she could not swim either, remember, Jean?'

'Yes, I recall that, but her companion said he was a capable swimmer. I thought it was remiss that he did not assist. She could have waited safely with us.'

'Very unheroic,' Jane said and blushed, 'even if that is an uncharitable thing to say.'

Lilly smiled and tried to rein in the interview. 'So you recall seeing this very same lady in the photograph and speaking with her?' Lilly clarified. 'It's very important to our investigative piece.'

The sisters looked at each other, and Jane gave Jean a small nod as if authorising her to speak.

'Miss Lewis, I can confirm that we saw this lady and spoke with her and her handsome friend,' Jean said. 'She was a lovely young lady and seemed so caring.'

'She wore a beautiful dress,' Jane added, 'very expensive fabric.'

'Very expensive,' the twin agreed.

Lilly tried not to look as frustrated as she felt at the twins' back-and-forth banter. 'Her name is Mrs Elizabeth Rowe. Did she introduce herself by name or introduce her male companion?'

'No, I'm sorry to say,' Jean shook her head. 'We just started talking and did not undertake formal introductions.'

'There was too much going on,' Jane explained.

'But she called him by his first name, so they must have been closely acquainted. It was an unusual name. Irish. I can't recall it,' Jean said.

'It will come to me,' Jane mused, 'I am good with names.'

'You are very good with names, Jane. I am not,' Jean said, 'but I am good with numbers.'

'That is a good skill,' Lilly said as Fergus waited to record a quote or two. 'What did you speak of in particular?'

'Oh, just the drama unfolding before us,' Jean said. 'The horror of it. She wanted to help, and the young man suggested they move closer to the river bank to see if they could assist.'

'Did he now?' Lilly asked with a raised eyebrow, and Fergus scribbled that fact down with great interest.

'She wore a wedding ring, but he didn't,' Jane added. 'He might have been her brother. What was his name... it will come to me.'

Lilly and Fergus did not want to offer it for fear they might place the suggestion in the ladies' minds, so they waited patiently.

'Was she intending to catch that ferry and missed it by any chance?' Lilly prompted.

'She did not say that, so I could not confirm or deny it,' Jean said.

'Donahue!' Jane exclaimed and smiled, and Jean clapped her hands together.

'That was it. Jane, you are truly amazing with names,' Jean smiled at her twin with great admiration.

'Excellent, Miss Daniher, that is truly appreciated. Is there anything else you can think of about the couple?' Lilly prompted. 'For example, did you see them depart, and in which direction?'

'Or see them again later that evening?' Fergus added.

'They did depart before us,' Jean said, looking to Jane, who nodded her agreement. 'They headed down to the waterline and were soon out of sight. Many people were there; one could have easily been lost amongst them.'

'Many,' Jane agreed.

'Ladies, you have been so helpful. Thank you very much,' Lilly said. 'If only all our witnesses were as forthcoming', and Fergus echoed her thanks. They backed out of the store and got away after several farewells with much praise bestowed upon them.

Lilly squealed with delight once out of the ladies' sight and hearing range. 'Oh my goodness, Fergus, we have a witness to Donahue Marsh being on the scene and in the company of Mrs Elizabeth Rowe. That is just what the detectives need to corner him.'

'But did he kill her?' Fergus asked. 'There is still no evidence of that.'

'No, but he encouraged her to come to the water's edge when he knew she could not swim.'

'It will certainly help the detectives' case,' Fergus agreed and chuckled. 'What an interesting pair.'

Lilly grinned. 'The detectives will have their work cut out for them. I am sure the sisters will adore them. I didn't mention the detectives intended to call; the ladies would be so excited, and if they didn't, well...'

'A disaster,' Fergus agreed with a huff of laughter. 'Perhaps, time permitting, you should call on the detectives and brief them. I'm sure they would appreciate being spared the visit.'

'You are right. A good deed will work in our favour down the track.' Lilly took a deep breath. 'Onward then, let's visit the next witness, but maybe after their account, we will have enough to write our story. It will be hard to better the Misses Jean and Jane Daniher.'

Burying the dead did not affect Julius Astin as it did when he first began his business, *The Economic Undertaker*. In those early days, every parent buried was his own, and he felt the emotions of the moment. Every grandparent buried was his one day in the future, and his heart would be heavy. Burying young people and children only highlighted to him what suffering families endure. But now, after nearly a decade in the industry, and with his siblings and grandfather joining him in the business, he was more pragmatic. Numb to the grief of others around him, he was pleased about that.

Julius cast an eye over everything to ensure it was in order as he and Ambrose stepped away from the gravesite. They had a brief reprieve while the priest delivered his blessings, and the mourners said their last farewells to the deceased. Julius's gaze settled on his brother. Ambrose did not look tormented or anguished as one would expect after the loss of love; in fact, many of the mourners who claimed to be only acquaintances of the dead were grieving more than Ambrose.

'What am I to do now?' Ambrose mumbled and sighed. 'I was making plans and looking to buy a house.'

'Then you should continue to do so,' Julius said in a low voice. 'Go out with Lucian, throw yourself into your work, and do your best not to linger on what might have been.'

'Should I sit on our parents' grave and drink too much like you did when you lost Violet once?' Ambrose asked.

Julius smarted at his tone. 'You asked me what you should do. I did not offer my advice unsolicited. If it makes you feel better, visit Mum and Dad and get drunk. Or continue to be angry with me, if that helps.'

'I am sorry, brother, that was unnecessarily cruel of me,' Ambrose said sincerely and sighed again.

'I understand; think nothing of it. But, Ambrose, are you truly heartbroken?'

'Of course I am,' Ambrose said indignantly, and Julius hushed him. 'Why would you ask me that?'

'Because your heart never seemed to be completely with Miss Kirby. Did she keep you awake at night, drifting through your thoughts? Did you feel passionate about protecting her and providing for her?'

Ambrose did not answer, but he bit his lower lip in thought.

Julius continued, 'Can you say, in all honesty, that you are devastated by the loss of Miss Kirby's affection? What if you met a young lady like Miss Lewis and were engaged to Miss Kirby? Would you regret that? Perhaps it is a blessing in disguise for you both that it ended as it did. You are a free man, Ambrose.'

Again, Ambrose did not respond, but Julius could tell from his brother's expression that his mind was racing.

Eventually, Ambrose said, 'It is hard to meet women in our profession, and I don't wish to attend dances.'

'And yet, I am married, as are Claude, Will and Grandpa. There are attractive women at every funeral, many swooning and needing your assistance.'

'They do look striking in black,' Ambrose agreed.

'I met a young lady on the omnibus this week. I don't know if she has a beau, but she wasn't wearing rings. I will introduce you,' Julius said.

'How?' Ambrose asked, looking directly at Julius. 'Did you exchange details? Violet will not be pleased.'

'Nothing like that; what do you take me for?' Julius frowned. 'She introduced herself as we are in the same profession – Miss Billie Prout—Willamina, but she informs me she will not answer to that name.'

'Prout?' Ambrose said, recognising the name and squinting as he thought about it.

Julius did not have time to explain. The priest finished, and Julius nudged Ambrose; the two men stepped forward to lower the deceased into the grave as the priest sprinkled holy water on the coffin. They then stepped back, allowing the family room to throw in dirt, flowers, or themselves, as happened on rare occasions.

Twenty minutes later, with the family and priest departed and grave diggers present to fill in the dirt plot, Ambrose exclaimed, 'Prout, the monumental masons.'

'Precisely. A very attractive and sassy young lady she was, too; she reminded me of Miss Lewis with her confidence and ambition. Miss Prout is coming in to present some of her designs. I'll be sure to let you know when. Perhaps you would like to handle the meeting as you are the Operations Manager.'

Ambrose smiled. 'I would indeed. Billie... hmm, most interesting. Who does she look like? Violet, Miss Lewis or our sister? Or some other beauty in our acquaintance?'

'I could not say. I didn't study her a great deal, but she made a favourable impression,' Julius said as they walked towards the now empty hearse to make their journey back to the office.

'Very diplomatic of you, brother,' Ambrose said with a smile. 'Perhaps you are right. I thought I loved Kate, but maybe I was just in love with how she adored me.'

Julius hid a smile; the real Ambrose was back, and the trip home was much brighter.

'I never thought Mrs Rowe might have used a false name with Miss Glasson, Sir,' Gilbert admitted.

'It just occurred to me while we were there. Perhaps she was worried Donahue might have mentioned her or his former employer. So she took precautions and used her maiden name, Jenkins.'

'Very astute,' Gilbert said, writing the details on their board.

Harland looked up at the clock and was momentarily excited to know he would finish work on time to walk Phoebe home, and then he remembered she had an emergency *Vexed Vixens* gathering. Ambrose's fault for breaking Miss Kirby's heart, according to Gilbert, who received a note from Miss Emily Yalden, his belle, this morning, breaking their plans for the night.

Returning his mind to work, he addressed the young detective. 'Tomorrow, Gilbert, first thing, I believe we are ready to speak with Donahue Marsh.' He sat back at his desk, opened one of the packs of sweets he bought from Miss Glasson at BonBon's Confectionary, offered one to Gilbert, who politely declined, and popped a caramel into his mouth.

'Excellent, Sir. You don't wish to speak with the witnesses themselves?'

'No. Thanks to Miss Lewis, we have dodged a bullet there, as they say. However, we will need to get formal statements from them if we arrest Mr Marsh.'

'What if he denies everything, Sir?' Gilbert asked.

'I expect he will. But he is associated with all the parties, and if we need to bluff a little, we will do so to corner him. It is most unfortunate that both of our victims are dead and cannot identify him.'

'Do you think Mrs Elizabeth Rowe could confirm his involvement if you asked Miss Astin to summon her?' Gilbert gasped as an idea came to him. 'Sir, if he does not confess, we could set a trap.'

'Do tell?' Harland had another caramel and then closed the box before he ate more.

'What if we tell Donahue Marsh that the undertakers found a tin with cash and a note meant for him on the body of Mrs Elizabeth Rowe? He will then have to explain what the money was for if he wants it returned.'

'It is a good plan, but I would not mention *The Economic Undertaker* business. We don't want him showing up there and trying to speak with the Astin family. Perhaps we could say it was found at the coroner's office,' Harland mused. 'We will warn Tavish, and we can follow Mr Marsh to see if he will go there.'

'I still doubt he will tell us the truth.'

'As do I,' Harland agreed. 'Here is another idea, Gilbert. Should we meet resistance – we could ask Ernest Rowe to visit Donahue, and we can secretly listen to that discussion.'

'That would be interesting, Sir, especially as Mr Rowe now knows Donahue is not his wife's cousin.'

'Indeed. Let us mull on it overnight,' Harland said. 'Enjoy your evening.'

'It is my poetry meeting night, Sir. I did have plans with Miss Yalden for a walk, but as she is absent now, I will stop thinking like a criminal and think like a poet.'

'I can't imagine,' Harland said with a smile, and once Gilbert departed, he paced the office, going back over the case. Maybe he would catch up with Julius and see what he thought. His wife would also be at the *Vexed Vixens* tonight, and the men could share a drink.

He grabbed his hat and departed, hoping to find Julius still at the office.

Chapter 27

AMBROSE DEPARTED TO MEET Cousin Lucian in a cheerier mood than when he had arrived this morning. Mrs. Dobbs packed and left for the day, the thanks of the men ringing in her ears. Phoebe and Violet headed to their *Vexed Vixens'* emergency dinner, and at last, Julius and his grandfather were alone.

'Do not spare me, lad,' Randolph said. 'I have long wondered what drove Reggie from home, and telling me the whole story is the greatest favour you can do for me.'

The men sat in the tearoom, sharing a pot of tea that Mrs Dobbs had left them before departing, believing they were reviewing the pending shift in office for the ladies' next door. It was a small white lie, but one that allowed them privacy.

Julius inhaled and started, as his Uncle Reggie did, with Maria and Reggie's friendship. His grandfather relayed no emotion until

Julius spoke of Reggie introducing Maria to his brother and knowing, in that moment, he had lost any chance of gaining her affection. Randolph gave a small groan but nodded for his grandson to continue.

Julius avoided looking at his uncle, who appeared behind Randolph. Reggie paced, watching his brother's face. He disappeared before reappearing again, concern etching his ghostly countenance and unable to stay away.

'When you had your first child and asked him to be godfather, he was honoured and confessed to being jealous beyond all measure,' Julius continued. Randolph rubbed his hand over his jaw before pressing his knuckles to his mouth in contemplation of that event so long ago.

'Shall I continue, Grandpa?'

'Yes, please, Julius, tell me everything,' Randolph said.

'He believed himself in love at one stage and that he had moved on from Grandma,' Julius continued.

'I remember hearing of his engagement, but he never brought the young lady to meet Maria and me,' Randolph said.

'No, Reggie said he knew it was not love and was dishonourable, calling off the wedding.'

Randolph nodded but did not speak. Both men were silent by nature, and Julius mused that if his uncle was expecting an outpouring of emotion or grief, he didn't know his brother as well as he thought.

Julius continued, 'It was twenty years after your marriage when Uncle Reggie returned for my christening that his actions became rash,' Julius said, coming to the last details of Reggie's story.

'I remember,' Randolph said. 'I begged him to come. But surely after twenty years the flame he held for Maria must have been extinguished.'

'I believe his ardour had long since cooled, but when he held me in his arms and saw your beautiful family, he felt his loss more heavily. He said it could have all been his, and despair and jealousy saw him take to his horse that afternoon.'

Randolph rose, paced for a few moments, and then sat again. 'I would never have begged him to come had I known how painful it was for him. He must have thought I was rubbing my happiness in his face,' he said, distressed. The ghost of Reggie dropped into a seat opposite him, begging him not to think like that.

It was wasted. Randolph could not see or hear anyone but Julius, who ignored Reggie, believing that acknowledging his presence would heighten his grandfather's pain. He wanted to relay the story while maintaining some distance from his uncle's despair.

'Uncle Reggie wanted you to know that he never blamed you. He wanted you to know how deeply sorry he is for the pain caused by his weakness and claimed he was a petty man.'

'No, Reggie, was never that. My poor, dear brother.'

'He said he should have put his feelings for you above all else.' Julius finished. 'That is all I have to tell you, Grandpa. Except he called you a name I have never heard. Rone.'

Randolph inhaled sharply and then smiled. 'I have not heard that for such a long time.' He straightened in the chair and looked at his grandson. 'Thank you, Julius. I know the sacrifice you have made to recount that story to me when you did not want to be a channel for the other side.'

'I am glad I could assist Uncle Reggie, but I am unsure how knowing this benefits you. Are you all right, Grandpa? Can I see you home?'

'No, no,' Randolph said with a smile and, rising, took their cups to the sink to wash them before Mrs Dobbs returned in the morning. 'As you have bared your soul to Maria, I will share the account with her this evening. But do not fear, lad; I am made of sturdy matter.'

Julius smiled, and a quick rap on the front door had both men peering around the doorway. Julius went to answer and found Detective Harland Stone on the doorstep.

'Julius, Mr Astin, the lights were still on; I was hoping you were in,' he said.

'Harland, hello. Phoebe has gone to the emergency *Vexed Vixens* dinner with Violet,' Julius said, assuming Phoebe's beau had forgotten.

'I know. So, I have come to collect you for a drink and to discuss my case. Are you free?'

'Perfect timing, Detective,' Randolph said, adding to his grandson, 'Go and relax, Julius; I shall see you first thing in the morning.'

'If you are sure?'

'Very sure, I am leaving now too. I will lock up.'

Julius grabbed his hat and saw his uncle hovering near his grandfather, but there was nothing more to say. The living must live on, and the dead must remain so.

Miss Lilly Lewis was the last to arrive and rushed in with apologies, carrying an egg and bacon pie that her mother had made for the *Vexed Vixens'* dinner that evening. Since Lilly began her courtship with Mr Bennet Martin, her parents were much more content for Lilly to pursue her reporter role as long as it did not stop her from accepting his hand in marriage or having a family when that time came.

Miss Emily Yalden was hosting the dinner, as she was the only group member with her own premises. The students of the *Miss Emily Yalden School of Deportment* had gone for the day after their lessons in elocution, dancing, manners, and hosting duties, to name but a few of the classes on offer. As no less than a dozen of Emily's girls had made excellent matches and were well received at their debuts, Emily's skills were in great demand by mothers keen to marry off their daughters. At night, Emily was pleased to have the premises to herself. Her beau, Detective Gilbert Payne, had not yet been to the home unchaperoned, although he had attended a dinner dance she hosted for the *Vexed Vixens* and friends before they began courting.

While Lilly had rushed in late, Phoebe and Violet had arrived together earlier, keen to be on hand when Kate arrived. Phoebe felt responsible for her friend's grief. She came bearing one of her grandmother's desserts and a reasonable wave of anger towards her brother, Ambrose.

Not long after, a despondent Miss Kate Kirby arrived and accepted their commiserations.

The ladies with drinks in hand hovered around the sitting room. It was an awkward gathering, and while they were quite hungry, Kate was not. It would appear unseemly for them to tuck in with great abandon, so they restrained themselves to drinks and conversation. They did not discuss Kate's broken heart until Emily officially welcomed the group.

'I am so sorry to have called this emergency meeting on such a sad occasion, but, dear Kate, we are here for you.'

Kate gave Emily a teary smile. 'Thank you, Emily, and do not fret, ladies, I do not intend to be a wet blanket this evening, although I am grateful for the chance to gather.'

'You may be as miserable as you wish, Kate,' Emily said. 'We understand and are most upset for you and with you.'

'Thank you, Emily,' Kate sat near the window, and the ladies followed suit, selecting chairs nearby. 'I have had a day and night of solid crying and am feeling much better, even if I do not look it. I was quite strong before I arrived, but your hugs and well wishes made me teary again.'

Phoebe, who sat on one side of Kate, took her hand. 'I am so terribly sorry, Kate. I hope you will forgive me, and we may remain close friends despite my brother's insensitivity.'

'Forgive you? For what, Phoebe?' Kate said, squeezing her hand. 'And yes, we will be friends forever, I am sure of it. It came as a shock, I confess. But I blame myself.'

'But you mustn't, Kate,' Violet said. 'My mother, God rest her soul, often quoted the poet Tennyson:

'Tis better to have loved and lost
Than never to have loved at all.*

'I believe that,' Violet continued, 'despite how raw your heart must be feeling now.'

'So true,' Lilly agreed. 'Some people never experience love or romance. That would be tragic. You have opened your heart, Kate, and when the pain is gone, the happy times will always be yours to remember.'

'I hope that is true, but right now, I can't conceive it will ever be that way,' Kate said. 'I was childish in love. My heart fell out of rhythm when Ambrose looked at me; I imagined a future with him.' Her voice caught, and she cleared her throat. 'It would be so easy to write and ask Ambrose to forget my declaration and to come back, and I will accept his heart no matter how strong his feelings are or aren't for me, but I cannot do that. I wish I could.'

The ladies murmured their sympathy, trying to understand why the relationship had ended. Emily knew only because she had called on Kate this morning, and Phoebe had been informed by her brother himself.

Kate dabbed her eyes and continued. 'I am to blame, not Ambrose,' she said bravely. 'I should not have rushed into the relationship. I should have been more circumspect and cautious.'

'But how could you be so?' Lilly asked, studying her teary friend, a little confused. 'If a man shows his affections and requests the pleasure of your company, and you know he is from a good family,' she added with a glance at Phoebe, 'why would you need to be cautious, dear Kate?'

Kate bit her lower lip, and Emily attempted to change the subject, but Lilly, a reporter by day and by nature, was now curious.

'Kate, please tell us what happened. I am concerned now. Why did you need to be circumspect about...' she stopped herself from saying his name, 'about your relationship?'

'Well,' Kate started, seeking diplomatic words, which proved challenging given that she was the most impulsive of the *Vexed Vixens* and known for blurting out what was on her mind. 'I should have taken things more slowly; that's all I meant.'

Lilly looked unconvinced as she studied the faces around the table, who were not making eye contact. She locked eyes with Emily, the hostess.

'He loves you, Lilly,' Emily cut to the chase. 'I am sorry, Kate, but it is bound to come out eventually, and best to clear the air. Ambrose loves you, Lilly.'

'No!' Lilly exclaimed and looked at Kate and then at Phoebe, who nodded in agreement. 'But why?' she asked and rose, rushing to kneel before Kate and take her hand. She hurried on. 'I would never have accepted his ride to *The Courier* office if I had known. I promise you I did not flirt with him or lead him on.'

'I know, my friend, do not stress,' Kate said, squeezing her hands reassuringly.

'But why? Oh, Kate, I have never...' she shook her head, recalling all the times she spoke with Ambrose. She turned to the ladies. 'In truth, and I think you all know, I was in love with an Astin, but it was Julius, and I assure you, Violet, it was purely infatuation and not reciprocated, not for a moment. Now I have met my match in Bennet, and I give you my word, Kate, I did not encourage Ambrose.'

Kate held up her hands. 'Do not fret, dear Lilly, I know. It is not your fault. It is no one's fault whom we lose our hearts to. I know Dr McGregor was fond of me, but I could not reciprocate his feelings, and now he is finding happiness with Emily's delightful cousin, Isabelle. That is how it goes sometimes.'

'You are being very generous and worldly, Kate,' Phoebe said, 'but Lilly and I can't help but shoulder guilt for your unhappiness.'

'Then we shall speak of it no more,' Kate declared, raising her chin with defiance. 'It is done. As Violet said, in time, I am sure I will think fondly of those memories. So please let us eat if that is all right with our hostess, and I shall tell you my plans.'

'You have plans?' Emily asked, surprised. She indicated everyone should enter the dining room, where their meal awaited. Lilly rose, and Kate once more assured her friend that she was not to feel responsible. Emily removed the covers and revealed the dinner dishes each had brought.

'Please do sit,' Emily said, 'and we shall serve ourselves.'

Once they had done so, Emily said, 'Now, Kate, what are these plans, and will the *Vexed Vixens* agree with them?' She teased, and Kate laughed.

'I am sure you will,' Kate said, smiling with genuine enthusiasm. 'I have accepted a position in Ingham.'

There was a stunned silence before Lilly said, 'But that is the end of the earth, Kate, is it not?'

'Where is Ingham?' Phoebe asked.

'It is farther north, I believe,' Violet said.

'But you are so fair, and it will be horrendously hot,' Emily added.

Kate laughed. 'I am not the first woman ever to head north. I have an opportunity, and some might say it was fate.'

The *Vexed Vixens* were so relieved to see Kate's genuine smile and enthusiasm that they adopted the same.

'Do tell then, a new adventure,' Phoebe said, clapping her hands together. 'How exciting.'

'You are a lady explorer, Kate,' Violet exclaimed, making Kate laugh.

'I think the area has already been settled,' Kate teased Violet.

'So, what is the opportunity? How did it come about? When do you leave?' Lilly fired questions at Kate, and she held up her hands.

'As declared, it was fate, truly. I was buying supplies for my studio when the salesman, Mr Owen, pinned a notice to his board from a woman in Ingham, Mrs Harriett Brims. She was seeking another photographer to assist her at her burgeoning studio. I asked Mr Owen to show me where Ingham was, and he pulled a map out from under his desk and pointed to it. It is a reasonable distance, but what a challenge! So I immediately sent a telegram to Mrs Brims, and she invited me to come as soon as possible.'

'Goodness gracious, you are brave, Kate!' Violet exclaimed. 'What if you get there and do not like it?'

Kate shrugged. 'It is not as if I have given up a great deal. My studio will be leased, and I live at home. In Ingham, I will be paid a salary and may choose to stay for a year or five. Who knows where it will lead me?'

'I can tell you are genuinely excited,' Phoebe said. 'But have you given it enough thought? Are you not running away from your pain?' she asked as gently as she could.

'I know it seems that way, Phoebe, and maybe that is true, but I am excited by the chance to do something so unexpected. I have always lived here, never gone further than my neighbourhood. Imagine what I will see and photograph,' she said enthusiastically. 'I leave this Friday.'

All the ladies reacted with surprise and shock, and Kate continued. 'I will take the train to Gladstone, a steamer further north to Townsville, and then travel overland by coach to Ingham. Mrs Brims has paid my fare on the basis I stay at least six months, no less, or I have to pay her back.'

'That seems fair. So you are happy with this choice then?' Lilly asked.

'I am excited about the change. I will miss you all and be sorry to miss the *Vexed Vixen* meetings, but I will come home to visit and imagine our reunions.'

'To grand adventures,' Emily said, raising her glass.

'To Kate,' the *Vexed Vixen*s said, and for that evening, no one was vexed. Well, that was not quite true. Five *Vexed Vixens* were still very vexed with Ambrose Astin.

Harland returned with the first round of drinks that he had elected to buy, to hear Tavish congratulating Julius.

'What have you done now?' Harland asked, cocking an eyebrow at the man who would be his future brother-in-law if Harland had his way.

'I'm here; that is apparently a feat in itself,' Julius said with a smile, accepting a beer.

Tavish agreed. 'I congratulated him on escaping the bonds of marital bliss to step out with his dear friends. I didn't expect to see you for some time, Julius, being a newlywed.'

'As pleasant as it is at home with my wife, Violet is busy this evening, along with Phoebe and Miss Lewis,' Julius said with a nod to Harland and Bennet.

'Oh, I am a poor second choice,' Tavish sighed. 'Never mind, I am pleased to see you all.' He raised a glass in a toast. 'To the boys.'

The men clinked glasses and turned their attention to the fight about to start.

'Are you fighting this evening, Harland?' Bennet asked.

'No. Now that I am courting,' he said with a glance to Julius, 'I am conscious of not presenting a battered face any more than necessary.'

'Yes, that nose is crooked enough,' Tavish agreed. 'Speaking of courting, I am pleased that the ferry disaster is over and we can return to normal. I have not caught up with Miss Yalden for some time, and it is a sad state of affairs when the dead outnumber my visitors.'

'Oddly, we all benefitted from it though, did we not?' Bennet said, then glanced to Harland. 'Except for the police, of course. Lilly has written some very interesting pieces about your investigation.'

'Indeed. It is a complicated case,' Harland said. 'But Mrs Elizabeth Rowe appearing in Miss Kirby's photographs of people on the hill made our case for us.' He discreetly refrained from mentioning Phoebe's involvement.

'Ah, poor Miss Kirby,' Bennet said, and their small party glanced toward Ambrose and Lucian, who were entertaining several ladies on the other side of the club. 'Is he not upset?' Bennet asked Julius.

'He was initially shocked and despondent, but I believe his feelings never ran as deep as Miss Kirby's, sadly,' Julius said diplomatically.

'Then best it ends before years of marriage wear down any regard they hold for each other,' Harland said as if he had first-hand experience. Julius wondered if that reflected Harland's parents' marriage. His own role models—his grandparents—were as committed to each other as ever.

'I have great sympathy for Miss Kirby,' Julius said, 'but I am pleased my brother is not in pain.'

Again, the party looked to Ambrose, who locked eyes with Julius at that moment. A raised eyebrow from Julius got a nod from Ambrose before he turned to speak with Lucian.

'What went on then?' Bennet said. 'It was as if you were communicating. I do not have a brother to share such intimacies.'

'Nor do I, nor a sister,' Harland said. 'Perhaps siblings have their own means of communicating.'

Bennet shook his head. 'I have a sister, and we don't communicate through looks.'

'I am one of nine,' Tavish said. 'My twin brother and I can speak without words. But I can't say the same of my other siblings.'

'I said to him he is working tomorrow; do not imbibe to excess,' Julius said, 'and Ambrose nodded his understanding.'

Bennet put his drink down on the table. 'I will speak with Ambrose immediately and ask him what was said. We shall see if you two speak the same unspoken language,' he said with a grin and hurriedly departed to find Ambrose.

'Is your twin intending to visit you here in Australia?' Julius asked Tavish.

'He threatens to often enough, but I will believe it when he knocks on my door,' Tavish said. 'Back on your case, Harland, do you have a suspect?'

'Yes, and tomorrow Gilbert and I intend to interview him. We've been lining up our evidence.' Harland shook his head as one of the boxers swung awkwardly and hit the ground. 'I am still not sure we have enough to put him away yet.'

'What will you do if you can't get him to fold and admit his part?' Julius asked. 'For the love of God, I've seen better swings in a playground,' he said, shaking his head at the boxers and making Tavish and Harland laugh.

'I will have to try to trap him into a confession, and as to how to do that, I am not sure yet,' Harland said.

'Maybe your clever little sidekick will come up with an idea,' Tavish said.

'Gilbert has already shared his knowledge of ironbark timber, thus proving Mrs Rowe's first husband might not have met an accidental death,' Harland said.

A roar went up as the referee ended the fight and raised one of the boxers' arms in victory.

Bennet pushed through the crowds and sat back at the men's table. 'Well, I never,' he said with a smile. 'Ambrose said you were telling him to go light on the drink and be at work on time.' Bennet laughed.

Julius smiled. 'Exactly so. Whether he does so is a whole other matter.'

Taking advantage of Tavish and Bennet engaging in a lively discussion, Julius leant closer to Harland and said quietly, 'In regards to your case, my uncle met Mr Tyson, who claimed his death was by foul play.'

'This is your uncle in the afterlife?' Harland said, now alert but speaking in a voice low enough for Julius's ears only.

'Yes, I meant to pass the message onto you, but I forgot,' Julius said. He hurriedly added, 'From Phoebe, of course; the message is from Phoebe.'

'Of course,' Harland said. 'For a moment there, I thought you had started talking to spirits too.'

Julius gave a small laugh and looked away uncomfortably. But a seasoned detective well versed in reading expressions studied him for a moment longer before adding, 'Your information is welcomed and timely, thank you. I was just thinking about my case. It appears you can read me as well as Ambrose.'

Julius smiled. 'Be careful then; that might work against you.'

Harland laughed and muttered, 'Lord help me.'

Chapter 28

IT WAS A BRIGHT but cool May morning, and Harland wished he had imbibed a little less and slept a lot better, but the case had kept going around in his head, along with the thought that he would see Phoebe and walk her home tonight. He wondered how Ambrose had fared this morning and if he had met his brother's expectations. Gilbert, as always, was alert, neat, and keen to work.

The men had decided to arrive at Mr Donahue Marsh's residence early in case the contract labourer had secured himself work and departed before they had a chance to question him. Unfortunately, it also meant encountering the early morning workforce. Harland was just about to give up on getting aboard the omnibus and resort to hailing a hansom cab when two seats became available at their stop, and they hurried into the carriage.

Lowering his voice, Harland said to his protégé, 'If for any reason Mr Marsh becomes violent, do not challenge him. He is a solid man who is strong from labouring, and we do not need to be heroes. We will return with reinforcements.'

'Yes, Sir,' Gilbert said. 'If he is capable of murdering a lady, then I doubt he will come without a fight.'

'Some men do if they know they are beaten,' Harland said. 'We should be so lucky.'

Alighting at the stop nearest Donahue Marsh's boarding house in Fortitude Valley, they soon realised they need not have arrived so early.

'Mr Marsh is in his room,' the landlady said, pointing to the first room near the entranceway. 'You were here last time, weren't you? He hasn't worked all week, so tell him I'm still expecting rent on the usual day.' She walked off and left the men outside Donahue's door. Harland rapped on it.

'Perhaps I should watch the front window in case he tries to exit,' Gilbert said just as the door swung open and Donahue Marsh stood in the doorway in his bed wear, unshaven, and with his hair unkempt.

'It's a bit early for social calls, isn't it, detectives?' he said and stepped away, allowing them to enter. Harland closed the door behind them. The bedsit flat was large, and everything was in one room except for a screen that hid the ablution area.

'We have come to arrest you, Mr Marsh,' Harland said confidently, and the cocky young man whirled around in surprise.

'For what?' He regained his confidence and asked drily, 'For not working this week? Take me away then, detectives.'

'I suggest you put some clothes on and then sit down,' Harland said, indicating the couch and remaining near the door. Gilbert moved to the window and watched his superior in action.

Harland did not drop his gaze as Donahue Marsh glared at him. Then, the labourer gave a small sigh of resignation and went to the wardrobe, grabbing some long pants and a shirt and hurriedly dressing. He slipped his feet into black shoes and, running his hands through his hair, dropped onto the couch.

'Righto, what have I done?' he asked, crossing his arms in front of him.

'We know quite a lot about you, Mr Marsh,' Harland said, moving closer now. 'We know of your relationship with the late Mrs Elizabeth Rowe and why you were dismissed from her first husband's employ.'

Donahue scoffed. 'Jealous husbands are a dime a dozen. So what?'

'The very same husband, Mr Richard Tyson, who fell to his death from a new bridge constructed with ironbark timber that would have easily withstood his weight had it not been tampered with.'

Donahue looked impressed. 'Bravo, detectives, that's very good. But if it was tampered with, why would I have done so? Perhaps it was bad workmanship, or someone else held a grudge against him.'

Harland continued hoping that Donahue Marsh would reveal himself as the murderer.

'You tampered with it because you wanted Richard Tyson gone. You hoped to win the hand of his wife, Elizabeth, or Mrs Rowe as you know her by now – a very wealthy widow with the death of her husband.'

'If that were the case, I would be with her, detectives, and not contracting out my labour services, would I not?'

'Not if you took advantage of her and her feelings were not reciprocated,' Gilbert pointed out.

'I could have had Mrs Rowe as easily as this,' he said and clicked his fingers. 'But I only ever wanted a dalliance. Is that all you've got?'

Harland had not felt like boxing last evening in the company of his friends, but he did right now. His hand itched to wipe that smirk off the labourer's smug face.

'You obviously don't read the newspaper, Mr Marsh,' Harland continued, calm and in control. 'There's a lovely photograph of yourself and Mrs Rowe on the hill watching as the *River Lady* ferry sank before you. So she was not a victim of the ferry accident but died by your hand soon after. Did she refuse your advances and ruin your plan to be a wealthy, kept husband?'

'Woah, woah, go back,' Donahue Marsh raised his hands. 'I saw that photograph. That wasn't me; that was her husband.'

Harland nodded to Gilbert, who said, 'No, Sir. Mr Ernest Rowe was at work then and was seen by his colleagues. You were identified by several witnesses, one of whom recalled your name.'

'Those stupid old biddies,' he muttered and then stretched out on the couch, putting his arms on the headrest. 'So what? I met with Elizabeth. We were friends.'

'Then why not say so? Why lie to us?' Harland asked, and the young man before him shrugged casually. Harland continued, 'You knew she couldn't swim; she told you so according to our witnesses, but you still insisted that the pair of you go to the water's edge and assist those in distress.'

'That doesn't mean I told her to get in the water or I drowned her.'

'Why didn't you help the victims if you were a capable swimmer, Mr Marsh?' Gilbert asked.

'I did go to help, but I could do little to assist. Elizabeth and I bid each other farewell, and I went on my way.'

'You did not enter the water at all?' Gilbert asked.

'No, as I said, there was no need at that point.'

'And you left Elizabeth Rowe there at the scene of that terrible disaster?' Harland asked.

'She knew her way home,' Donahue said with a shrug. 'Besides, I had places to be.'

'Why did you both decide to tell her second husband, Ernest, you were cousins?' Harland asked.

Donahue smiled. 'My, you two have been busy. Because Elizabeth and I were friends, and her first husband couldn't handle that. It was better to say we were cousins to avoid drama with her second husband. Ernest bought that hook, line and sinker.'

'Friends don't passionately kiss as you were sacked from your workplace for doing,' Harland said.

'Jealous husband, as I said. You can't blame us for taking precautions when Elizabeth remarried. Although Ernest is a good bloke, that first husband thought he was better than everyone.'

'Your ex-fiancée, Miss Charlotte Glasson, said your wedding was cancelled because she caught you kissing a barmaid. It seems that husbands have a right to be wary of you, Mr Marsh. Then you tried to steal back Miss Glasson's engagement ring.'

'It was my ring. I paid for it for my bride, and she had no right to it now,' he snapped, then realised he had not denied trying to steal it. 'I told you I didn't have it on your first visit; I still don't.'

'No, but Mrs Rowe was getting it for you, wasn't she?' Harland asked. 'Deed done.'

Donahue looked genuinely confused or played the role very convincingly. 'What do you mean, "Deed done"? Why would Elizabeth be involved in trying to get my ring back?'

Harland nodded to Gilbert.

'We found a tin on Mrs Elizabeth Rowe's body containing a large wad of money, a ruby engagement ring, and a note saying "Deed Done" signed by Mrs Rowe. Are you saying it has nothing to do with you, Mr Marsh? We thought the cash and ring might be yours,' Gilbert continued. 'Why did Mrs Elizabeth Rowe have your ex-fiancée's engagement ring on her person?'

He was momentarily silent, scrambling for some conclusion, something to say, before blurting out, 'I know nothing of that, but it should be returned to me as the rightful owner.'

'You don't know who owns the cash then or what the deed done was?' Harland pushed, desperate to get a confession and expecting the man's greed.

'The cash is mine too,' he blurted out. 'Where's the tin?'

'How can it be yours?' Harland asked. 'Perhaps Mrs Rowe found it.'

Donahue scoffed. 'So she found a ring that belonged to my ex-fiancée and knows I want it back. Highly unlikely, don't you think, detectives?'

'We do indeed, Mr Marsh,' Harland said cooly. 'So we intend to arrest you and make the case that you killed Richard Tyson when he fired you for kissing his wife. You then carried on an affair with Mrs Rowe, right under her husband's nose, meeting on the pretence that you were close cousins. You encouraged Mrs Rowe to steal back the engagement ring from Miss Glasson, who told us she gave Mrs Rowe access to her bedroom and jewellery box, and you killed Mrs Rowe in a fit of anger when she would not leave her current husband for you and wear your ring. By the time we bring forward all our witnesses and the tin with its contents, we will convince any jury that you are despicable and not to be trusted. You have, after all, lied to us several times in this interview.'

'And you are most likely the last person to have seen Mrs Rowe alive,' Gilbert added.

'Just hold on there,' Donahue Marsh said, rising.

'Sit down,' Harland barked, and the man dropped back on the couch. He felt he had the man now and wanted to keep the pressure on.

'Just wait a moment,' Donahue said, his voice a little more conciliatory.

Harland knew they didn't have one proven fact, but they had enough circumstantial evidence to create reasonable doubt, and cases had been won on less.

'Just give me a moment,' Donahue said, pushing his hands through his hair.

'To do what, Mr Marsh? Make up some more excuses?' Harland asked. 'It's time to come with us.'

'No, wait. That's not what happened. Some of that happened, but it's not what you think. It's not that black and white,' he said, speaking quickly, his mind racing.

'Where is the suit you wore that day the ferry sank, Sir?' Gilbert asked.

Donahue looked confused. 'My suit?'

'Yes, where are the suit and shoes you wore that day you met Mrs Rowe on the rise?' Gilbert made his way to the large wardrobe with no door.

'I threw them out,' he said, turning to watch Gilbert's progress.

'You threw out a suit and shoes? Sir, you must be doing very well as a contract labourer,' Gilbert said, sniffing inside the wardrobe.

'What are you looking for in there? Get out?' Donahue said, rising. Harland was at his side in a moment, pushing him back onto the couch.

'Don't get up.'

'Something smells damp in here,' Gilbert said, sniffing. He reached to the back of the wardrobe and pulled out a pair of dry but water-damaged shoes that smelt of the river. 'It looks as if these have been submerged in water recently.'

'I got caught in the rain a week back,' Donahue said.

'I don't recall any recent rainy days,' Harland said.

'Nor do I, Sir,' Gilbert said from the cupboard. He found a pair of dry trousers that smelled of the river and had not been cleaned. 'Is this the suit pants you threw out?'

The suspect made a huffing sound and turned away.

'Gilbert, please pack up the trousers and shoes, and we shall take them for evidence,' Harland said. Seeing the landlady in the front garden, he pushed open the window, not taking his eyes from Donahue for more than a few moments, and beckoned her. 'Madam, may I have a word?'

She came over to the window, annoyed at being interrupted. 'What is it, Sir?'

'I need you to do your civic duty, please, Madam, and rest assured, Mr Marsh's rent will be paid. Please go to the nearest police box or hail the first police officer you see and request two constables to return here with you. Tell them Detective Stone is requesting their presence.'

'Goodness, that is not good for business,' she said, alarmed.

'Then the sooner done and over, the better, Madam.'

She nodded. 'Right now.' With that, she headed down the path to the nearby main street, where several police resources were on hand.

'Just stop, I can explain... let me tell you the truth,' Donahue Marsh said in a panicked voice. 'It's not what you think. I'm not to blame.'

'I'm sure you are not, Mr Marsh. The gaols are full of innocent men. You can tell us your truth from a police cell,' Harland said. Not long after, he opened the door to two constables, one bearing handcuffs.

Julius and Rufus the hound arrived at work shortly after Randolph, and Rufus made his way around the office, sniffing in case some fresh scents had presented themselves overnight.

'You are in early, Grandpa. Are you all right? Did our talk keep you awake?' Julius asked, hanging his hat on the rack and carefully studying his grandfather.

'It did, but do not be concerned. I had much to consider, and your grandmother was a good sounding board.'

'She knew,' Julius said.

'Yes, but she did not know the extent of Reggie's feelings and that it would have kept him away or continued for so long. I wish we could have dealt with these emotions all those years ago, but I don't know how we would have done that,' Randolph sighed.

'Nor do I,' Julius agreed.

'Was Ambrose with you last night? He came home at a reasonable hour.' Randolph changed the subject, and Julius assumed it was still too raw to speak about.

'He and Lucian were at the Brunswick Club for a while, but I left before them. I'm glad he didn't wallow and stay out too late. Lucian is good for him.'

'They are firm friends and cousins,' Randolph agreed.

'How does our day look?' Julius asked.

'Back to normal, thank goodness. There are two funerals today, and I have appointments with three bereaved clients. Mid-afternoon, I booked a meeting for you with a lovely young lady who dropped in to make an appointment. She claimed to have met you on an omnibus.'

'Ah, Miss Prout. Yes, I meant to mention her. She would like us to consider offering our clients the Prout Monumental Mason catalogue. I told her we had been loyal to one company for a long time, and to her credit, she suggested we look at some of her modern designs that would not infringe on our current relationship with Mr Busby as he does not offer the same.'

'Most fair of her.'

'I thought so,' Julius agreed. 'Would you be open to our offering additional products?'

'We have no signed agreement with Mr Busby for monumental mason supplies; it has always been goodwill and habit. If he has nothing similar on his books, we are just offering an alternative, and that is always good business,' Randolph said.

'I agree. If we do opt to offer Miss Prout's designs, I will advise Mr Busby as a courtesy. Mind you, he supplies all the funeral homes, so he is not reliant on us. Are you available to attend the meeting with Miss Prout?'

'If you wish. I have a couple coming in just beforehand, but I will hopefully be free by the time Miss Prout arrives.'

'I thought she might also like to meet Ambrose. He is our Operations Manager, and they may liaise regularly should we offer her products.'

'Good Lord, lad, don't tell me you are matchmaking? What is the world coming to?' Randolph asked, feigning shock, and Julius chuckled.

'Perhaps. Uncle Reggie's tale worried me, so I want to see Ambrose happy and settled. I don't know if Miss Prout has a beau, but she was not wearing any rings and is a lively character.'

'She is that and a most attractive young lady,' Randolph agreed. 'Let's hope for fireworks then and some interesting options for our clients as well.'

With that, the backdoor opened, and Phoebe entered wearing a pale blue dress. Julius assumed Harland was walking her home today as Phoebe saved her newest dresses for those days.

'Hello, Julius. Grandpa! You left well before me today,' she said, closing the door and removing her hat.

'I was keen to get my day in order, dearest,' Randolph said and offered to call her for a cup of tea when Mrs Dobbs arrived.

Julius headed downstairs with Phoebe to find Rufus lolling on the leather couch in the morning sun streaming in from Phoebe's top window. He jumped up and enthusiastically greeted Phoebe, and after a reasonable session of patting and attention, he returned to his position.

As Phoebe organised her table and set up her powders and brushes, Julius inquired after the *Vexed Vixen* dinner. 'How was Miss Kirby last evening?'

'Upset but putting on a brave face. She is going away to Ingham to work for a lady photographer. I am pleased to say she was excited about it.'

'Ingham! That is extreme, but maybe the best way to get over a broken heart,' he said, thinking of Reggie leaving when his heart was broken.

'Kate claims it is her fault for falling too quickly for Ambrose. If that is the case, I better guard my heart too.'

'You need not concern yourself in that regard; Harland is very dedicated to you. Speaking of Harland, he told me last night that an arrest would occur this morning – Mr Donahue Marsh, the man in the photograph with Mrs Rowe.'

Phoebe's eyes widened. 'Is that so? I am surprised.'

'Why?' Julius asked, squeezing onto the couch and patting Rufus. 'This used to be my seat, Rufus, you couch stealer!'

Phoebe laughed but sobered as she spoke of the crime afoot. 'All is not as it seems, brother. Why would Elizabeth Rowe not return to discuss her murder with me, and why did she disappear when I began questioning her? Even Rufus growled at her, and I am finding him to be an excellent judge of character.'

'Well done, Rufus,' Julius patted him, and the large black dog's tail thumped with pleasure.

Phoebe shook her head. 'There is something untoward about it all, but no doubt I shall hear more from Harland.'

'Speaking of which, I forgot to mention that Uncle Reggie met Mr Tyson in the afterlife,' Julius told of their discussion. 'I accidentally told Harland, and he asked if I had your skills. I said you informed me. I confess I was quite alarmed by my slip.'

'Good thing you told me then,' Phoebe said, 'but I will always try to cover for you.'

Julius sighed. 'I feared this.'

'I know,' Phoebe gave him a sympathetic look and changed the subject. 'How is Ambrose? Faring better than Kate, I imagine.'

'Yes, which I am relieved about, if honest. Have you heard of Prout Monumental Masons?'

'Of course. They do very good work, I believe. Are we to work with them?'

'Maybe. Miss Billie Prout is coming to meet with us this afternoon. Do come in and meet her if time permits. I will ensure Ambrose does.'

'So soon after Kate?' Phoebe said, understanding his motive but regarding her brother with great indignation. 'It feels most unfair.'

'Miss Kirby must rely on her family and friends to rally her; my duty is to our brother,' Julius said. 'I will have neither of you suffering if I can prevent it.'

Phoebe softened. 'Oh, Julius, even now, with a wife and family of your own,' she said with a smile at Rufus, 'you still look after us.'

'I just don't want you both moping around and making the place miserable,' Julius said in jest. Given they worked in a funeral home, the idea was laughable, and Phoebe did just that.

Rising, he suggested his sister start work, earning him a grimace and a grin as he ascended the stairs to begin the day's work.

Chapter 29

DESPITE HIS SHADY NATURE and slick appearance, Donahue Marsh was unfamiliar with a cell and did not want to know it any better. For most of the morning of his confinement, he paced, declined food, and demanded to be let out. Harland had left his interview until the afternoon to give Donahue time to rally his thoughts; he imagined the normally confident labourer would be full of justification.

'You would think he was innocent of all wrongdoing,' the warden said, leading Detectives Harland Stone and Gilbert Payne to the interview room. 'Do you want him left in cuffs?'

'No, as long as he can't make a break for it,' Harland said.

The warden laughed. 'He'd come up against at least four locked doors, not to mention the guards, before he saw the light of day.'

'When can I get out?' he asked as the detectives entered the room and the warden released the suspect from his handcuffs.

'That depends on your confession and crime, Mr Marsh,' Harland said, indicating the seat. 'If you do not remain seated, we will request that you be restrained again.'

Donahue held up his hands in a surrender motion and sat. Harland sat opposite, and Gilbert took a seat at the end of the table, opening his notebook, ready to take notes.

'You wanted to tell us your story?' Harland said.

'The truth, detectives. I want to tell you the truth,' he said earnestly.

Harland nodded for Donahue Marsh to begin, and the prisoner drew a deep breath and started.

'It began because I was choosing where next to work. I heard Richard Tyson was a local developer looking for employees, and as I had experience, he promptly took me on. I didn't notice Mrs Tyson for some time, but she regularly walked through the building and always sought me out and asked a question each time.'

Harland held up his hand. 'Mr Marsh, this is not a stage production. I do not need your misguided memories, and Detective Payne and I can see right through your embellishments. You are not the first person we have interviewed. Please start again and tell us the facts only. Our time is limited.'

Donahue Marsh silently fumed. Harland suspected he had been preparing his speech for hours and would paint himself as the victim and hero where possible.

'Fine then,' he said with frustration. 'I needed a job, and Richard Tyson took me on to do his bidding, not labour work. I was to deliver contracts, collect anything he needed, and drive him where he needed to go; in short, I was at his beck and call.'

'Surely that meant he trusted you, and it would have been an easier job than labouring,' Harland said.

'I would prefer to labour – that's good, honest work, and you earn your pay. Tyson said he had no labouring jobs but liked to call me "his man" like I was his servant – bloody snob. I regularly saw Elizabeth—Mrs Tyson—because I had to drop him home and pick him up in his carriage, then take it to his stable and find my own way home. He'd tell me to collect papers from his home office, and Elizabeth would help me find them. He used us both, and that drew us together. Because of his work and being ten years older than Elizabeth, he had no time for her; she was a pretty ornament in his life. I loved her.'

'Were you engaged at that time to Miss Glasson?' Gilbert asked.

'No, but we were dating. Charlotte was sweet on me, and I was pleased for some company,' he shrugged.

'Did Mrs Tyson feel the same about you as you felt towards her?' Harland asked.

'I thought she did; I would have done anything for her.'

'You killed Richard Tyson so you could be together?' Harland moved the suspect along.

'It wasn't like that. Elizabeth didn't love him. She never loved him,' Donahue said. 'The wedding was arranged by their families, who were old friends. This is God's honest truth – Elizabeth asked me to get rid of him and make it look like an accident. Then, she would be a very rich and available widow; she offered me a sizeable fee to do the job.'

'So you hit Richard Tyson on the back of the head, pushed him over the landing, and damaged the floor to make it look like he fell to his death,' Gilbert said.

'In a manner of speaking,' Donahue admitted to Harland's surprise. 'You've got to understand I was in love, under her influence and always broke. She promised me the world; you can't imagine that kind of salvation to someone who has never known love or had money.'

'Yes, we can, Mr Marsh. We are all tempted throughout our lives, but that's where our moral compass comes in and guides us,' Gilbert said.

'Survival and the chance to have her was all that kicked in for me. It wasn't easy to break the new timber, like you said,' Donahue continued. 'So I gave him a good push and made it look like the timber had cracked, and he'd tripped on the broken pieces. It worked until now. But I was just the messenger, sent to do the work,' he hurriedly added.

'Save that argument for the judge, Mr Marsh. He might take mercy on you. Did you kill Elizabeth because she didn't fall in love with you but instead married Ernest Rowe?'

'Well, that's the thing. I didn't know she and Ernest Rowe loved each other before her marriage to Richard Tyson or that they weren't allowed to marry. She didn't mention that while she was manipulating me,' he said, his tone sharp and his face flushed. 'She told me after I had done the job. Elizabeth was done with me, so I took her money and left. I heard she married Ernest, so I moved on and asked Charlotte to marry me. She's a lovely girl.'

'But you were disloyal to her,' Harland said.

'Well, that's because of Elizabeth, again. She was Elizabeth Rowe now, and she found me. All the same feelings returned, and she was so vulnerable and sweet. She said it wasn't working with Ernest; he was too clingy and needy, and she couldn't breathe. She said their marriage was a mistake, and she thought about me constantly.'

'Did she want to run away with you?' Gilbert asked.

'That is what she had me believe. Elizabeth wanted us to have a chance at love and life, as she put it. It was what I had wanted to hear and had waited to hear. Charlotte was no match for Elizabeth, who was a lady and so beautiful. I would have done anything for her, and I thought maybe I would have a chance to make her my wife if Ernest wasn't around. I became disinterested in Charlotte, and I confess I made sure she saw me kissing the barmaid; I didn't want to sully Elizabeth's name or reputation by having Charlotte find out about her. Sure enough, Charlotte called it off, and I was a free man again. But she wouldn't give the ring back.'

Harland glanced at Gilbert. He had a hunch about where this was going.

'You struck another bargain with Mrs Rowe?' Harland asked.

'Yes. She would get the ring back for me and pay me a sum if I could make it appear like Ernest had had an accident. To find out his routine, she introduced me as her cousin, allowing us to continue our romance right under his nose. He was a good bloke, though, I have to say. I liked him.'

'But you did not like him enough to deny Mrs Rowe her request and spare his life,' Harland pointed out.

'But I did, Detective,' Donahue Marsh said. 'I did.'

'Go on,' Harland nodded.

'Elizabeth messaged me she had done her part of the bargain and to meet her that fateful day that the *River Lady* sank. That's why we were on the rise.'

'The note reading "Deed done, E.R." was meant for you along with the cash payment and the return of your engagement ring, which she had stolen from a trusting Miss Glasson?' Gilbert summed up.

'Right, you are, detective. Now, it was up to me to deliver my side of the bargain, and I intended to do it that evening, running down Ernest on his way home from work and leaving the scene as quickly as I could. I knew the route he walked home and where no one would see me hit him with my horse trap.'

Harland's eyes narrowed, knowing that was how Phoebe had lost her parents and seeing the lifelong distress it brought to the family.

'So why did your plans change?' Gilbert asked.

'When I met Elizabeth on the hill, she wouldn't give me the tin with the ring and money until after I did my part of the job. I couldn't believe it – Elizabeth contacted me and rekindled our love, but now, she had no faith in me! My blood boiled, and I realised she was playing me again. I was putty in her hands. I thought of Charlotte keeping the ring and how manipulative these women were, always getting their own way. People like Richard Tyson, who was hardworking and provided for Elizabeth, Ernest, who loved her passionately, and me, who moved mountains for her, were just pawns.'

'So you invited Mrs Rowe to the water's edge?' Harland asked.

'Yes. I determined I would set things right. I would take her life in revenge for all men who were manipulated, and I'd spare Ernest Rowe. The timing could not be better. The ferry sinking before us provided a perfect decoy for Elizabeth's death. It took minutes to end her life in the river with no one the wiser, and then I pushed her into the turbulent swirl and did not feel any regret as she went under. Except I couldn't find that tin on her and ran out of time, so I had to give up on it. I assumed she was lying and did not have it with her in the first instance.'

'Which is a great shame for you, Mr Marsh, because had you found it, there might have been no investigation. It appears Mrs Rowe claimed another victory over you from her grave,' Harland said, thinking the man despicable.

Donahue leant forward. 'Surely you can see I am innocent, detective. The Tysons hired me, and I did their bidding, his wife manipulating me with beauty and money. Then, I saved Ernest Rowe's life by refusing to kill him, instead, murdering his murderer.'

Harland pursed his lips as he thought. 'You know, Mr Marsh, you might just persuade someone with that argument, but not me.'

The detectives rose, and Donahue Marsh was re-cuffed and returned to his cell, yelling about brotherhood and rising as one.

Out in the afternoon sunlight, Gilbert smiled. 'The case is solved, Sir.'

'Indeed, it is Gilbert, and well done to you for your part in it. What a sordid tale.'

'I think they deserved each other – Mrs Rowe and Mr Marsh. But he won't be the first man to have killed for love or jealousy.'

'No, sadly, and he may just find a sympathetic judge.' Harland looked up. 'A lovely afternoon for strolling; I shall depart on time to walk Miss Astin home today. What are your plans for the evening?' he asked as they began their walk to the omnibus.

'Miss Yalden is coming to dinner to meet my mother. I believe I am more nervous than she is for the meeting.'

'Congratulations, Gilbert. Is it serious, then? She is a charming young lady and very accomplished.'

'She is, Sir, thank you. I am sure my mother will agree. I hope so,' he added under his breath.

Harland did his best not to smile at the gentle young detective's dilemma. It was one that he would never experience; years of boarding school had reduced his relationship with his parents to a formal catch-up, and their opinion of the woman he chose held no weight.

Thinking of Miss Phoebe Astin, he smiled again.

Chapter 30

WILLIMENA PROUT, WHO ONLY answered to the name Billie and was the son her father never had, kissed her father on the cheek as she departed.

'Are you sure you do not wish me to accompany you and pay my respects to the Astin family?' Mr George Prout asked.

'Pa, I shall pass on your regards, and in normal circumstances, I agree it would be fitting that you were there. But Mr Astin was cautious not to offend his supplier, and I only got my foot in the door because I said we had modern designs that Busby Monumental Masons did not.'

He nodded and sighed. 'Modern designs, goodness.'

'Don't be so old-fashioned, Pa,' she teased him, and he smiled, having always been wrapped around his daughter's little finger.

'Good luck then, my dear, and I look forward to building a relationship with the Astin family and *The Economic Undertaker*.'

'Thank you for the vote of confidence; I shan't let you down.' With that, Miss Billie Prout tucked her folder of modern design headstones under her arm, straightened her hat and departed with her head held high.

As the omnibus neared the stop closest to *The Economic Undertaker*, she did not feel as confident and hoped the meeting group was not too large. Billie was confident around men; working in the industry exposed her to businessmen and clients, and her father had always supported her working in the business. Even so, she knew nothing of the Astins and their attitude toward women. It would have been nice to have had her father on hand.

Several gentlemen offered their hands to help her alight, as often happened with Billie, and she thanked them with her sweetest smile. There was no opportunity to fix her hair or check her appearance before arriving at the door of *The Economic Undertaker*, so she hoped she looked professional and not too askew from the carriage ride.

As Billie approached the business, the door opened, and a very handsome young man rushed out, nearly knocking over a mature woman passing by.

'My apologies, Madam,' he said and hurried down the street, umbrella in hand, the door closing behind him. Billie arrived, took a deep breath, and entered, finding Julius Astin behind a large reception desk.

'Miss Prout, welcome,' Julius said. 'I hope my brother did not bowl you over.'

'Mr Astin, hello. It was a near miss.'

'He is attempting to return an umbrella to a client who just left. I like to keep him on his toes. Won't you come into our meeting room?' Julius said, indicating the doorway of a large room behind him.

Billie entered, adding, 'Thank you for seeing me today and for this opportunity.' She took the seat offered, admiring the tastefully decorated room and the vase of fresh flowers in the window.

'It's a pleasure. I am keen for the business to be progressive, so I welcome the opportunity to see your work. My grandfather, Randolph, who co-manages the business with me, will be here shortly; he is just putting away some paperwork. Ambrose will return, hopefully, without the umbrella. I have asked him to sit in as he is our Operations Manager, and there is no doubt you will deal with each other should we partner. And this is my sister, Phoebe, our mortician,' Julius said, looking at the door where Phoebe had arrived.

Billie rose from her chair, and the ladies greeted each other. She was relieved to have another lady present and of similar age, which was most unusual in the industry.

'Goodness, are we not rare birds, Miss Astin?' Billie joked.

'Indeed, Miss Prout. I have never met another lady mortician or monumental mason for that matter.'

'I shall hurry the men,' Julius said, leaving them momentarily alone.

'I do love that pale pink dress, Miss Astin; it is truly becoming,' Billie said.

'Thank you, Miss Prout,' Phoebe said, slipping into the seat next to her as the ladies sat again. 'Your mint green dress is very fashionable this season and looks delightful on you.'

'I am partial to green,' Billie said. 'Pa says some days when we check our headstones in the cemetery, he has trouble seeing me against the green backdrop.'

Phoebe laughed as Julius re-entered the room. Billie sensed his mind was elsewhere, and he wished the meeting was over. She understood a distracted mind and was often punished in class with a rap on the knuckles for drawing when she should have been concentrating on her French, Latin, or algebra lessons.

'I'm afraid Mrs Dobbs, our wonderful kitchen manager, had to depart early this afternoon, but would you like a cup of tea?' Phoebe asked, filling in the time as they waited for Ambrose and Randolph to join them.

'Please do not trouble yourself on my behalf. I expect this will be a short meeting,' she said with a glance to Julius, who appeared to be studying something he could see from his seat facing the reception area. 'Shall I begin then, or would you prefer I wait,

Mr Astin?' No sooner had Billie asked, Randolph appeared, and introductions were done.

'I shan't stay, Miss Prout. I don't want you to be overwhelmed and outnumbered,' Randolph said politely.

'Oh, please do not be concerned on my behalf, Mr Astin,' Billie said. 'It is very considerate of you, but as Miss Astin is here, I am sure the numbers will be balanced, and I won't feel too nervous.' Truth be known, she was not nervous at all now and very confident of her designs, but she felt it was best to appear a little demure.

The front door slammed, and Ambrose came in, panting and brushing his hand through his hair. 'Good Lord, for an old girl, she can move fast,' he said. 'Umbrella returned, Julius. Oh, hello.' He stopped short on seeing Billie, and again, she could see the look of admiration in his eyes, a familiar sight for the blonde, well-proportioned beauty.

'Brother, this is Miss Billie Prout, who has come to show us her designs,' Julius said. 'Miss Prout, our Operations Manager, Ambrose Astin.'

Ambrose could not recall having ever seen such beauty. While he could not see her full figure as Miss Prout sat at the meeting table, he was like most men, taken by the impact of a face so pretty with her bright, wide brown eyes, fulsome lips, a smile that would level any man alive, and blonde tresses boasting curls. There was the promise of a perfect hourglass figure as a small waist and well-proportioned chest were visible – Miss Billie Prout was a great beauty.

Ambrose cleared his throat as he took the vacant seat next to Phoebe. 'Miss Prout, your family name is as well known as ours is in the industry.'

'Thank you, Mr Astin. Father started the business close to fifteen years ago and has never looked back.' She looked to Julius and Randolph. 'He sends his regards and would have liked to attend but was mindful of your existing business partner, and I would not allow him,' she added with a smile.

Julius smiled. 'Very considerate, thank you.'

'You must have him well trained, Miss Prout,' Randolph said in jest, and Billie laughed.

'It is a never-ending job, Mr Astin,' she replied in fun. 'You are all busy, so please allow me to present my modern monument designs,' she said, opening her folder.

Ambrose realised he had been staring, watching her lips as she spoke and her eyes sparkle, and he sat up with more attention.

'Oh, you have photographs, not illustrations,' Phoebe exclaimed. 'How wonderful.'

'I hoped it makes seeing my designs and their application easier. I have permission from the families to include their loved one's monuments in my folder.'

'Of course,' Phoebe said as Billie spread the photographs over the table.

'I had them taken by Miss Kate Kirby of Kirby Studio,' Billie said, startling Ambrose, who broke into a coughing fitting. He raised a hand to excuse himself, and Randolph poured his grandson a glass of water, pushing it toward him.

'Forgive me, did I say something wrong?' she asked with a raised eyebrow.

'Not at all,' Julius assured her. 'We are well familiar with Miss Kirby's work. She took the photographs of our business that you might have seen in our foyer or advertising. She is very talented.'

'I think so too,' Billie said.

'And a dear friend of mine,' Phoebe added loyally.

Billie looked surprised. 'Yes! She did mention a dear friend in my industry, but I didn't make the connection.'

'These designs are lovely and very dignified,' Randolph said, studying one and handing it to Julius.

'Thank you, Mr Astin. My father calls this the "golden age" of grave monuments, as we are getting more and more requests for variety and grandeur in the choice of stone. In the last year, we have produced quite a few large marble statues and columns.'

'Is that so?' Julius asked. 'A display of grief and wealth?'

'Indeed, Mr Astin,' Billie said, 'and if the family can afford it, they naturally wish to convey their grief with a monument for all time.'

'That is not our market, Miss Prout,' Ambrose said, finding his voice and sounding more curt than he meant to come across.

'Of course. I am mindful that you are the "economic" undertaker,' Billie said abruptly. 'So while some of these designs appear in marble, they can be replicated in cheaper stone if your clients want something different but have restricted budgets. I always work to a client's budget,' she said directly to Ambrose as if she were insulted by his stating the obvious.

'We get very few clients who could afford these columns and statues,' Ambrose continued, and he felt his family looking at him. He knew he was being obnoxious but could not say why. Was he disappointed that her designs missed their mark, or was he seeking her attention and to be memorable to her when she left the meeting at *The Economic Undertaker?*

Billie Prout pulled a black diary from her folder and opened a page with prices and calculations scribbled upon it. She selected half a dozen photographs from the table where they were scattered, bringing them to the front and attention of the group present.

'I found six of your recent burials in South Brisbane Cemetery and roughly costed the headstones. Mr Busby's prices are quite similar to ours,' she explained. 'While these six headstones of mine are different designs to the ones your clients selected from Mr

Busby, they are all within the same price range when made with more economical stone.'

'That is exciting, Miss Prout,' Phoebe said, and Randolph agreed.

'You are very well prepared, Miss Prout, thank you,' Julius said, and Ambrose felt his brother's stare as if he expected him to make amends for his abrupt behaviour earlier.

'I understand you are busy and don't wish to waste your time,' she said with a side glance at Ambrose, reflecting her displeasure at his earlier tone and attempt to dismiss her.

'I see this working quite well with some of our younger clients who may wish to express their own style,' Randolph said.

'And those who request a financial division for the funeral,' Julius said.

Ambrose read the look his brother gave him and, as then requested, explained their business model. 'It's when the immediate family pays for the funeral and chooses our economic option, but the grandparents, a benefactor, or fundraising covers the cost of the headstone. Hence, having these options will be fortuitous,' he added the latter to appease his brother.

'Exactly so, Ambrose,' Phoebe agreed. 'I love the stone roses you have created around this headstone; they look so real.'

'They are my favourite,' Billie said with a smile. 'Well, I need not take up any more of your time, gentlemen, Miss Astin. I have prepared a costing and illustration sheet to leave with you for consideration. I do hope to hear from you, and we might work together.'

She presented the document to Julius, who thanked her again for her professional preparation and passed it to Ambrose. A look of disappointment flashed across her face as if she believed her cause was lost if it were up to the younger Astin brother.

But quite the contrary. Ambrose was sold and wanted to speak with her again without everyone present. Could he work with Miss Billie Prout? He wasn't sure it would be easy, but it would be fiery, to say the least.

'Will you see Miss Prout out, Ambrose?' Julius asked, and Ambrose hurried to his feet.

'Miss Prout, can I hail you a hansom?' he asked.

'Thank you, Mr Astin, but I can...' she appeared to bite her tongue, 'that would be appreciated.'

The pair gave each other a tight smile, oblivious to the looks the family exchanged behind Ambrose's back.

Chapter 31

PLACING HIMSELF ON THE street-side of Miss Phoebe Astin and carrying her umbrella and the small basket she had brought to work this morning for the mail, Harland Stone felt at ease for the first time that day. He was constantly amazed that the petite, beautiful Miss Phoebe Astin found him handsome and interesting enough to accept his court. She had shown no interest in Bennet, who was not only an attractive man by anyone's standards but also wealthy and cultured. For any young lady needing to secure her position in the world, Bennet's affection toward her must have been an attractive proposition compared to a detective with a passion for boxing and a middle-class upbringing, even if he did attend a very good private school.

'What happened behind the doors of *The Economic Undertaker* today?' Harland asked as they moved away from the noisy street.

He admired her feminine dress and hat and longed to kiss her. It was most distracting.

'Oh, business as usual except for a visit from a lady monumental mason,' Phoebe said with a smile. 'Can you imagine?'

'Is that as rare as a lady mortician?'

'Every bit so,' Phoebe assured him. 'Miss Billy Prout from Prout Monumental Masons, a very reputable company. She met Julius on an omnibus and requested to show us some of their modern designs.'

'There is so much to say about that, I don't know where to start,' Harland joked. 'How does one meet Julius on an omnibus? He is hardly the most talkative and friendly fellow, and to be talking with a lady as well. It is most out of character. Are you alarmed?'

Phoebe laughed. 'I have grounds to be,' she agreed. 'But Miss Prout is no shrinking violet, so I suspect she introduced herself and won him over. We all think she will be perfect for Ambrose.'

'Ambrose? So soon?' Harland said, shocked. 'If you decide to abandon me to a life of despair without you, I hope you do not date for at least five years.'

Phoebe laughed and squeezed his arm, where her hand rested. 'Five years! You are silly. How could I abandon you? We are perfectly suited with my odd visitors, strange predictions, and your random hours and complex cases.'

'And no one could love you as much as I do,' he said, looking down upon her. She snapped to look at him and blushed, looking away just as quickly, but her hand tightened on his arm.

'Fortunately for us, our hearts are in agreement,' she said, smiling and not making eye contact. 'But should you fall out of love...'

'That will never happen,' he said quickly, and she looked up to study him.

'Kate thought Ambrose loved her, and he thought he did too. But it wasn't deep enough.'

'Ambrose's heart was with someone else from the beginning. Mine is firmly planted and very much at home here.'

Phoebe smiled. 'I shall look after it, I promise.'

He kissed her hand and, not wishing to make her uncomfortable, continued their previous conversation. 'You ladies are so progressive. So, a monumental mason, you say? What did you make of her work then?'

'Oh, it was very impressive,' Phoebe said. 'Columns and statues that can be made to budget and capture one's grief and sentiment so perfectly.'

'That is a skill, and like your work, it must comfort the bereaved.'

'Thank you for saying so. It is all we can do in the face of despair, but I believe it provides comfort. And what of your day?' Phoebe asked.

'We made an arrest today, and we have you to thank for the lead. Donahue Marsh confessed in a round-about fashion to the murder of Mrs Elizabeth Rowe and her first husband, Mr Richard Tyson.'

'No! The first husband as well,' Phoebe said. 'Can you tell me what he owned to doing?'

'With pleasure,' Harland said. He rarely hid details of his cases from Phoebe, as quite a few resulted from a tip-off she had passed on from the recently departed. He told of Donahue's love for Elizabeth and her treachery, concluding, 'So he was meant to kill Ernest but could not do it and killed Mrs Rowe instead.'

'Well, I am truly surprised,' Phoebe said as they reached the bench seat under a tree marking halfway in their journey and sat as they did each time, for a small reprieve. 'No wonder Mrs Rowe did not come back to see me. She was murdered, but she did not want to admit that she had brought it upon herself. I am most cranky with her.'

'I am pleased, as Donahue Marsh would have gotten away with murder twice if Mrs Rowe had not visited you and advised that she was not on the *River Lady* ferry.'

'I guess so,' Phoebe said, 'but I feel like she has manipulated me. She wanted Mr Marsh found guilty with no recourse for her actions.'

'True, but what recourse can there be now if she is dead?' Harland asked. 'She has escaped punishment.'

Phoebe huffed with frustration. 'I guess she has paid with her life, but there is still her name.'

Harland chuckled. 'Goodness, remind me not to get on your bad side.'

Phoebe laughed. 'I am a woman; we have our ways.'

'No doubt. On a brighter note,' Harland said, smiling, 'this evening, Gilbert is introducing the two most influential women in his life to each other.'

Phoebe clapped her hands together. 'Oh yes, Emily told me she was dining with Mrs Payne. Between ourselves, she found the idea somewhat daunting.'

'Understandable, if Mrs Payne is anything like her son.'

Phoebe grinned at the thought. 'Speaking of which, Grandma hoped you might come to dinner next week too. And now you must look delighted with the invitation,' she teased.

'I am delighted with the invitation; my thanks to Mrs Astin. I would be happy to attend.'

'We shall see after she quizzes you on your understanding of the Bible,' Phoebe said, laughing at Harland's alarmed expression. 'I am teasing you; Grandma would not do that, but I might.'

'Miss Astin,' Harland said formally, 'may I remind you that you will also be invited to meet my parents?'

'Yes,' she sobered, 'in that case, I assure you I will smooth your journey.'

He grinned. 'That was easily won. Fortunately, I have met your grandparents on several occasions, but if they are testing my table manners, I am quite confident. As a boarder, many of my school friends and I had our knuckles rapped by Mr Mooney during meal time until we met his standards, which would give Miss Emily Yalden's school of deportment a run for its money.'

Phoebe laughed. 'Excellent. I shall put my family on notice and hope I do not look wanting beside you.'

Across town, Miss Emily Yalden had worn her Sunday best and arrived with flowers for Mrs Margaret Payne, mother of the young man who had won Emily's heart.

As expected, Mrs. Payne greeted her at the door, and by her side, Gilbert looked like a man desperately in love and wishing to show off his belle to a mother who was not to be won over easily. After all, Gilbert was her only child – this shining beacon of success and manhood.

But Emily was not daunted. When invited, she entered the premises at the expected time and removed her hat. Momentarily, she used the hallway mirror to fix her hair and saw Mrs Payne nod approvingly. Like her son, she was a compact woman – neat, groomed, and of a sensible weight. Her clothes were of good quality and style.

Emily was surprised that Mrs Payne was not as stern as expected but rather lively. She was a woman of wit with good conversation skills, and Emily could see the likeness between mother and son. However, Mrs Margaret Payne was much more liberal with her opinions than her conservative son.

'You have a lovely home, Mrs Payne. Thank you for your kind dinner invitation,' Emily said as they entered the dining room. Emily admired the furnishings and tasteful fixtures.

'Thank you, Miss Yalden. If I were not so sensible, I would refurbish my home completely to reflect my latest interests, but I cannot bear fashions that come and go.'

'Nor I,' Emily said in agreement. 'I cannot keep up with them. Quite wearisome.'

They spoke of current matters, literature, and theatre, all of which Emily was comfortable discussing. After all, her trade was preparing young ladies for social occasions.

'If I may be so bold to ask, Miss Yalden, will you continue your deportment business when you marry?'

'No, Mrs Payne. I wish to keep house and care for my husband and young family. The ladies will have to get by without me.'

Mrs Payne smiled. 'I imagine that will be a loss as so many young girls need guidance.'

'That is very kind of you to say, and yes, my girls never cease to surprise me with what they come out with some days,' Emily said.

Margaret Payne looked at her son. 'A detective's salary is not what every young lady would be comfortable living on,' she continued, pressing the questions that Emily suspected were well prepared and discussed with Gilbert as he showed no shock at his mother's directness.

'Fortunately, Mrs Payne, a dear aunt bequeathed me her townhome, so I am in a position to bring a residence into my union. That should make life comfortable and allow for a good-sized family.'

'Indeed,' Mrs Payne said, eyes widening.

Emily was surprised at Gilbert's discretion in that he had not shared this with his mother, and it reassured her that his feelings were genuine. He had not presumed to earn her assets. She felt a little weepy at the thought but, naturally, took hold of her emotions.

'Mind you, Gilbert will most likely rise in the police force to the inspector role or beyond, so he will be reliably able to look after his wife and family, as well as his mother in her old age.' She said the latter with a wink and laugh at her son.

Gilbert chuckled. 'My mother is very ambitious for me. I am barely a competent detective yet.'

Both ladies went to refute that and smiled at each other; they had one thing in common: their love of Gilbert Payne.

The ladies laughed and talked about many topics. Gilbert breathed easily for the first time that evening, and then, sitting to dine, Emily said the one thing that convinced Mrs Margaret Payne there was no one else for her son.

'Forgive me for being so bold, Mrs Payne, but I must declare my admiration for you. You have raised a gentleman. Beautiful manners, so considerate and so thoughtful of my comfort. I am honoured to be in his company.'

From that day on, Gilbert reliably advised Emily that his mother thought no other young lady could be as suited to her son as Miss Emily Yalden and that he would be a fool to let her go, which he was not.

Chapter 32

As JULIUS AND AMBROSE waited for the Redford men—father and son gravediggers—to fill the grave on a cool and comfortable late May afternoon, Julius brushed the horses with long, sweeping strokes to smooth their coats. The younger of the two horses nudged him, and Julius found a couple of carrots that Charlie packed in the hearse and fed them both.

'You are putting Charlie out of work. Grooming is one of his roles now.'

'I find it relaxing, and I don't get to spend much time with my horses these days,' Julius said. 'Is Charlie proving himself to be useful?'

'He does much more than expected,' Ambrose said. 'Saving him from a gaol cell when he stabbed you and giving him a job has created a slave of him.'

Julius shook his head. 'No, I have spoken with him about that. He owes me nothing. I think he genuinely likes his work and training with Phoebe.'

'We may need two morticians at this rate, with so many more people not wishing to mourn the dead in their homes. At least Charlie will be ready to take over from Phoebe when she leaves to raise a family,' Ambrose said. 'I can't imagine what Harland and Phoebe's offspring will look like.' Ambrose chuckled at the thought.

'If she marries him,' Julius said, standing back to study his work.

'Why shouldn't she? Do you know something?' Ambrose asked suspiciously.

'No, I suspect they'll marry, but you have proven this week that everything can change in a day,' Julius said, straightening and putting away the brush.

'We are all done, Mr Astin,' the senior gravedigger, Mr Redford, called. The Astin brothers thanked them both. Julius paid the men and wished them well until the next job brought them together.

Julius shrugged his suit jacket back on, returned his hat to his head and climbed into the carriage, nudging Ambrose – who had attempted to take the reins — back across the seat. Julius drove the horses out of the cemetery. 'You drive too fast,' he said by way of explanation.

'I don't know how, since I never have a chance to drive,' Ambrose grumbled.

'Such a hard life you have,' Julius said with false sympathy. 'Have you decided if we will offer our clients the Prout Monumental Masonry designs?'

'Is it my decision?' Ambrose asked, surprised, turning to look at his brother.

'Are you not the Operations Manager? Grandpa and I have enough on our plates managing stock, bookings, advertising, renovations, and the other businesses. However, I am happy to offer an opinion, as is Grandpa.'

'Then give me your opinion,' Ambrose invited him to do so.

'I think you were abrupt and quite harsh on Miss Prout.'

'I meant your opinion of the product,' Ambrose said.

'Ah, that. I think the product is an outstanding option for our clients; I believe Grandpa felt the same, but it would be respectful to ask him yourself. As for Miss Prout, I found her to be a very astute businesswoman, and her respect for our business and time said a great deal about her character.'

'That's exactly what I thought,' Ambrose said and did not see his brother hide his smile. 'I might have been a little abrupt, but I wanted to test her mettle. And it was true; the products she showed us in marble were not for us. However, she certainly did her preparation.'

'Then, I suggest you speak with Grandpa. After hearing his thoughts, add your own and advise Miss Prout if we intend to work with her.'

'I think we will be working with Prout Monumental Masons,' Ambrose said confidently.

'Good. Then call in person and make sure you speak with her first and not her father.'

'Why? It is a family business,' Ambrose said.

'Imagine if you were presenting our business to a client, and they came in and advised me of their decision; how would you feel about that?' Julius asked.

'I see. You are correct.'

Julius nodded, knowing Ambrose would want to speak with Miss Prout anyway. He continued, 'Once you have told her we would like to partner, lock down prices for at least a half dozen designs to begin with and prepare a catalogue that we can show clients. Check her delivery times, too.'

'I will. Can you say all that again?' Ambrose asked, and then, seeing his brother's exasperated expression, he grinned, adding, 'I have it in hand, do not worry.'

Julius groaned. 'Ambrose, Ambrose, Ambrose. You know what I found most interesting?'

'Do tell?' Ambrose dipped his hat at several young ladies who looked up at them as they passed a city corner.

'Miss Prout reminded me of someone... I think it is Miss Lilly Lewis. I know they do not look similar, but their drive and ambition are very similar.'

'Yes, I see that too,' Ambrose said. 'I suspect Miss Prout has more front; she was quite bold approaching you in the first instance.'

'Well, it is her product to sell and promote; understandably, she would take the opportunity that presented itself that day on the omnibus. You could learn from her!'

Ambrose grunted.

As they turned into the backyard of *The Economic Undertaker*, Ambrose hurriedly descended from the hearse, calling to Claude that Julius had done Charlie's job for him.

'Charlie is with Miss Astin. Has Ambrose forgotten something?' Will asked, coming out of the carriage shed with Claude and seeing Ambrose hurry off.

'No, he is fired up with a new project,' Julius said with a small smile. And then, thanking the men present and leaving the horses and hearse in their care, he headed towards the back door of the next-door dress store, keen to see his wife, even for only a moment or two.

Phoebe watched Charlie's application of powder on the young man lying on the table and nodded her approval. There were several marks and bruises on the corpse and a discolouration extending over the whole of the lower neck.

'He has taken a nasty fall,' Charlie said, concentrating on the deceased's cheek.

'He has indeed, poor man,' Phoebe said, ignoring the young man who stood nearby watching their work on his body. She would not admit his presence in Charlie's company, but Phoebe hoped to wish him well for his next journey when she was alone.

Charlie stood back and looked at the man's skin colour in death and the powders. He screwed the lid onto the tin he was using and selected a different shade.

'Miss Astin, I think this shade might be more appropriate,' he said.

'You have done very well, Charlie,' Phoebe said, smiling. 'That is the colour I would have chosen too.'

As Phoebe prepared the young man's hair, Charlie covered the bruisings and fixed the clothing as best as possible to hide the trauma from the mourners who would attend tomorrow's viewing. The pair finished within the half hour and stood back.

'Lovely, I believe we have done our best by this gentleman,' Phoebe said, and in the corner, the young man agreed with a smile and nod. 'Well done, Charlie. I shall see you in a few days, and we will work together on whoever is on the table and discuss your next study chapter.'

'Thank you, Miss Astin,' Charlie said, refusing to call Julius or Phoebe by their first names as he was the youngest staff member and he held them in high regard.

No sooner had Charlie departed than Julius came down the stairs, having just visited Violet.

'You are back,' Phoebe said. 'Did all go according to plan?'

'Yes, the dead are buried,' Julius said with a small smile. 'How was Charlie's lesson?'

'Very good. He is most conscientious and a natural. So let me test you, brother,' she teased.

'Uh oh.'

'This is Mr Yardley,' Phoebe said, introducing the spirit in the corner. 'I am Miss Phoebe Astin, and this is my eldest brother, Mr Julius Astin.'

'My goodness, you can see me!' he exclaimed.

'Mr Yardley,' Julius acknowledged the man of his age. 'I am sorry that you have departed this earth.'

'Thank you, Mr Astin. I am not.' That told the Astin siblings all they needed to know: Mr Yardley most likely left this world by his own hand.

'Now, brother, which powder would you have chosen to conceal the bruising?' Phoebe asked and lowered Mr Yardley's shirt enough to show an untreated area.

Julius took the question most seriously, as Phoebe was training him and Charlie to step in and take her role or assist as needed.

'I believe I would use this one as it is the closest match to Mr Yardley's skin, but I would most likely use a darker base to begin with,' he said, tapping on two tins, then frowning, considered another, but returned to his original choice.

Phoebe clapped her hands. 'How lucky I am to have such clever students. I hope you are pleased with the result, Mr Yardley.'

'Miss Astin, Mr Astin, I am, and I thank you. It will be easier for my mother to see me this way. Could the other young man not see me?'

'No, not that we know of, at least,' Phoebe said. 'Charlie is not family.'

'Ah. Well, thank you both.' With that, he gave a small bow and faded away.

'Most sad,' Julius said, and Phoebe sighed. 'On a brighter note, I believe Ambrose will call on Miss Prout and advise we shall do business.'

Phoebe grinned, 'I was never in doubt despite his performance in the meeting. Speaking of performances, Harland told me about Mrs. Elizabeth Rowe on our walk home last evening. I am most cranky at her duplicity.'

No sooner had Phoebe made her declaration than Mrs Rowe appeared, slight, pretty and smiling.

'Thank you for your help in locking up Donahue Marsh, Miss Astin,' she said smugly.

'Mrs Rowe, you did not tell me the entire story,' Phoebe said. 'You too are complicit in several terrible crimes.'

Elizabeth Rowe laughed. 'You are too naïve, Miss Astin, is she not?' The attractive young woman, who had secured the love of three men and played Donahue Marsh to do her bidding, looked to Julius for a response.

'No, she is too trusting,' Julius said. 'And sadly, you will have removed some of that trust and innocence from my sister in all her future dealings.'

'Never mind, the deed is done, and so be it,' Elizabeth smiled.

'No, it is not Mrs Rowe. My beau said there was no recourse for your actions now, but my dear friend is a journalist, and I will ensure she writes a story in the paper about your part in the murders. She will mention you by name and by your maiden name, and all who know you will realise what your true character was like.'

'You cannot do that. I am deceased. You cannot disparage my name when I am not there to defend it!' she declared angrily. 'How dare you!'

'She dares, as do I,' Julius said. 'Being dead is no excuse for letting a crime go unpunished.'

She disappeared with a scream of frustration and a scowl at both Astins. Phoebe and Julius exhaled.

'Goodness me,' Phoebe said, her hand on her heart. 'Thank goodness you were here, Julius.'

In the corner, another spirit appeared, and both Phoebe and Julius jumped slightly, ready for another barrage from Mrs Rowe, but she had not returned.

'Uncle Reggie, it is good to see you,' Phoebe said, delighted with the newly arriving guest.

Julius agreed. 'I was worried we had seen the last of you.'

'Why did you think that?' Phoebe asked, unaware that Reggie had bared his soul and reason for lingering in this world.

'Because of his absence,' Julius said, which was somewhat true.

'No,' Uncle Reggie smiled. 'I think I shall always visit my favourite people.'

The men exchanged a look that Phoebe did not see as Julius gave a small shake of his head; his grandfather was not yet ready to provide a message to his brother as he worked through his disappointment and guilt.

'I would miss you if you were not around, Uncle,' Phoebe continued.

Reggie bucked up. 'If for any reason I must depart permanently, I will endeavour to say goodbye,' he assured her of his loyalty. 'Now, do not worry about Mrs Elizabeth Rowe; she has gone somewhere to pay for her sins and will not return.'

'So there is a heaven and hell?' Phoebe asked.

Uncle Reggie tapped his nose. 'I cannot say, but I know I will see you in heaven, Phoebe. I'm not as sure about your brother,' he teased and laughed at Julius's grimace.

'If you are there, Uncle, there is hope for us all,' Julius said in jest, making Reggie laugh.

'Do not fear; I shall put in a good word for you both,' Phoebe told them, having the last word on the subject, and as gentlemen, they allowed it.

Chapter 33

THE HIGHS AND LOWS of human emotions were displayed at the Roma Street Railway Station mid-afternoon in Brisbane. A woman and her young child excitedly waited for the train to take them home, wherever that might be. Several gentlemen stood with small bags indicating a brief business trip was necessary, families waited with restless children keen to board, and a group of senior ladies appeared to be heading off on an adventure equipped with their reading material and goodies for the journey. Also waiting for the call to board were the five members of the *Vexed Vixens*—Phoebe, Emily, Lilly, Violet and the departing, Kate—all doing their best not to appear sombre.

Kate checked again to see if she had her ticket, straightened her hat, and fiddled with her bag, knowing that today would be difficult. She would relax only when the train pulled out of the station, and the next stage of her journey began.

'I am surprised your mother did not insist on coming,' Lilly said.

'Oh, she did, but as it required juggling other commitments, I told her it was best she did not come in case I became hysterical with tears; we said a private goodbye, and I assured her my dear friends would see me away. My sisters are at school; I could not bear to say goodbye to them here either. Even my father was teary-eyed on departing this morning,' Kate said, with a small smile masking her sadness.

'You are the first to leave home, and it is not as if they can drop in for a cup of tea to see how you fare,' Emily said. 'Nor can we.' This was accompanied by a hurried dab of her eyes and a quick chin raise as Emily gained control. 'Remember, you can come home anytime.'

'Yes, that's very true,' Kate nodded. 'But my father says it is best to give any new location or job at least six months before decisions about the future are made.'

'That is sound advice,' Lilly agreed, 'but I always follow my instincts, rightly or wrongly. So, do not hesitate to return if you are miserable, Kate.'

'I will. It is so good of you all to come, especially as you are all working,' Kate said, a handkerchief at the ready, 'but I refuse to cry as this is an exciting day. Imagine what lies ahead!'

'Oh, Kate, it will not be the same without you,' Phoebe said, her voice hitched. 'I rue the day you started courting my brother.'

'Perhaps I should thank him, Phoebe, for being my first love and now, for this new adventure,' Kate said. 'I have always admired him, for years, and to think for a brief time...'

She looked away, and all the ladies harnessed their emotions, pretending to watch and enjoy the antics of several of the children on the station platform, who provided a welcomed noisy distraction.

Kate continued, now under control. 'This new role is an opportunity I never imagined; I should not have considered it if... well, you know.'

'That is very kind of you to say, Kate,' Phoebe said, 'and I hope a grand adventure awaits. We look forward to all your letters, which we will read aloud at our gatherings.'

'You must put in something that vexes you, though, just to be in the spirit of the gathering,' Lilly reminded her. 'So if nothing does, do make up something. Heat, nasty beasts and insects – I'm sure there will be something.'

Kate laughed. 'I will do my best.' Then, her breath hitched as she looked over Phoebe's shoulder. The ladies turned to see what had caught her attention; Ambrose Astin approached, looking remarkably handsome, and removed his hat as he neared them. He turned a few ladies' heads, and knowing he would never be hers,

Kate faltered a little; she straightened, pushing her shoulders back and masking her emotions at seeing him.

'Ladies,' he said, with a nod in the direction of the *Vexed Vixens*, who were, at this moment, most vexed.

They responded curtly, but Phoebe touched his arm. 'It was brave of you to come,' she said to her brother.

'It is my duty,' he said.

'No, it was good of you to come, Ambrose, thank you,' Kate said graciously, her face flushed and her discomfort obvious.

'May I have a word?' Ambrose asked.

The pair excused themselves and moved a little away from the *Vexed Vixens*, Kate leaving her luggage behind with the ladies.

'Please forgive me, Kate,' Ambrose said in a low voice, his hat in hand.

'There is nothing to forgive,' she began, but Ambrose cut her off with a quick shake of his head, taking her hands in his and looking down upon the woman he once spoke with of love and marriage.

'Kate. I let you down. You put me first, and I am never first. Julius is my grandfather's favourite and the ladies' favourite too. Phoebe is kind and loveable and the only girl, but I am this child in the middle with nothing special to recommend me. But you saw me and found something in me, and I did not give you the same special treatment you so deserve.'

Tears ran down her face, and she swallowed, unable to speak.

'So, let me see you off on your next grand assignment, and I hope you will remember some of our times with fondness. We had fun, Kate,' he said with a grin.

Kate laughed, enjoying the slight relief from the ache inside her that Ambrose created by his appearance. 'We did, Ambrose. It was great fun.'

'All aboard!' the porter yelled.

He kissed her on the cheek, and Kate held his gaze momentarily. Ambrose released her hands, which she knew he would never hold again.

'Thank you for coming,' she whispered as it was all she could manage, and Ambrose walked her back to the ladies.

Kate said goodbye to the ladies in the order she had met them – last to first: a hug and kiss for Violet, her newest friend; then Lilly, whom she had met through Phoebe as their work overlapped; next came Emily, whom Kate met when Emily asked her to photograph her debutants; and last, standing next to Ambrose, Phoebe. They had met at school and stayed close, but Ambrose did not even consider his sister's friend romantically until recently.

'I will miss you so much,' Phoebe whispered, and Kate shuddered with tears. Pulling away and seeing Ambrose had her luggage, she followed him to a carriage. Once settled, Ambrose alighted and rejoined the ladies.

The steam train began with its customary puff and noise and soon began chugging out of the station. Kate waved until she was out of sight. Then she fell back into the chair and allowed herself to cry briefly before declaring it was time to dry her eyes and look to the future.

Ambrose looked at the bereft ladies around him and, knowing he was most unpopular, decided his best defence was charm and humour. He was very good at both.

'Well, ladies, who needs a lift back? I have the hearse handy, and if you would like to play dead, I'm sure we can get away with it,' he declared and surprised all four ladies, who burst out laughing.

'I refuse to play dead,' Violet declared. 'I will lean out the window, yelling I am alive, and ask to be saved.'

Ambrose laughed. 'You are an Astin now, Sister,' he said, waggling a finger at her. 'You must think of the business first.'

'Oh, drat, you are right,' she agreed.

'It is an enticing offer,' Emily said with a smile. 'I have never ridden in a hearse.'

'And most likely won't get a chance to do so while you are alive,' Ambrose agreed. 'You are fortunate that I left Rufus at work. He likes to hang out the window and pretend he is one of the hounds of hell and scare people into repenting for their souls.'

Again, his welcomed humour provided relief. He slipped his hat onto his head and could tell he had not only brightened the mood, but they were looking at him with a lot less severity, maybe even fondness. He hoped for understanding in time.

'Thank you, Ambrose,' his sister, Phoebe, said, 'but I think I would like to go to a tearoom and have tea and cake to help me recover from this afternoon's gathering. *Brews and Bouquets Tea House* is just around the corner. Is anyone free to join me?'

'I will,' Emily said. 'My girls are gone for the day, and I am in no rush to return.'

'So will I,' Violet agreed. 'Now that I am married to the boss, I am sure I can get away with that,' she joked.

'Excellent. We will face his wrath together,' Phoebe said in jest, tucking her hand through the crook of Violet's arm. The new sisters smiled at each other.

'I wish I could,' Lilly moaned, 'but Mr Cowan expects us all back in the office for the late edition deadline.'

'Then I shall drop you off at the office of *The Courier*, Miss Lewis, and then go back to work and cover for my sister and sister-in-law.'

Lilly looked in the direction of the departed train. 'I guess there is no harm in that now, Mr Astin,' she agreed, and the group exchanged awkward looks as Ambrose cleared his throat uncomfortably. Phoebe hurried everyone along with another round of hugs before Lilly departed with Ambrose.

'I shall sit up front with you if I may, rather than be delivered to work in the hearse and risk becoming a headline,' she said with a small laugh.

'Of course. That's probably the best course of action to avoid alarm,' he agreed with a grin, offering to assist her, but Lilly had already climbed up and settled into the seat.

Ambrose went around the front of the hearse, thanked the stable lad at the station, tipped him, and leapt up beside her, starting the horses on their way.

After a short while, Lilly spoke, addressing Phoebe's brother informally. 'Ambrose, do you think we should speak of... uh, your declaration of feelings...'

He shook his head and smiled at her. 'No, but thank you, Lilly. Not today. Today, I am just thinking about Kate.'

Chapter 34

The Courier – Morning Edition

"FERRY VICTIM" MURDERED
WOMAN HIRES LOVER TO KILL TWO HUSBANDS
SENSATIONAL CASE COMES TO AN END
An exclusive report by Lilly Lewis and Fergus Griffiths.

Mrs Elizabeth Rowe, formerly Mrs Elizabeth Tyson, nee Jenkins, had the love of two good men and was raised in a respectable family – her father a banker, her mother a nurse. But her death, at first believed to result from being aboard the stricken ferry, *River Lady*, has now been proven to be murdered in a sensational investigation conducted by Detectives Harland Stone and Gilbert Payne of the Roma Street Police Headquarters.

Were Mrs Rowe alive, she would be arrested for being complicit with her former lover, Mr Donahue Marsh, in the murder of her first husband, Mr Richard Tyson, and the attempted murder of her second husband, Mr Ernest Rowe. But in a strange twist of fate, the man who loved her held Mrs Rowe below the swirling waters of the Brisbane River until she was drowned, thus saving the life of her husband, Mr Ernest Rowe, whom he had been paid to murder.

The story begins in...

Harland placed the newspaper down, sat back, pulled his teacup closer and sighed.

'Just when I think people can no longer surprise me,' he said with a shake of his head to his protégé, Gilbert Payne.

'They always surprise me, Sir – especially the female of the species. One expects them to be nurturers by nature, but Mrs Rowe appeared to lack any sentiment towards her first and second husbands. Fascinating.'

Harland lifted some correspondence from his desk and added, 'We have received a thank-you letter from Mr and Mrs Tyson for proving their son, Richard, did not die accidentally but at the hands of Elizabeth Rowe.' He picked up another. 'And here is a letter from Ernest Rowe's brother, Leslie, thanking us for our work, which saved his brother's life. He mentions Ernest will write himself when sufficiently recovered.'

'I imagine his mourning period will be over now that he knows his wife wanted to kill him,' Gilbert said pragmatically.

'I imagine so,' Harland said with a smile. 'As he is a wealthy, widowed gentleman—and quite the dandy—he will not want for company.'

'No one could describe us as such, Sir,' Gilbert said as he packed up the case notes, and Harland laughed.

'Correct on all accounts, Gilbert.' He lifted another note from his desk. 'And this is from the inspector saying well done and hurry with the report. He is pleased we uncovered two murders for the price of one.'

'There is one more thing about this case that bothers me, Sir,' Gilbert said, lifting the notes into a file box as Harland decided to get started on the report. 'It kept me awake last night for some time.'

'What's that then?' Harland asked, pausing. He had learnt never to disregard the hunches and ramble collection of knowledge that his young partner stored in his brain.

'We never determined why Elizabeth Rowe was paying Donahue to murder her husband? They each had a deed to do. She was to retrieve the engagement ring, which was worth a considerable sum, and he was to make her husband's death look like an accident. Then, they could be together, or so he said. Mrs Rowe delivered her part of the agreement. Did he think he should be paid as his role was worth more? And why would money change hands if they were to embark on a life together?'

'That is a worrying loose end,' Harland said and sat thinking for a brief time. Gilbert knew better than to interrupt him. Then, Harland rose quickly, surprising the young detective. 'Come, Gilbert, let us go and ask.' He grabbed his hat, and Gilbert did the same, hurrying to catch up.

Exiting the building, Harland hailed one of the hansom cabs that regularly serviced the area. 'To Boggo Road Gaol, if you will?'

'Right away, Sir,' the driver responded.

As the hansom departed from the police station, the two men speculated on how honest Mr Donahue Marsh would be when asked whether there was a logical reason for the payment. On arrival, they were shown into a room and told to wait while the prisoner was fetched. He appeared ten minutes later and sighed upon seeing the detectives. Harland noted the cocky young man had come down a peg with his greasy hair and prison wear.

'Unless you have come to release me, I confess to not being excited to see you,' Donahue said.

'That's a great pity, Mr Marsh, as we aim to bring joy to our offenders' days, whether at large or in prison,' Harland answered drily. Nodding for Gilbert to ask his question, he saw the young man suppress a smile.

'Mr Marsh, what was your payment for killing Mr Rowe?'

'What? No small talk or niceties? You don't wish to tell me how the weather is today or ask how I slept?' he joked.

Harland tapped on the table. 'We are busy men, Mr Marsh, unlike yourself. Please answer the question.'

'You saw my payment in the tin. I was getting the ring in return for getting her job done.'

'And the cash?' Gilbert asked.

'Oh yeah, and the cash, too,' he added as an afterthought.

Harland studied him, leaving a moment's silence to see if Donahue would fill it, but he didn't, and Gilbert knew not to proceed until he got the nod from his superior, which came next.

'Allow me to clarify the agreement, Mr Marsh. You and Mrs Rowe had a deed to do, but you were getting paid cash on top of your deed. Is that correct?' Gilbert asked.

'What does it matter now?' Donahue asked with a shrug.

'Because when we first spoke with you and again now when we mentioned the cash, you did not seem to recall it or associate it with this deed you agreed to do,' Gilbert said.

'Which leads us to think, Mr Marsh, that Mrs Rowe asked something more of you and brought the cash hoping to persuade you to do her bidding again,' Harland said, studying the prisoner before him.

Donahue Marsh scoffed, and Gilbert looked slightly surprised. He had not thought of that but leaned forward for the answer.

'No, the cash was for me to get rid of Ernest.'

'But if you and Mrs Rowe were lovers and intended to be together, why would Mrs Rowe pay you when you would soon inherit her wealth by marriage?' Harland asked, and again, the detectives waited in silence before Harland said, 'Perhaps the truth, Mr Marsh, it will save you coming up with a story, and as you are in for two murders now; you will not be seeing the light of day anytime soon.'

'I have a good lawyer now,' Donahue said with a satisfied smirk.

'You can trust me on this, Mr Marsh; your lawyer might save you from the rope but not from gaol time. This will be your home for a long time,' Harland told the man a truth that Donahue Marsh did not want to contemplate.

The prisoner looked toward the window and the blue sky beyond it. They waited, and eventually, he grimaced, looked back at the detectives, and put his hands flat on the table.

'She tried to buy me off,' he said, his eyes narrowed, and Harland saw the vicious side of the labourer in his glare and how he now fisted his hands. 'Elizabeth said that she had fallen in love with Ernest's brother, Leslie, and that they didn't mean to, but it just happened. She still wanted me to get rid of Ernest because that was what we agreed on, and she did her deed and got the ring back for me. But Leslie wanted me to have the money to start over. In other words, he was saying get lost; she's mine. Well, if I wasn't having her, no one was.'

'And that is why you drowned her,' Harland nodded, fully understanding the passion of the crime now. His mind processed the information, and Gilbert shuffled beside him, bursting with a thousand thoughts and questions. Harland nodded for him to proceed while he thought about Donahue Marsh's admittance.

'Did Leslie Rowe know you were going to kill his brother?'

'I'm guessing so, but I don't know when he found out. Elizabeth and I were going to be together when we first made plans, but now I wonder if this was always Leslie and Elizabeth's plan. They thought they could trap me into doing their dirty work if she pretended to want me, as she did when married to her first husband, Tyson.' He shrugged, 'But maybe Leslie didn't know until recently and suggested the money would shut me up, and I'd go away.'

'Well, it worked,' Gilbert said. 'You didn't mention Leslie Rowe in your confession. Although you still have Richard Tyson's death on your hands, regardless.'

'Ah,' Harland said with a better understanding of the situation. 'Leslie Rowe is paying for your lawyer and believes he can get you off. He has bought your silence.'

'He said the lawyer's the best money can buy,' Donahue boasted, 'so I won't be saying anything against him under oath.'

Then Harland landed another truth on the man Elizabeth Rowe had so well manipulated.

'You killed the woman he loved, Mr Marsh. He is not going to get you off. He's hired a good lawyer to bury you.'

Lilly Lewis had dropped in to thank the detectives for involving her in another astonishing case, but she could not believe her ears.

'Another twist! Have you arrested Leslie Rowe?' she exclaimed.

'He is waiting for us in a cell block as we speak,' Gilbert said.

'He is summoning his lawyer,' Harland said. 'Sadly, I doubt we can charge him with anything. It is the word of Donahue Marsh—a murderer—over the respectable Mr Leslie Rowe, and his brother is still alive after all.'

'Despicable,' she answered. 'I feel very sorry for Ernest. He appeared to love his wife only to find out Elizabeth tried to kill him, and now he learns she was in love with his brother, and they might have both plotted his death. Goodness gracious, what a melodrama!'

'My thoughts exactly, Miss Lewis,' Harland said with a smile. 'Mrs Rowe was quite the manipulator, playing three men as if they were putty in her hands.'

'Well, I am grateful for another exciting twist to the story, and thank you, as always, Detectives, for letting me run with it.' With her quotes for the next edition in hand and in a rush, as always, to meet a deadline, Lilly Lewis departed, and Harland rose.

'Let's get this arrest over with, Gilbert; I am keen to close this case once and for all.' He put his hat on and added, 'Well done. It was worth your while to lose sleep over that loose end last night.'

'Thank you, Sir,' Gilbert grinned, 'but I would never have thought for a moment that Leslie Rowe was involved. I suspect you will be asked to discard that letter of thanks from him for saving his brother Ernest's life, given we are about to charge him.'

Harland chuckled at Gilbert's odd thought. 'Yes, I imagine we will no longer be held in high regard by him.' He gave a small sigh. 'Brotherly love. A strange thing.'

'As neither of us has brothers, Sir, we'll never know.'

Chapter 35

ONE MONTH TO THE day of the *River Lady* ferry tragedy, the newspaper issued an invitation to the citizens of Brisbane. Miss Lilly Lewis, who knew the sad event and its outcome better than anyone, was tasked with writing it by her editor.

THE *RIVER LADY* ONE-MONTH ANNIVERSARY
SPECIAL CEREMONY ON SITE THIS AFTERNOON

One month ago this evening, not only in Brisbane but in the uttermost parts of the British-speaking world, there was a thrill of horror and sympathy as the news spread that the ferry steamer *River Lady* had been overturned into the flood waters of the Brisbane River and that many persons were thereby instantly consigned to a watery grave.

One month to the day, the departed have been buried, and so many homes bear the impression of the shock and sadness. A special remembrance and blessing will occur at 4pm this afternoon at the site of the tragedy, concluding with a hymn at the time of the heart-rending sinking. All are welcome.

Hundreds of people gathered on the banks of the Brisbane River that afternoon to pay their respects to the victims of the *River Lady* tragedy. The captain was not among them. By the waterline stood the bereaved families, a priest, and a choir of a dozen singers donned in blue robes: friends, the sympathetic public and the curious spread around the riverbank.

Julius Astin, with his wife, Violet, and his siblings, Ambrose and Phoebe, arrived, representing *The Economic Undertaker* and *In Mourning – Attire for the Family,* which played a large role in seeing the deceased on their next journey and their relatives appropriately dressed in black. They stayed on the rise, close to where Mrs Elizabeth Rowe was photographed on the last day of her life. Here, they could hear the priest and individual readings from the bereaved families. Candles were lit, and the choir sang a hymn.

'There's Miss Lewis and Mr Griffiths,' Julius said, nudging Phoebe, who subtly raised her hand to attract Lilly's attention.

As the two reporters joined them, one of an elderly pair of ladies nearby could be heard saying to Lilly, 'We saw our names in the newspaper, Miss Lewis.' The other, who looked just like her, added, 'A wonderful report you did, too.'

Lilly whispered, 'Thank you, Miss Jane, Miss Jean. I hope to see you again soon,' she said with a small wave as she moved closer to Phoebe and Violet. The party greeted each other.

'Are you reporting tonight?' Ambrose asked Fergus.

'Yes, I will return to the newspaper afterwards to write a few paragraphs about the memorial gathering,' Fergus said, shaking Julius and Ambrose's outstretched hands. 'But just me; Lilly is not working and is here to pay her respects.'

'Hopefully, we're not working either if everyone could stay away from the water's edge,' Julius said drily, making the group hide their smiles.

Julius then raised his hand slightly to acknowledge someone, and Phoebe turned to see Harland and Gilbert arriving. The senior detective locked eyes with Phoebe and smiled before sobering, given the occasion's solemnity. The detectives approached the Astin group and were greeted by the family and two reporters.

'A very good turnout,' Gilbert said.

'Indeed,' Harland agreed, standing next to Phoebe. 'Did we miss anything?'

'A few readings and a song by the choir.'

'Good,' Harland said, and Julius huffed as Phoebe playfully scolded Harland, telling him, 'The choir is very good.'

'No doubt,' Harland said, and again, they looked at each other until Julius cleared his throat to get their attention and broke their concentration on each other. Julius rolled his eyes at the pair, and Phoebe poked him.

'Do not be such a stick in the mud.'

'It is his job, and he is very good at it,' Ambrose said, teasing his brother.

The priest raised his voice, and they ceased their low conversation as he spoke of the apostle Paul's address to the Romans, saying, 'We have been raised out of the watery grave of baptism a new man, empowered to bear righteous fruit in service to God...'

Gilbert seemed to be the only one in their party familiar with the apostle Paul's teaching. The priest, whom Julius had not recalled seeing before at any of their funerals, explained Paul's meaning to the gathering in a fire and brimstone voice: 'After being raised from the water in newness of life, the repentant sinner stands before God perfect, holy, and sinless.'

'That is comforting,' Gilbert agreed, 'if not an odd choice given the victims were not baptised by the flood waters but had their lives extinguished.'

'True,' Phoebe agreed. 'But perhaps the thought of them arriving for judgement cleansed by the waters as one is with baptism, will comfort the families,' and the young detective and lady mortician agreed, smiled and strengthened their friendship.

Harland supported their comments, even if he was not overly comforted by the thought himself, and earned a raised eyebrow from Julius. Harland gave a small shrug.

The choir burst into song, and then, at the exact time of day when the *River Lady* sank, the crowd joined in one more prayer before dispersing. The twins bid Lilly farewell, and several people acknowledged the Astin family on departing.

'Well, a sad affair indeed,' Harland said, watching relatives of the deceased clinging onto each other as hugs and well wishes were exchanged.

'There's Miss Prout,' Ambrose said, nodding towards an attractive young lady talking with several other women. She caught his eye simultaneously and, excusing herself, came over.

'Mr Astin, Mr Astin, Miss Astin,' Billie said. 'I see you are here too to thank the dead for their patronage.'

'Eloquently put, Miss Prout,' Julius chuckled, and Ambrose did the introductions.

'Oh, I love your articles,' Billie said to Lilly. 'My father gets the paper daily, and I always point out to him that women can do anything they put their minds to, which he supports.'

'I completely agree, Miss Prout,' Detective Gilbert Payne said.

'That is because you are a true gentleman, Detective Payne,' Lilly told the man who loved their friend, Miss Emily Yalden. 'And thank you, Miss Prout, for reading our work,' she included Fergus beside her. 'Phoebe tells me your monuments are beautiful.'

'Too kind,' Billie said with a gracious nod and smile to Phoebe.

'They are exceptional,' Julius said, 'don't you agree, Ambrose?'

Ambrose smirked at his brother's attempt to make him acknowledge Miss Prout in a manner more gracious than he was at her presentation. He nodded, answering, 'Yes, which is why we are now partnering in business.'

'Please, Mr Astin, do not be so effusive about my work; I fear it will go to my head, and it might swell so my hat will not fit,' Billie said cheekily to Ambrose, creating much amusement at Ambrose's expense.

'A busy time for Prout Monumental Masons too, I'm guessing, Miss Prout?' Harland asked Billie, saving Ambrose from a retort.

'Indeed, Detective,' Billie agreed, 'but our workload will increase some time from now when the ground has settled and the headstone can be placed upon it. That is when our orders come in.'

'Well, it has been lovely to see you all again despite the sad occasion,' Gilbert said, turning to Harland and announcing, 'If there is nothing more, Sir, I shall depart. Miss Yalden and I have a recital this evening.'

'By all means,' Harland said.

'How lovely,' Phoebe added, and the group bid Detective Payne goodbye.

'I must hurry too,' Lilly said. 'Bennet is coming to dinner tonight. My parents like to see him occasionally to assure themselves he is still around and hasn't abandoned me,' she said with a laugh. 'Goodbye for now.'

'And I have a story to file. Good day to you all,' Fergus added and hurried down to the water's edge to get the correct spelling of the priest's name and details of the choir before rushing off to write up his small story for the morning edition of *The Courier*.

The Astin family, Detective Stone and Miss Prout remained.

'Well, I am sure we shall see each other again now that we are in business, and it is very good to meet you, Mrs Astin and Detective,' Billie said to Violet and Harland. 'I shall be going.'

'Miss Prout, do you like ice cream?' Phoebe asked before Billie could depart. 'It is just that we are all here, and while it is nearing dinner time, it has been some time since Julius treated us to ice cream. Could we not have dessert first this evening?'

Julius laughed, drawing the admiration of those present – his handsomeness enhanced by the rare laugh he shared with friends.

'We are finished for the day,' he agreed, 'and you have all worked so hard of late. I think that is a fine idea.'

'And we are alive and should celebrate that after such a solemn occasion,' Violet agreed. 'Besides, Spilsbury's confectionery shop is on our way.'

'I do love ice cream,' Billie agreed, 'but of course, I will pay for my own.'

'Absolutely not, Miss Prout,' Julius insisted. 'You will detract from the pleasure of me shouting everyone, including you, Harland.'

'Excellent, my favourite is vanilla,' he said. 'Oh, that's your favourite too, isn't it, Phoebe?' he teased, and she laughed.

'Banana ice cream for me,' Violet said, looking up at Julius, 'it is nothing short of divine.'

'Then you can have two serves,' he joked as the party started walking towards Spilsbury's confectionery shop. Julius saw the pleased look on Ambrose's face at the inclusion of Miss Prout.

'I love chocolate ice cream. It is by far the best,' Billie declared.

'That is my favourite too,' Ambrose said, looking at her suspiciously. 'I am sure I like it more than you.'

'I doubt that,' Billie huffed. 'It has been my favourite since I was a young girl. My mother used to make it.'

Julius looked at Violet and shook his head as she laughed at their antics. He glanced back to check on his sister on Harland Stone's arm and gave them a menacing look to behave, which made Phoebe laugh. With a wink, Violet distracted her husband, leaving Phoebe in Harland's care.

As she walked beside the handsome detective, Phoebe felt as if her heart might burst with happiness. Here, on this solemn occasion, she could walk away with the people she loved and, with a glance to the river, she silently wished the dead eternal rest.

Harland acknowledged people who passed them and recognised him from his duties, while Phoebe felt herself floating between conversations. She heard Julius and Violet talking about dinner this evening.

'Tom is cooking for us tonight. He was quite excited to do so,' Violet said of her brother.

'Good Lord,' Julius said, alarmed, 'should we eat something before we get home?'

She heard Violet's laugh and turned her attention to her brother, Ambrose, walking with the lively and beautiful Miss Billie Prout.

'As I am older than you, I have liked chocolate ice cream for longer, so you cannot claim to like it more,' Ambrose said competitively.

'How do you know you are older? That is quite an assumption, Mr Astin.'

'I am a gentleman and would not dare ask your age. I can only go by your appearance, and you are much younger than myself, without a doubt.'

'Mr Astin, I have been charmed by some of the best. You will have to work harder if you think you can win an argument with me using your manners and good looks,' Billie teased.

'I am sure you have, Miss Prout, but the good looks in my family belong to my brother, so the ladies tell me.'

Phoebe heard the edge of vulnerability in his voice; he had loved Lilly, who admired Julius, and Ambrose always seemed to be in Julius's shadow.

Billie looked at the eldest Astin brother, who walked ahead with his wife. 'He is beautiful, of that there is no doubt, but I have never sought the Byronic types – dark, quiet and considered. I prefer a man who is one of the lads – playful, irreverent and full of character,' she declared. 'And where is your lady today, Mr Astin, so I might discern your excellent tastes?'

He laughed. 'Thank you for that compliment, but alas, I am a single man. But I do like a woman with a bit of sass.'

A small tug on her hand saw Phoebe turning her attention to Harland, who gazed down at her.

'This is promising,' he said in a low voice, nodding at the pair ahead.

'It is indeed,' Phoebe smiled and flushed at having been caught listening to their conversation.

But apparently, Harland had been as well, and he asked most formally, 'I do hope you like those Byronic types, Miss Astin. Tall, dark, and extremely handsome?'

She grinned up at him. 'They are my favourite types, Detective,' she responded in kind. 'And pray tell, what sort of lady attracts your attention?'

'Oh, I like a girl with spirit,' he said, making Phoebe laugh.

'How fortunate,' she said, and with a last glance at the river, she was pleased to see no spirits lost or despairing, only the living.

THE END

From the author:

THANK YOU ONCE AGAIN for spending time with the Astin family and all they hold dear. I try to be as factual as possible when writing about the period (1891), and you might find the following interesting.

It is not surprising that Julius's mourning wear store was feeling the pinch, as there were quite a few dressmakers in Brisbane. Queen Street retailer Finney and Isles opened a dedicated mourning department in 1871 that expanded to three dedicated mourning departments.[1] Mourning jewellery was also a big business, and Flavelle Brothers of Queen Street was one of several Brisbane jewellers who catered to this market.

The terrible sinking of the *River Lady* ferry was inspired by the sinking of the *Pearl* Ferry in Brisbane on 14 February 1896. The inquest found the captain to be under the influence of alcohol, but he was not the owner or in financial trouble; that was fiction. Amazingly, the actual captain went home, changed, and returned despite all the tragedy unfolding around him. Unimaginable.

The wording of many of the news accounts and the inquest stories included in this book were based on factual accounts reported in *The Courier*, including the captain's version of events, which was an interview granted to the newspaper at the time.[2] The real Captain James Chard lived to the ripe old age of 83. He tried to go down with his ferry but survived. It was a terrible maritime disaster, and in my nonfiction book, *Grave Tales: Brisbane*, jointly written with journalist Chris Adams, we feature the story of *The Pearl* and the loss of lives, in particular Miss Grace Yorsten, 27, and Mr Harry Jarman, 21. Do read it if you have time to remember them.

A small piece ran in the *Brisbane Courier* one year after the Pearl disaster, similar to the piece Lilly wrote one month after the tragedy. I have used the wording (out of copyright) as I found the manner of reporting and choice of words fascinating, such as "a thrill of horror and sympathy". At the hour of the tragedy, the Ida Newman Cot was dedicated at the Children's Hospital in remembrance of a life that was cut short. Miss Newman was a dance teacher. (My fictional character was Miss Ida Nielsen). If you are interested in reading the original news piece, the link is below.[3]

Julius's idea of having dedicated train carriages for the coffin and mourners existed. There were "mortuary stations" in Sydney but not in Brisbane, where this book is set. As early as 1867, the train brought mourners and coffins to Rookwood Necropolis (Cemetery) in Sydney. Eventually, special trains from Sydney stopped twice a day at pre-arranged stations to pick up mourners and coffins, with some stations having dedicated waiting areas for funeral parties. The corpse travelled free. The service had halted by the late 1930s.[4]

I hope you were not too disappointed in the love match ending between Ambrose and Kate. Our dear Kate has headed to Ingham for a new opportunity with a fellow lady photographer. I'm pleased to write that Harriett Brims existed and was a pioneer female commercial photographer in Queensland, Australia. She opened a photographic studio in the late 1890s in Ingham and later moved to Mareeba, opening a studio there in 1904, until she moved to Brisbane in 1914. She captured pioneer people and places. Harriett died in 1939, aged 75.[5] What a trailblazer!

There were monument masons by the name of Prout in 1890. Prout and Thumm made a beautiful monument to the murdered siblings of the Murphy family in Gatton, another story that is featured in our *Grave Tales* book and believed to be Queensland's oldest cold case – a great tragedy. Monuments were becoming more creative toward the end of the 19th century, but

Billie (Willimena) is a fictitious character, full of sass and fun (hopefully). More to come from Billy.

And more Astin adventures to follow. Go carefully until we catch up again.

About the author

Helen is a hybrid-published, Amazon best-selling author. After studying English literature, media, and communications at universities in Queensland, Australia, and obtaining a counselling diploma, Helen has worked as a journalist, producer and marketer in print, TV, radio and public relations. Born in Toowoomba, she has made her home in Brisbane, Australia, with her journalist husband, Chris, and Boxer dog, Baxter. She is published by Next Chapter, Podium Entertainment, and her own imprint, Atlas Productions.

Connect with Helen:

Website: www.helengoltz.com

BookBub:www.bookbub.com/authors/helen-goltz

Facebook: www.facebook.com/HelenGoltz.Author

Instagram: https://www.instagram.com/helengoltz1/

Also by Helen Goltz

I**F YOU LIKE THE** Astin family, you might enjoy:

Miss Hayward & the Detective Series (historical mystery/romance):

Murder at the Carnival

The Artist's Missing Muse

Mystery at the Asylum

The Mortician's Clue (introducing Phoebe and staff from *The Economic Undertaker*)

Murder in Bridal Lane

The Clairvoyant's Glasses (supernatural/romance)

Volume 1 – A vision unexpected

Volume 2 – Time has a shadow

Volume 3 – Love knows no bounds

Volume 4 – Fate comes to call
Volume 5 & 6 – The Raven's son (coming soon)

The Jesse Clarke series (cosy mystery):
Death by Sugar
Death by Disguise
Death by Reunion

The Mitchell Parker series published by Next Chapter (crime thrillers):
Mastermind
Graveyard of the Atlantic
The Fourth Reich

Writing as Jack Adams (psychological mystery/suspense):
Poster Girl
Delaney and Murphy childhood friends series:
Asylum
Stalker
Cult
Hitched
Carnival
Forgotten (coming soon).

With journalist Chris Adams, *The Grave Tales* series (non-fiction) x 9 titles:

Grave Tales: Brisbane Vol.1

Grave Tales: Great Ocean Road – Geelong to Port Fairy

Grave Tales: Sydney Vol.1

Grave Tales: Bruce Highway

Grave Tales: True Crime Vol.1

Grave Tales: Queensland's Great South West

Grave Tales: Melbourne Vol.1

Grave Tales: Queensland's Scenic Rim & Surrounds

Grave Tales: Tasmania.

Grave Tales: Cold Cases (an amalgamation of stories from existing titles)

The Lady Mortician's Visions (historical mystery/romance/paranormal twist)

The Missing Brides

The Fake Child

The Dastardly Debutante

The Deathly Dolls

The Potent Perfume

The Watery Grave

The Vanishing Groom

The Fallen Angel

More to come....

Writing as Ally Adams:

The Saints team (contemporary romance):

Team Lucas

Team Tomas

Team Niklas

Team Alex

Stand-alone titles:

The House on Findlater Lane (mystery/romance paranormal)

The Forgotten House (historical romance)

Three Parts Truth (mystery suspense)

Morphers (middle grade fiction).

1. Maclean, Hilda Erica, *Funerary consumption in the second half of the 19th century in Brisbane, Queensland.* A thesis submitted for the degree of Doctor of Philosophy at The University of Queensland in 2015.

2. The Pearl Disaster. (1896, February 18). *Gympie Times and Mary River Mining Gazette (Qld. : 1868 - 1919)*, p. 3. Retrieved August 11, 2024, from http://nla.gov.au/nla.news-article171451093

3. Pearl Anniversary. (1897, February 13). *The Telegraph (Brisbane, Qld. : 1872 - 1947)*, p. 4. Retrieved September 8, 2024, from http://nla.gov.au/nla.news-article172152290

4. McKillop, Bob, Funeral Trains, 2016. Retrieved from: https://dictionaryofsydney.org/entry/funeral_trains River Lady Ferry disaster reports and eye-witness accounts:Sydney Morning Herald, 15 February 1896, p.9.The Queenslander, 22 February 1896, p.376Evening Observer, 4 February 1896

5. Late Mrs. Harriett Brims (1939, October 26). *The Telegraph (Brisbane, Qld. : 1872 - 1947)*, p. 16 (CITY FINAL LAST MINUTE NEWS). Retrieved August 27, 2024, from http://nla.gov.au/nla.news-article188025739